Debra Adelaide is an author and academic who has published five works of fiction, including *The Household Guide to Dying*, *Letter to George Clooney*, and *The Women's Pages*, as well as many edited collections, the most recent of which is *The Simple Act of Reading*. She works at the University of Technology Sydney, where she is an associate professor in creative writing.

Also by Debra Adelaide

Novels

The Hotel Albatross

Serpent Dust

The Household Guide to Dying

The Women's Pages

Short Story Collections

Letter to George Clooney

Anthologies

Motherlove

Motherlove 2

Cutting the Cord

Acts of Dog

Non-Fiction

A Bright and Fiery Troop (ed)

Australian Women Writers: A Bibliographic Guide

A Window in the Dark (ed)

Bibliography of Australian Women's Literature

Stories from the Tower (ed with P. Asthon and A. Salt)

The Simple Act of Reading (ed)

DEBRA ADELAIDE

ZEBRA

AND OTHER STORIES

PICADOR
Pan Macmillan Australia

First published 2019 in Picador by Pan Macmillan Australia Pty Ltd
1 Market Street, Sydney, New South Wales, Australia, 2000

Cataloguing-in-Publication entry is available
from the National Library of Australia
http://catalogue.nla.gov.au

Typeset in 12.2/17 pt Adobe Garamond Pro by Post Pre-press Group
Printed by McPherson's Printing Group
Edited by: Emma Schwarcz
Designed by: Debra Billson
Cover illustration: Heather Gauthier

For my father, who always loved a joke.

Contents

FIRST

Dismembering 3

Welcome to Country 21

A Fine Day 33

SECOND

Festive Food for the Whole Family 55

How to Mend a Broken Heart 65

Migraine for Beginners 71

The Master Shavers' Association of Paradise 95

THIRD

Carry Your Heart 117

I am at Home Now 131

No Hot Drinks in the Ward 143

Nourishment 157

The Recovery Position 171

Wipe Away Your Tears 185

Zebra 203

Acknowledgements 327

FIRST

Dismembering

THE DREAM WAS so vivid I woke in a sweat of fear and went straight down the backyard, but the ground between the garden shed and the fence was as innocent as a lamb. Which could also have been grazing there, so green and dewy was the patch. There was no sign the ground had been disturbed in years.

Or perhaps it had, and perhaps I had no idea how quickly lawn could regrow into a smooth carpet. After all, lawn had never been my responsibility. Carpet, yes.

But I still had doubts, and these were so strong that I went inside to the home phone and called my ex-husband. I rarely phoned him from my mobile, on principle. He laughed at me down through the copper cables, after complaining I'd rung him at 6.30 am.

'You're sure?' I said.

'Of course I'm sure. I think I'd remember a dead body.' He laughed again, which was so much better than not laughing, or whatever it was he did for the first few years after we parted. I was so pleased to hear this laugh I didn't mind that it was directed at me.

I stared out the kitchen window towards the shed, trying to remember. Much of the dream was already fading away, as dreams do, but aspects of it were still clear. The cutting off of the head. The removal of the arms and legs. The red checked flannelette shirt it wore. The fact that it was undeniably a man, middle-aged.

What was also clear in the dream was that while my then-husband and I were co-conspirators, it was his action that we were now covering up, though for what reason I could not tell. But somehow I was his assistant, fearful yet compliant. I could see myself in that dream, sawing away at a knee joint with the bush saw and wondering aloud if the tenon saw would do a better job, and that it was a shame we could not use the chainsaw, while he concentrated on digging the hole. But the chainsaw was cinematically clichéd, messy, and far too noisy. The neighbours would be flicking their back lights on: no one used a chainsaw at night.

This hole, when my ex-husband climbed out of it, sprinkled with black soil, turned out to be deep but not quite long enough, hence the careful sectioning of the head and limbs so the pieces could be stacked. Then he said that this would be better anyway, as it would not risk leaving the outline of a regular grave, however faint it might be in years to come. Perhaps we would plant a grevillea or a hybrid ficifolia over the top. At the time I quite liked the cultivar Corymbia 'Summer Red'.

I went outside again after I had taken the children to school. There was no ficifolia, cultivar or not. There was nothing out there but lawn, recently mown by Sam of Jim's Mowing, who came twice a month in summer. I trod all over the patch where in my dream I had been arranging arms neatly upon a torso, while my ex-husband leaned on the shovel and wiped a dirty hand across his brow. It was firm. I jumped up and down a few times, then went to the shed and looked inside.

There was the very shovel from my dream, the square-mouth shovel stacked inside the door next to the spade and a few old star posts, which my ex-husband had got when repairing the back fence. He had taken most of the tools and implements, apart from a few, like the shovel and the green spade. I hardly ever used them since discovering – even though my mother had already pointed this out – that a vegetable patch offered little return for hard labour. There was also the Flymo, which Simon and I were both too scared to use (hence Sam, from Jim's Mowing) and a broken blower vac, which I would never have used anyway.

Anything useful, shed-wise, had been taken out and added to all the other things we had divided up when the split occurred. His *Star Wars* DVDs. My boxed sets of BBC historical dramas. His gym equipment, dismantled after the first child arrived. Half each of the wedding-present dinner-service cream stoneware, though I kept the gravy boat and sugar bowl. We were gracious about the items we owned together, civilised. He ceded me the blender and espresso machine; I gave him the matching Russell Hobbs toaster and kettle.

While our arguments generally had been spectacular, I could not remember any argument over this final division of possessions, not a single thing, unless I counted the one over the crockpot, of which I was dismissive and contemptuous and he protective, seeing as his older sister had given it as an engagement present. Not that he wanted or ever used it either: it was the principle. Afterwards, I remember taking it to the Salvation Army along with various items, harmless in themselves, but which would only remind me of my failed marriage. Three small framed prints of cacti (anniversary present). A set of satin-edged blankets, new but never used in favour of doonas. A Zyliss mandoline grater (the last anniversary present) with too many attachments to be practical, and indeed requiring a firmer wrist than I had to work properly. A cut-glass vase that only looked good when unoccupied, and in any case was useless for most flowers, excepting those loose bunches of buxom roses that you see in paintings, but which I had never received as a present.

We did not divide the children. We agreed he would keep Corky. My mother helped me with the property, and when that settlement was signed and paid for, the only contact I had with my ex-husband was every other weekend when he would come from Windsor to fetch Oscar and Nancy, waiting on the front porch, stow them and their backpacks into his Prius and return them the next day by 5 pm.

There were these dreams, though. In one of them I was on a train – what is it about trains and dreams? someone must know – and I met him at a country town after a long journey. He was wearing a blue stripey shirt, the sort of shirt that boys the age of three or four wear, and was hiding under the platform bench seat. I leaned down and pulled him out by the hand and he dusted himself off and said, We have to go, come on, I've got to get back to work. I'd arrived to help him run some business, but he did not seem all that pleased to see me. Another dream involved a deep, dark swimming pool somewhere, and I was perched on the ladder that vanished into the water's mysterious depths. Just as I acquired the courage to go deeper he always appeared and hauled me back, away from the water.

These dreams, and others, I re-dreamed over the years, sometimes with variations but not enough to make them more interesting or intelligible. They were just dreams as far as I could see. But if I woke in the morning and these dreams were fresh I would be annoyed. Even in the early days, with Simon beside me, not yet awake, and our new children in their cot at the foot of our bed, I would have these dreams and wonder why, given my new life, my happy life. Had I not moved on? Or did I attribute too much psychological power to such dreams, more than they or he deserved?

But now, there was this new dream.

During that week I couldn't help myself: I kept walking down the backyard to gaze at that plot of lawn between the garden shed and the fence. I was even thinking of it as a plot, when all it was – all it could possibly be – was an empty space. A stretch of lawn, buffalo grass, or kikuyu. Something I might have turned into another shed, or a pond, or a sandpit for the children, if I had wanted. But its blank innocence mocked me. Why was it so smooth, much smoother, I thought, than the rest of the lawn? And why had the grass there grown so well over the years? Regarded in certain lights, it was distinctly greener.

I started noticing things around the house. The little one-drawer desk in the hall which I had asked my ex-husband to take, several times, but he refused. It had belonged to his side of the family, not mine. I want to travel light, he would say, you hang on to it. The implication being that the life he was leaving had been . . . Well, I don't need to spell it out.

Then there was the wardrobe in the spare room, now Oscar's room, which was dark and impractical, and the children complained that it smelled of other people's clothes, old people's clothes. Poking my head into the wardrobe and breathing in, I would have to agree, and that something lighter and larger, with wire baskets and maybe those modular white fabric boxes, would be so much better for kids on the verge of teenagehood. But their father disagreed, reminding me that it was valuable, flame mahogany, and that his grandmother had given it to him and not to get rid of it. He did not want it himself, saying he needed very little, that furniture was mostly an encumbrance. You keep them, he'd say with a wave of his hand as he disappeared into his car after returning Oscar and Nancy every other weekend. He somehow managed me into being responsible for his belongings while at the same time making me feel

I was a shallow materialist nailed down by things; his life, meanwhile, was now free and floating. When I thought it through I became enraged. Wasn't he the one with a huge place out there at Windsor, with plenty of room in the house for old wardrobes?

Enough of this, I thought. I would get tough. That weekend was when he was due to take the children. I put the hallway desk onto the front porch and then, when Simon came home from work on the Friday night, we dragged the ugly old people–smelling wardrobe out beside it. This time I texted my ex-husband, suggesting he might need to hire a utility instead of coming in the Prius. I almost never texted him, since messages tended to provoke responses. I found the old landline so much simpler for post-post-nuptial negotiations. There was also the undeniable satisfaction of real hanging up: no matter how hard one jabbed an end button with one's thumb, it was no substitute for crashing a receiver down.

Simon, the twins, and I went away for that weekend too, returning on the Sunday afternoon to find a sullen Oscar and Nancy sitting on the desk with the wardrobe standing guard.

The next day I noticed a stack of prints against the wall in the spare room. Norman Lindsays, unframed. How had they escaped our divvying-up years back? I had always hated the goggle-eyed, preposterously breasted female figures that Lindsay sketched. You would not catch me hanging them in my house. There was also the roll of posters that represented my ex-husband's brief period as a student activist. I packed them onto the desk on the front porch then went back inside the house. A room-by-room search was required. The rest of the spare room, the space under our king bed, the top of the children's toy closet, the laundry, right through to the cupboard on the back verandah: they all yielded tarnished marriage spoils that each of us had overlooked all those years back, and which I certainly did not want, perhaps never had. A stack of LP records which contained such eccentric artists I knew they could never have been mine, including a radiator coolant–green vinyl actually called *The World's Worst Record*. A three-piece EPNS coffee set (cricket prize? company farewell gift?) nestled in purple satin in a fake velvet box. A black wooden photo frame still in its plastic wrapping, containing a trio of oval shapes, ones that would never be filled. A nest of laminex tables, small, medium and large. Why was everything in threes? As if the drama of marriage were in three acts. Well, this was the coda, the encore, the next play.

We were lucky, the house was large, but even so I could not understand how these items had escaped my scrutiny all those years back. Now I regarded them with new and uncompromising eyes, eyes that had seen strange things, albeit in a dream. A monkey-pod salad bowl and servers I found in the dining room dresser, not mine and never used. What was monkey pod anyway – was that even a real type of tree? More prints from the days he fancied collecting botanical ephemera. Butterflies pinned and framed in little glass boxes. Magnificent butterflies. I did not gaze at them too long. It would perhaps inspire metaphor, and I had no need of metaphor, being on such a practical mission.

I dragged everything out to the front porch and stacked it as neatly as I could and, when I was done, went around inside and outside once again, just to be sure. I added a garden rake that I remember him buying back when Bunnings was Hardware House and raking the lawn an altogether different activity, somehow homely and bonding. Now the job never invoked images of autumnal joy: Corky chasing flurrying leaves, silly wheelbarrow rides, red cheeks and post-gardening beers. Perhaps it never had. Perhaps I was remembering a storybook marriage, the Ladybird book cover one, and not the one that really existed? Anyway, after the rake, all that was left was the shed down the back. Before doing that I texted him. He didn't respond within five minutes so I rang, intending to leave a voicemail, but he actually answered.

I told him what I had done and where he would find everything. A couple of old coats from the hall cupboard, and the rolled-up, supposedly Persian rug from the garage. His kayak, which I'd found lying forgotten beside the fence, covered in morning glory. The box of broken medicine bottles, doubtless old, possibly antique, but broken all the same.

'You've told me not to enter the house. It's why I wait in the driveway to pick up the kids.'

'I'm making an exception.'

'I think this is your problem, not mine.'

'Including that dead body in the backyard,' I said.

But he had already hung up.

*

I inspected the garden shed dispassionately. He had taken his toolbox with the good saw, screwdriver set and assorted fixings. Also the whipper snipper, chainsaw and hedge trimmer, along with the smaller electrical tools: the orbital sander, belt sander, angle grinder, and the good cordless drill. He had left the bad cordless drill but I didn't mind because it was fine for small jobs around the house. The shed had never been my domain but I had always prided myself on keeping it neat. Now dead leaves littered the ground and dust covered everything. The potato vine on the back fence had sneaked its way inside and cobwebs obscured the window, danced from the naked light fitting, and covered a precarious stack of milk crates. Amongst sagging cardboard boxes and scraps of old towels and paint-splattered sheets there was very little that could be considered functional. A grease-black vice was still clamped to the bench, never used as far as I remembered. The naked outlines of shapes on the hand-tool wall looked both sinister and forlorn, as if a forensic team had done its job then quickly moved on.

Over the years I had become accustomed to simply reaching in for whatever garden implement I needed then putting it back beside the door. I had long promoted the bad cordless drill, the rusty but serviceable claw hammer, and a handy little screwdriver set to the laundry, for ease of use. I switched off the light that did not work, and struggled with the bolt that barely slid. If I looked at this sad, broken-down place any longer I would start to see metaphor.

Busy for the next few days with the twins' birthday party and the older kids' end-of-term school play, I handwrote invitations and ticked names off lists, and attended meetings to determine the craft roster. I shopped and cleaned and cooked. I iced cupcakes and fashioned real sausage rolls. Using empty pineapple juice tins, I baked the chocolate cake for a spectacular medieval castle. The twins had stipulated turrets, drawbridge and a moat. I knew I could do a lot with chocolate icing but was still not sure about the moat. Then I stuffed octopus arms and sewed them onto a leotard. I spent hours on my knees with the good scissors cutting blue and purple satin into shapes to pass on to the next mother in the process line, I think for stitching into enormous padded bubbles. So it was a few days before I had time to ring again. The items on the front porch, and now the front path, were depressing me, and, besides, I didn't want the clutter when all those parents were coming by on Saturday to drop off Miles and Ricky's friends. I told him I didn't care that it was not his designated weekend, I wanted the lot gone.

'And another thing,' I said. 'Don't forget that dead body of yours in the backyard.'

'There's no dead body.'

'Yes, there is.'

'No, there isn't, Genevieve.'

Then he hung up. Bastard. He knew how much I hated anything but Gen.

To be honest, I hadn't wanted Corky at the time. She had diabetes and he had suggested that living with him would be easier. There was also the advantage of the vast freedom of his new place. And it would provide some continuity for the children, who were only little, for their weekend stays. We had both agreed on that.

But I wanted Corky now. In fact just thinking about her made me feel almost bereft, which was strange so many years later. She would be nine or ten by now. I began to imagine he was not looking after her properly, not feeding her high-protein kibble, and failing to administer her daily injections of insulin. Had he kept her vaccinations up to date? Remembered to inspect her ears? Perhaps she would succumb to a tick out there on that property, which, I was told, included a large stretch of unimproved ground. I was always reminding the children of the hazards of this. But I did not feel I could interrogate them about Corky, and aside from my bland questions about how she was doing, and their bland answers that she was great or okay or slept a lot or hardly ever dug holes now (probably because the place was intimidatingly huge), I felt uncomfortable about probing.

Now at nights when I wasn't lying awake thinking about the body in the backyard, I was worrying about Corky. At nights I was awake a lot, which had one advantage in that at least I was not dreaming weird dreams. And it gave me time to think thoroughly, to review the dreams I was now not dreaming, to examine all the details I could remember. Why the body was dressed in a red checked shirt, and why I didn't know if it wore trousers or shorts. Which I should have, if I had been sawing the legs off at the knee. You would think you would notice a detail like that. I thought it was shorts, actually. Grey. Or maybe khaki. Then I considered the rest of the dismembering, what I had done with the arms.

Had I sawn them off at the elbow or shoulder? I considered the whole dismembering thing. Then I wondered if dismembering had anything to do with remembering. Was it remembering's antonym? Its evil twin? Or good one? In the morning I would have to look that up, but for the present, getting out of bed at 3 am, switching on the light and going to the *Shorter Oxford English Dictionary* represented too much of an admission of defeat in the battle to sleep.

Miles and Ricky had just blown out their candles and I was standing with the knife poised with one each of their hands planted on top of mine, ready to slice through the first turret, when I noticed the table. I paused and Simon looked at me.

'What's wrong?' But all the kids were still hip-hipping and hooraying.

'I'll tell you later.'

We pushed the knife in, knocking the turret down altogether into the excellently slimy moat (green and blue jelly combined). Oscar had supplied Lego maidens which fell into the jelly while all the knights on the wafer drawbridge dropped as one. The kids cheered and hoorayed again.

Afterwards, when we were clearing up, Simon asked me again.

'It's this table,' I said, speaking in a low voice though the children were in the front room watching TV. 'He bought it. I remember now. I always thought it was ours but it's definitely his.'

'Gen, does this really matter? I mean, if you hate it that much we can get rid of it and buy another, but . . .'

'It's not that I hate it.' Actually it was a lovable table: some honey-coloured timber, with a nice grain and a finish that resisted almost everything the family had managed to do to it. 'It's just that it's his. He needs to take responsibility for it.'

Simon almost sighed. 'Well, let's put an ad on Gumtree.'

'No. He's got to take it. And everything else.'

I thought that I would feel better after dragging the table out to the front, but later when we all sat around the empty space on the dining chairs – and I had definitely bought them, each one a happy mismatch from op shops – I just felt stupid. Simon had made the children macaroni cheese, easy to manage in bowls, but he ended up taking them to eat in front of the TV. I pushed the chairs back against the walls and brought out a rug and coffee table from our study. We could eat sitting on beanbags and lounge chairs for a while, and it would still be warm enough to have dinner outside for a few weeks to come.

After raising the topic of the table, I finally mentioned Corky. My ex-husband laughed again, and it was not a nice laugh.

'You hate anything to do with injections.'

'Not anymore.' Which was the truth: with four children, immunisation seemed to happen every other week and I had become quite okay around needles.

'I'm not exchanging one dog for that pile of rubbish you've got out the front of your place.'

'It's yours. And just because I don't want it doesn't mean it's rubbish.'

I was offended by the thought that I would degrade the

front of my house with rubbish. And everything was as neat as I could make it, in the circumstances.

'And that dead body is yours too,' I reminded him.

'You dug it up yet? Genevieve?'

This time I got to hang up on him. I had to get the children up anyway.

As it happened, the children did not want Corky here, and Simon's loyalties were with the twins, who of course had never even met the dog. Discussing this over breakfast, they expressed interest in having a new dog, not a second-hand one, while Oscar and Nancy looked so troubled that I dropped the topic and went to make their lunches. I was thinking about that challenge to dig the body up, and wondering why I had not actually mentioned this body to Simon yet, and if I ought, when I realised I had squeezed chocolate sauce instead of barbecue onto the sausage sandwiches, and had to start again. And because I had left the children eating their cereal in front of the TV, we were running late for school and I had to drive them. I buckled Miles in first, then Ricky, then checked Miles, who after all these years still resisted seat harnesses, while the older two chattered about the bed Corky had in the garage and another in the closed-off verandah at the back, for when the weather was cold, and how every second Saturday she knew even before she heard the Prius turning the corner, and would run all the way down the driveway to be waiting for them at the gate. They loved that. She loved that.

'So there's a gate? Which means there's a fence? A secure one, I hope?'

The severity of my tone made them both stop and look at me before they got into the car, and their look was just like the one Simon had given me over the table. The drive to school took about two minutes so thankfully the discussion about new or old dogs ended there.

I had intended to ring him again, but when I got home the appearance of the front struck me anew as soon as I pulled up. The table had encroached on the driveway and despite my denials I could admit that it all did look like rubbish. Falling leaves had settled onto the dust covers I had draped over the items of furniture, tools and prints. The front door was flanked by stacks of boxes and crates, and the smelly wardrobe had been obscuring light through the twins' bedroom window for weeks. I backed the car out again and, outrage providing me with strength, dragged everything to the nature strip, even the wardrobe and dining table.

I got the broom and swept the porch and path clean, then cleared the dust and cobwebs from the front windows and shook out the doormat. Inside, starting from the hall, I worked my way back and spent the remainder of the day cleaning, even parts of the house that hadn't been messed up by the birthday party. The kids were in front of the TV again and I was mashing potatoes when Simon walked in and gave me a kiss, removing the sugar shaker from my hand.

'I think you meant to use salt,' he said.

No, I thought, I was right not to mention the body to him. I would work it out myself. I had to.

When I went to bed late that night I was sure I would fall asleep from exhaustion but my mind knew better. Eventually

I got out of bed, uncaring that it was well after midnight with no moon, and went down the backyard. But there is no such thing as complete darkness, not in the suburbs. In the ambient light, the plot of lawn looked the same as it always did, aside from a scattering of silvery leaves. I could have brought the torch but there was no need. I reached inside the shed where the square-mouth shovel always sat and turned around to face the lawn. After some initial resistance, the ground yielded and I marked out a rough rectangle and took off the layer of grass. Then I commenced digging, piling the earth neatly at first. The damp soil smelled wholesome in its earthiness. It was soft, friable, inviting me in. Soon I felt sweat itching in my armpits, down the small of my back, and then the work became difficult, the ground becoming colder and harder the deeper I dug.

Now I was tossing the loads of soil behind me, over me, anywhere, then throwing off my t-shirt, standing there in sleep shorts, soil and nothing else. I was only knee deep and I was covered in soil. It was such hard work, so much harder than when I was in my dream, and as I dug I wished more than anything that Corky were here to help me, and that made my chest begin to heave.

I only realised how much noise I must have been making when Simon appeared.

'What the hell are you doing?'

'It's mine,' I said, now sobbing from relief. I stabbed the shovel in again. 'And I know I'll find it if I just dig deep enough.'

Welcome to Country

LATER THAT NIGHT, I was sitting out the back smoking a rare cigarette and drinking a not so rare glass of wine. White, some sort of sav blanc. Not my usual preference but something left over from ages ago, the last time I'd had people over. It was dry enough, and cold enough. The day had been exceptionally hot but the breeze was nudging the humidity away. In another half-hour or so it could even be cool.

I lit a second cigarette and turned the radio up. Set on the sort of radio station that people like me find themselves listening to, in the end, it had been humming in the kitchen behind me, in the dark. Now I listened while I smoked and sipped my wine and thought. Eventually the muffled chatter clarified from background noise to actual words, and song. I could hear distinctly the wind from the desert town of a far-off country. A place where it would be hotter right now than here.

Earlier that afternoon I had taken a small load to the charity store. This is what people did at this time of year. In my case, cleaning out the other bedroom was a long overdue task, and still a difficult one. I had sorted through the remains of clothing, outgrown or discarded, and all the cards and folders, the trinkets, toys and games, the faulty or obsolete electronic gadgets, and finally the books that surface in every generation: school atlases, paperback dictionaries bursting with stray leaves, and those novels all kids seem to acquire, even those who aren't big readers. *American Psycho. To Kill a Mockingbird. Trainspotting.* All the Harry Potter books, though only the first three of these had been read.

There were old shoes, mostly stained sneakers and outgrown boots. The boots were good quality, and my size. Still, I packed them as well. I knew I would never wear them. I put them in cartons along with the old board games, including a backgammon set that was never used, and playing cards that were. There was also a guitar, several cartoon-character doona covers, and an empty CD stack.

What I had thought would take an hour or two took me most of the day. I have always considered myself a tidy sort of person, not obsessive but tidy enough, yet confronted with the entire room and its half-emptied wardrobe, I felt a mild sense of panic, as if I had no idea where to begin, or what to follow through with. I had a feeling that the task would never end. Some of the cartons which I had accumulated over the past months for this very purpose I filled with the belongings I had decided to keep, packing them neatly and marking the outsides with black texta before stacking them back into the wardrobe. I had already vacuumed the bottom of the wardrobe, and sprayed for insects. When that part of the task was done I made a coffee and, before I had even finished drinking it, went back to retrieve them, to take away too, because what was the point? I knew there was no point. But when I reopened the wardrobe door and saw the cartons I had only just marked SCHOOL STUFF and SPORT AWARDS ETC, I closed it again.

Loading up the car, I realised there was not that much. It all fitted comfortably in the boot. Despite my best intentions I had really only cleaned and rearranged most of it. And with all my dithering about, by the time I pulled up at the charity store the place was closed. In the parking bay beside the skip belonging to the store someone had already left the skeleton of a bike, a baby's cot and mattress and a pile of bulging green garbage bags. And a CD stack, just like the one I was bringing. The empty CD stack: symbol of the charity throw-out, wherever you went, the world over, I should imagine.

I unloaded an old suitcase that I'd filled with soft toys, some of them damaged, but it was unthinkable that these go in the garbage bin. As I placed it down I noticed a rabbit's ear sticking out of the side. Rosie. Rosie the rabbit. She had received a great deal of love once. Rosie the rabbit, she has a funny habit. I could still hear the childish refrain. What funny habit? I could not remember, or perhaps I never knew. I opened the suitcase and tucked Rosie's ear back. She had also lost an eye, and I did remember how that happened. The dog at the time, a lumbering beast with a devoted nature and an excess of enthusiasm that was never tempered by age, made off with Rosie and chewed away an eye before we could rescue her. I remembered the wails, which went on all night, the sobbing to sleep. The even fiercer love that ensued. I almost took Rosie back to the car before I realised the futility of that, as if keeping Rosie meant anything.

I unloaded the cartons and on top of the stack placed the guitar in its cheap vinyl cover. The guitar was missing two strings; it had been cheap too, but it was serviceable, or had been. A three-quarter size, it had been replaced by bigger and better ones, which themselves had long gone from the house. It always had a decent tone, at least I thought so. But then maybe I was just a sucker, back then, for the special sound of a child first learning a musical instrument. Standing there beside the charity store, I could almost hear the chords of 'House of the Rising Sun' floating in the early evening air.

There was no one about. The store was at the end of a lonely strip of shops that were always shut by 5 pm. I took the guitar down again and unzipped the cover. There was an inside pouch containing a spare set of strings. I took a pair of pliers out of the car's tool kit and sat on the kerb of the parking bay while I replaced the missing strings. I tuned the guitar, as well as I remembered how, replaced it in the cover and laid it on top of the stack of cartons. On the way home I stopped at the servo and bought cigarettes.

Halfway through the second cigarette, and I was contemplating a third. The movement of my arm from table to mouth was not enough to set off the light sensors, so the dark was now complete and, in the still night, the radio seemed even louder.

I hadn't even looked in that skip, I realised now. I'd assumed it was already full. But now I wondered if I hadn't wanted to look, in case of rats or something. I'd read about people sleeping in skips. Homeless kids and refugees. Town drunks. It seemed unlikely in this quiet part of the suburbs, but still, I wondered about it.

The background noise on the radio faded and the sound of someone speaking in soft accents filled the night. I realised the topic under discussion was the rebellion. Some people were even calling it war. Then I heard the call of a song, in another tongue, one both familiar and unknown. More words, then a request. The presenter commenting on the conflict. More singing, soft and plangent. A single musical instrument, something reedy-sounding, a wind instrument, but a primitive sort. It was playing a simple but unbearably beautiful tune over the desert wind, which could be heard murmuring in the background. Someone talking again, this time about desert conditions. About the wind itself. The hardship. The rebels. Instruments – but were they talking about weapons or musical ones? The beautiful reedy sound kicked in again, this time with a voice, pure, full-throated, urgent, almost angry. A woman's voice, I thought. It seemed to cut across the country and through the soundwaves and the thick humidity where I sat in the dark, my cigarette held in suspension, burning to the filter.

The words may have been in another language but I knew what they meant. One long note stretched out for what seemed like minutes, the singer's voice deep and resonant yet rising and falling like the desert wind. Then the presenter's voice kicked in again only to cut out, mid-sentence. I went to the radio in the kitchen to fiddle with the dial but I knew what had happened. It was becoming more common. Sometimes it was the wind, but more often the programs that got through were detected and shut down. After a few seconds an announcer came on air to state the time and then introduce a chat show about do-it-yourself home repairs, as if the previous program had never even happened.

I grabbed the wine from the fridge and went outside but even as I was pouring my third glass I knew what I had to do. People like me, we don't act often enough. Perhaps if I were not the kind of man I am I would not have been sitting there alone, contemplating an ashtray, an empty glass, and the prospect of drinking more or just leaving the bottle and going to bed to stare at the ceiling in the dark. I did not know which would be worse. I tossed the wine away into the garden instead, and went inside and shut the back door.

Getting into the car, I drove like crazy, but as I approached the charity store my headlights scanned the pile of discarded belongings and I sighed in relief. The guitar was exactly where I'd left it.

I made the last flight out. It was always a late flight to that country, as if the airline decided that only the bold or the foolish held that sort of commitment, would care enough to be leaving so late, so close to the airport curfew. As if they provided a flight to support the official stance – that the country was not inaccessible – but only as a token gesture. Because who would willingly go there, given all that had happened in the last decade? And given all that *had* happened, I wasn't even sure if I'd need my passport or not, but I took it just in case. Anyway, after I was finished there I might want to fly elsewhere, to a place even farther away.

At the check-in counter the assistant barely looked at my papers, uncaring who might be flying out there or why. She waved me and the guitar straight through to the boarding gate.

'You can take that on board,' she said. 'You'll have a whole row to yourself.'

It was probably deliberate that you had to fly through the night, the dark and the humming of the engine meant to lull you to sleep, so you didn't have to think about what would face you at the end. But I remained awake the entire time. The plane was barely a third full. I could have taken out the guitar and strummed a few chords if I wanted, if I could remember any.

We landed just before dawn and by the time I exited the terminal, light was seeping through the indigo sky. I had forgotten about the desert chill. I stopped and took a jacket out of my backpack, knowing that in another hour or so I'd be taking it off again.

You couldn't fly all the way to that country, of course. We had flown west for hours, but the place where I was heading was now east. To get to it we'd had to fly all the way over it, to the closest town to the border. Now I would have to wait for a supply truck, one authorised to take travellers, as there were no longer any coaches and private cars had long been banned. When one came along, seeming barely to pause to let me in, I realised we would be driving for hours with the rising sun in my eyes. Leaving in haste, at night, I had not thought to bring sunglasses. I threw my backpack and the guitar in the rear seat and climbed on board.

The truck driver did not speak, though he was not unfriendly. He clearly preferred his own company and the sound of whatever he was listening to through earpieces that attached to a player on the dashboard. I closed my eyes and tried to rest as we sped through the morning. We drove for hours in the unbroken silence, the road unexpectedly straight and hard and fast, though, when I thought about it, I supposed it needed to be. Now that the conflict had accelerated, troops would have to be able to get quickly from place to place.

'Checkpoint ahead,' the driver finally said, dislodging me from a near sleep.

By now the light was bright. I squinted and saw ahead the long glittering line that stretched as straight as the road we were on, seeming to cross it. But the road stopped at the checkpoint. The driver waved me out with him, spoke briefly to the security officer at the gate, and returned, tucking his ID card back into his wallet. I wondered if he needed a passport to get through. I wondered about the load he was carrying, what goods were now being allowed through, and why. I barely had time to get my things out of the back before he accelerated and drove through. The gates closed behind him and I stood in the road with the sun falling down like a blessing I did not need.

This was the infamous fence. Three sides of a square at the bottom of the autonomous state now just called Country, stretching to the ocean way up north. Forming a country within the country, as it now was. The cyclone wire fence so straight and neat: if it were a perforated map you could just tear this bit off and toss it away. There had been dingo fences and rabbit-proof fences before – now we had the ultimate fence. A see-through Berlin wall, containing all the people who refused to submit or conform, swept up out of every corner of the country and installed here, forever. Told they could live wherever they wanted in Country, do what they liked: hunt, sleep, fight, sing, make love and music wherever they liked, but they could never come back.

And at the start they literally did not get a thing more: not a ration of bacon, not a sack of flour, not a packet of Band-Aids or a single headache pill. You wanted your lands, you got them back, the government decided. You want your sovereignty, so take it. You wanted country, you now got country, they said. Welcome to Country, said signs posted at all the entry checkpoints along the fence, a message for every new load of people rounded up and brought in.

Except here, at the most accessible side, there was a war, with supplies drip-fed or smuggled through by sympathetic people outside Country. The entire coast, of course, was the weakness, despite fences on every landing point and razor wire on all the beaches. Charities or just charitable people regularly threw supplies over the fence all the way around. No one could ever stop that. And they had never been able to stop the music coming out over the airwaves, despite cutting off the electricity years ago, right at the start.

That community I'd heard singing on the program, that person asking for help, was located around this side of Country. It was probable that if I waited long enough or walked along enough of the fence near one of the checkpoints I would encounter someone on the other side. It happened all the time. People stationed to receive or pass on news and telegraph it back via smoke signals, runners, even just by coo-eeing across the desert lands.

I didn't have a hat, I didn't have anything much, but I had a bottle of water and there was a clump of mulgas, enough shade if I sat patiently. The security officers at the checkpoint, just a donga with an air-conditioning unit almost as big, stared indifferently through me. I wondered, if I was desperate for water or anything, would they help?

Luckily I didn't have to find out. In the early afternoon some figures appeared through the shimmering heat. I walked right up to the fence.

'You heard,' a woman said. 'You came all this way.' She had a couple of kids with her, teenagers.

I nodded and tossed the guitar as high as I could. For a moment I thought it was going to catch on the razor wire, but it only brushed the top of the fence, then wobbled, then fell down straight into her outstretched arms.

I knew not to wait for or expect thanks, so I turned to leave, then stopped, fished the packet of cigarettes out of my backpack and tossed them over too. One of the kids stretched out a hand and caught it like a pro. I hoisted my backpack again and was already walking away when she called out.

'Hey!'

I turned around.

'My boys will love this.' She was holding the guitar horizontally, in two hands, as if it were an offering.

'Good,' I said. 'My boy did. My son loved it too.'

A Fine Day

April, and already it felt like winter. I sat in the lounge room trembling. But Alex made no offer to turn the heater on, so I joined him at the kitchen door. Tried to resist his anxiety. He darted around, balancing plates and saucepan lids on sweaty hands. Thrust a fork into the steamy interior of a pot. I sipped my wine. This was always Alex's culinary style: endless prodding, the heat too high, the vegetables cooked way in advance of the meat. And talking. Lecturing, with tongs aloft, waving them in the air to make his points. Which were beyond me, faced with the prospect of burning poultry. The sacrilege of overcooked snow peas.

My eyes browsed over the rim of my glass. All the cupboard doors were flung wide. The cutlery drawer like an imbecile's jaw. The tap dribbling over congealed fat. Alex now employed a boning knife to slice the bread, then prise the lid off a tin. He fancied himself as the gourmet chef. I couldn't interfere, stood in the doorway instead sipping cask wine. Who'd have thought it. Cask wine this close to the 2020s.

'I don't think it needs salt?' He picked the shaker up but was looking for agreement, not dissent. I liked a lot of salt, but Alex had added health consciousness to his obsessions. He wasn't even paying attention to the meal, being far too preoccupied with work. He would never leave the public service, as much as he complained. Not so long as he could still complain about A, B or Z and find himself superior to them.

'What's Julia's husband like?' I mainly wanted to distract him from adding vinegar to a stir-fry that already looked acidic.

A pause. Alex transferred tongs from right to left hand. Poked his spectacles up his nose, placed the free hand on his hip.

'I like Evan.'

Could three words contain so much! But that was Alex: should have been an actor. Gesture, tone, timing – all impeccable. Three words which said: You know, Evan is difficult, a bit of a prick, really, but I am the only person sensitive and perspicacious enough to see the good points of this man, to see past the superficial irritations to value his character, whereas everyone else dislikes him or misunderstands him. Including his wife. Evan is not without his drawbacks, but I am prepared to forgive them while many others cannot.

I like Evan. I wanted to grab the tea towel dangling from his back pocket and whip him across the face. Sometimes I couldn't believe we were still friends.

'Anyway, they've split up.'

'Really?'

Julia. All the way back to our undergraduate years. I would have been closer to Julia if I'd remained in Canberra. I'd not even got to meet Julia's new husband and now the guy was history. It wasn't hard to make the necessary mental adjustment and delete Evan and return to thinking of Julia as single, but this wasn't the first time her name had come up in the conversation that night. Typical of Alex's little mental games. If I hadn't asked, he would have said nothing then later accused me of not knowing and therefore not caring. And succeeded in making me feel guilty for it. I was convinced we were still friends only because I left Canberra.

More pirouetting and poking, made even more ridiculous by Alex's general pudginess and short-armed movements. Finally he pronounced the chicken ready. He dished it out anxiously, peering over his spectacles, asking how much, was that enough rice, what about the peas, could I handle a few more, was I sure I didn't want the leg, until I could have jabbed him with my fork. What was I doing here, eating an indifferent meal in a cold house in a bleak satellite suburb of a city I no longer cared for? Was our friendship even still alive? This meal was like its wake.

After the first mouthful Alex leaped. 'Is it all right?'

The chicken was dry. The sauce somehow managed to taste both underdeveloped and burnt. The snow peas were khaki and flaccid.

'Good, mate. Lovely.'

I ate, not talking. Alex ate and talked. He dined in the American manner, transferring his fork to his right hand after cutting his food, making the meal more leisurely than it deserved, prolonging the whole sorry ordeal. I scooped up the plates as soon as possible and began the washing-up. Not only for this meal, and a spectacular number of dirtied utensils and dishes at that, but as many from the cupboards as I could disçreetly manage. Especially anything I'd likely be using during my stay. Everything was covered in a film of grease. Not that Alex didn't clean or wash up, but I'd seen him at the sink often. It was an incitement to murder. He'd throw in everything unrinsed, from wine glasses to cast-iron frypans, fill the sink with water, add a squirt of no-frills detergent, then jiggle things around with a finger while pouring another glass of wine. Even with spectacles Alex's eyes were weak, but too often I'd watched him fish items out, shake off the lardy bubbles, then stack them in the drainer, smeared and cloudy. I know I have a thing about dishwashing, a generally un-blokey, Zen kind of approach that savours the ritual. But Alex was far worse than anyone.

I Ajaxed the sink first. Hands sunk in the water, I tackled four worries, while in the next room Alex tinkered with his sound system. First, how much longer could I stay here, with someone constantly seeking approval for every domestic achievement? So far Alex had demanded admiration of: his Ikea bookshelves, a new shower curtain, and the pots of herbs on the back porch. I'd been here two hours and was already thinking of home.

Second, the problem of a departed wife. The main reason I had, between work commitments, agreed to come down for a few days. Not dearly departed, but she may as well have died and gone to the afterlife, the way Alex had been talking. And since I'd arrived he'd barely stopped talking about her and I didn't want to stay with Helen too. Or Alex's version of her. That meal, chicken and stir-fry – it was her dish, I knew, something she cooked all the time. Alex was only pretending.

Third . . .

'Do you want to listen to the news? Or that new Sigur Rós album? I could Spotify it.'

I really wanted to telephone Riley (he would be where?), get warm, preferably in a hot bath, then go to bed with a great book I'd begun the day before. Sigur Rós were from a cold country, weren't they? I shivered.

'News.'

'Good. Then we can keep talking if it gets boring.'

Not good. Third, there were more reasons by the minute why I was finding Alex and his house so repellent after years of friendship. The perpetually soggy bathroom floor, the hard towels, the insulting Palmolive Gold soap – did his guests need extra help in the hygiene department? – the lack of real coffee, the brown-leafed African violet on the kitchen windowsill that had sat there as long as I could remember and had never once flowered. All the credit I'd unconsciously allocated this friendship seemed used up. Things previously tolerated were now placing it seriously in the red.

I shivered again. Four worries: it was so cold in Canberra.

*

Alex wanted me to help him persuade Helen to return. But what was I thinking of, even agreeing to visit? My own partner was, I suspected, starting to stray. Perhaps it was work, which he couldn't discuss. Or perhaps it was something else. Only last week Riley had come home, disappeared again, returned, then gone off again after yet another late-night call. Alex had sounded so forlorn I agreed to go down and try to help him. I didn't have any ready excuse not to.

'It's perfect weather here at the moment,' he had lied. 'Beautiful. The trees are metamorphosing.' Alex would never use a normal word when there was a Latinate polysyllabic to hand. 'And I'm not so busy at work. We could go to a play. Or the movies.'

'I can't, my car's playing up,' I had lied in return. 'And Riley needs his.'

Then Alex had offered: 'I'll pay for your flight. You love plane trips.'

Now the price of that ticket was clear.

We sat in the frigid lounge room with the ABC on. Alex was perched on a velour pouffe. With his weight it looked like he was laying a large brown egg. Over the news reports, he commented and ranted and wobbled back and forth while I shivered and thought about escape to the spare room. Which would be even colder. I wanted to disappear and read *The Sparsholt Affair*, and Alex wanted Helen back, but as I thought longingly of Oxford in 1940 and he spoke passionately of Helen, I realised that he didn't want her back – he only wanted to talk about having her back. I finally got the point: it was not that he was devoted to her; rather she filled his need to have a problem. Several problems. Alex had a series of unhappy obsessions and this was what made him happy. Work, Helen, workmates, women generally, the council harassing him over his front fence: they were all part of the banquet of conflict and warfare that was Alex's entire life. He spread this out on the dining table of his personality years ago. When the odd morsel dropped on the carpet, like now, it was profoundly distressing.

No wonder I found him so irritating. No wonder Helen had left.

'Actually, I thought we could go to *Uncle Vanya*.' He killed the TV.

'When, tonight?' It was getting on for eight. 'Have you got tickets?'

'Oh, we could pick them up at the door. It's only a small theatre company, at the uni.'

Even under benign conditions, the idea of *Uncle Vanya* failed to excite me. For some reason I had always found the northern European dramatists depressing, even their comedies. Especially their comedies. *Uncle Vanya* tonight in the cold was unimaginable. To sit in an unheated theatre with student actors trotting out lines about the enchanting weather and one's unbounded happiness, or discussing the temperature of the samovar . . . Maybe in the original language it would sound better. But in Canberran Australian English, with the wind whipping down Northbourne Avenue sending gusty draughts into the theatre . . .

It *was* imaginable.

'Then again, it's running all week,' Alex said.

So complete escape was not in the bag. Though there was a strong possibility it would be cancelled due to lack of interest. I felt a tiny pang of guilt. Alex had majored in drama studies. Once auditioned for NIDA. His public service job was punishingly uncreative.

'I want you to find her.'

'What?' I was preoccupied with the thought of my lucky escape from the cynicism of Vomitski – no, Voitski – and long passionate speeches about the disappearing forests. Maybe the Russian would not sound that much brighter.

'Talk to her. Ask her to come back.' His gaze was earnest through his thick spectacles. And I hadn't been listening properly.

'You want me to get her back? Why me?'

'She won't talk to me. Hasn't for months.'

'But I hardly know her.'

I had met Helen three, four times. First time at the wedding. No, not wedding. Marriage. There was an occasion, true, and a certificate, but nothing approaching the white-dress, tiered-cake and keg-of-beer style of occasion. There was no ritual in their austere coupling in the park at the end of Alex's street: a Colorbond fence surrounding a parched lawn featuring grevilleas clipped too severely for native birds to bother visiting. This was followed by dinner at a near-empty Chinese restaurant where Alex's friends discovered we were all meeting Helen for the first time, though we knew that he kept the compartments of his life separate. We all pretended not to notice his parents bickering the entire night. To like the soggy dim sum entrée and tinned lychees for dessert. None of her family was present, County Cork being a long way off.

Now he wanted her back. The marital abode was too empty. He'd lived here long before they got together. I suspected that was part of the problem. But what about people who knew her better, closer friends, ones who lived here, people she worked with? Alex shook his head.

'The fact you don't know her well is so much better. She'll resent anyone closer getting involved.'

'I'm not sure about that.'

'I'll pay you.'

'Don't be a dick. I'm your friend.' Just.

'But you and Riley do this sort of thing? I'm happy to pay for a professional job.'

'Riley is in security, not surveillance. And I just do the books.' I'd explained this a million times. Was it the perennial dullness of public service life or did Alex believe there was more to Riley's spontaneous trips? He seemed convinced there was something cloak and dagger-ish about our lifestyle. Riley knew as much about retrieving lost spouses as he did about particle theory. 'We've never looked for a missing person before.'

'Oh, Helen's not missing.'

No wonder at times I wanted to kill him. 'Then why do you want me to find her?'

'I mean, I sort of know where she is. Here, in Canberra.'

'Then why can't you find her?' I still thought of the place

as an overgrown country town. Walk down the main street, hang about the Woden shops, go to the theatre, and you'd bump into everyone sooner or later. Helen was probably out at *Uncle Vanya* right now.

'She won't have anything to do with me. Yvonne at the lab hinted she was still in town. Now she won't talk to me either.' Helen worked as a research assistant in a laboratory somehow connected to the ANU.

Poor Alex. There were more than a dozen years of friendship between us but also a gulf of misunderstanding. Just how wide that gulf was hit me next.

'It was all failure from the start. We never slept together before we were married. Then afterwards . . . But we were always good friends, you know. Close. That's what counts in a marriage, don't you think?' He looked at me, pleading. Those glass-plated eyes were almost threatening.

Of course friendship counted. 'But doesn't sex count for something?' I said. 'Just a bit?'

'Not if the relationship's genuine. Not in an open marriage. You're so middle-class, Tasman.'

I refrained from pointing out the obvious – if it was so genuine then why had she left? – and instead leaped to the offensive.

'Middle-class! You're the one with the public service career and the three-bedroom house in the suburbs. Plus you drive a Volvo.' Alex slumped into his pouffe. 'Anyway, if you're trying to tell me that you and Helen pursued sexual relationships elsewhere then isn't it likely she's gone off with some lover? Hadn't you better find out who he is? And what about you? Are you having it off with someone? Maybe she's jealous, or hurt, or –'

'No!' He stood up. 'You don't get it.' He was almost shaking. Then he took a deep breath. 'Yes, it's likely Helen has gone off with someone. But it wouldn't be a him.'

Finally, a chink of light. Alex was close to tears so I patted the pouffe. 'Sit down. Maybe I don't understand, but you're not doing much to help.'

He shook his head again and sat. Sighed. 'There was no one else for me. And Helen . . . Well, Helen married me to stay in Australia. Otherwise she had to return to Cork, and the family. They're very strict. Catholics, of course. She got away because she couldn't bear it. All her sisters were married, with kids.'

The chink was getting wider. 'Do you think she's always been a lesbian?'

'Yeah, probably.'

'And marrying you might have been to try and escape that?'

'Cure it. That's what she said. Her family and everything.'

'And you married her knowing or suspecting all this?' He nodded. 'And despite the open marriage thing, you've been . . . faithful? Chaste?' He nodded again, looking at the floor.

I felt a prickle of pity. A marriage of some inconvenience to him. Or was it? And an agreement to dally down the primrose path, except in his case it had led nowhere. Alex had never had luck with women. At university he was appealing in a scholarly, bearded way, and plenty of young women were attracted to men who could quote Shakespeare as well as complete tax returns. But nothing ever seemed to work out. He would go cold after the first date. I wondered if he'd ever come to terms with his own sexuality, if there was something deep-seated and passionate about his suspicion of lesbians. And his evident belief that he could rescue them. Or at least one. Despite the fact that of all our friends I should be the one who could talk about this, I couldn't. I just couldn't ask Alex.

We met for lunch the next day on the corner of the Sydney building. Or the Melbourne one. I always mixed them up.

'They left . . . huh . . . huh . . . halfway through.' Alex was puffing after the walk from Marcus Clarke Street. Despite the cold wind he was unfit enough to produce a constellation of sweat across his forehead.

'What are you talking about?'

'The others, last night. They told me they left the play at interval.'

'What others? At *Uncle Vanya*?'

'Julia, and a couple of others from finance.'

'You didn't tell me there were others! That it was a definite arrangement.' In fact I wouldn't have minded seeing Julia. Maybe the others.

'Oh, it wasn't a firm commitment,' he said far too airily. 'Anyway, I explained that you were too tired and depressed. About Riley.'

'You what? What do you mean, about Riley?'

'He wouldn't come here with you.'

'He's got work.' I began to walk quickly. The wind was icy. Fuck him. He was the one with major marital problems.

'Look, I didn't mind. Really.'

'Good.' I walked faster. Alex puffed, catching up.

'Besides, you were right. She said the play was terrible.' He glanced at me. I said nothing. 'Anyway, I didn't really want to spend time with Julia. Not after work as well. Just splitting up with Evan. She's coming on a bit too heavy for me. I need my own space at the moment.'

I resisted the urge to punch him, and not just for the clichés. The very idea that Julia might have fancied him . . .

'Why was it so bad? The performance?' I couldn't help myself.

'Someone was reading from the script, a last-minute stand-in. And the one playing Telegin had a cold and kept blowing his nose.'

The wind propelled us along, towards Alex's club.

'A fine day to kill oneself.'

'What?'

'Just a line from the play,' I said. 'The only one I properly remember.' To be fair, it was years since we'd seen it, on another distinctly off-kilter Alex night.

Downstairs, the club was cosy enough. The menu was basic but the place was warm.

'Steak and chips and a beer,' I ordered. 'And you're paying.'

Alex conveyed high-minded disapproval by ordering a salad without dressing and a mineral water. He hated being both health-conscious and overweight. Normally I wouldn't drink at lunchtime but I was inclined to be provocative.

'Have you thought about talking to Helen?' Alex asked.

'I don't think there's much I can do. I suppose I could try, but . . .' Alex was looking too earnestly at me, his bullet-proof spectacles reflecting the potted palms of the club centrepiece behind me.

'What about her family? Have you tried there?'

He looked away. 'She's not in touch with them. And I've never spoken to them.'

'Never? What about the wedding?'

'None of them came. You remember.'

Along with his bickering parents and the dreadful Cantonese food, like we were eating out in Goulburn in 1965, I did remember that. And Helen's cold appraisal when Riley and I were first introduced to her, how she turned away and muttered something about our matching suits, which could have been complimentary but I found condescending.

'Did they even know you were married?'

'She told them.' He shrugged. 'She said she told them.'

I ate a chip. Alex was clearly leaving information out but then Helen was the black lamb of her family. And they were in Creagh, County Cork. Still, it was a global community and even villagers on the bottom of Ireland were just a Facebook click away. Alex and Helen had met in the library one night when he was finishing his master's. She'd been here for less than a year and was working in the lab while applying to take a science degree. At least, that was what Alex had always said.

'Are you sure this is the full story?'

'What do you mean? You think I'm making all this up?'

'Only asking if you've remembered everything. Names, phone numbers, addresses?'

'You're talking to a person who knows every Melbourne Cup winner since Archer in 1861. Ridden by John Cutts. Trainer, Etienne de Mestre.' I must have rolled my eyes. He leaned closer. 'Someone who memorised the periodic table of the elements in school. Primary school. Of course I remember!' His forehead was glistening again.

'Sorry.' I finished my beer. 'You're not eating?'

Alex had barely taken a mouthful of his salad. 'Not hungry.'

'Are you feeling all right?' His sweaty face looked paler than usual.

'Fine.' He pushed his plate away and tossed the napkin on top. 'I haven't forgotten anything, you know.'

There was no logic in this. Plenty of men knew the cricket scores for the last fifty years but never remembered where they put their keys. Riley was one of these men, though I was not. I was very good with keys, wallets, phones. Not so sure about missing wives.

'All right, what if I visit this Yvonne after lunch, see if she knows anything?'

'Good. Are you finished?'

'No.' I beckoned the waiter and ordered the cheese plate. 'And a strong flat white, thanks.'

Disapproval gleamed from behind Alex's spectacles but I ignored him. If I was going to be bullied into finding a wife I would at least obtain some small indulgences.

*

By the time I reached Helen's place of work, I was glad of them. It had taken me three buses through suburbs named Deakin, Hughes and Pearce, along streets called Kitchener, Hodgson and Mawson, and by the end of it I'd had enough of famous dead men. The lab was at a place called, incongruously, Bunda Bunda. The person I sought was working alone in one of the smaller buildings in the complex, a block like a school demountable. Yvonne appeared puzzled, then suspicious. When I mentioned Alex she leaped up off her stool.

'You're his friend!'

'It's all right, he's not contagious. A little toxic now and then.'

She thought for a moment, then sighed.

'Helen's not here. We had a drink after work last Friday, then yesterday she didn't turn up. I thought she was having a flexi day. She had to take the cat to the vet or something. Then today, no Helen. I've tried ringing but no answer. I thought I'd try her place after work, before ringing the police.'

The police? It hadn't occurred to me that it might be serious.

'Where's she staying?'

'You're his friend. She doesn't want him to know.'

'I promise I won't tell him.' I explained how we went back years, how Alex got on my nerves but was like a mild skin complaint, something you got used to and didn't bother trying to cure any more. How he was devastated by Helen leaving, how he wanted to talk to her.

'I know all about his desperation and desolation. I've answered enough calls in the past few months . . .'

'He told me he'd only rung once or twice.'

She shook her head. 'He rang here every day at first, then about two, three times a week until late last week, then nothing. Helen was furious. She told me not to tell him a thing, not even that she was still working here. She changed her number, of course.'

'But why? People break up all the time, it doesn't mean you don't talk to the other person. You have to talk about the house, the bank, the cat, something.'

'She wasn't angry at first, just fed up. He pestered the life out of her, always anxious about everything. Used to ring her every minute of the day, for the stupidest reasons.'

'That sounds like someone who cares a lot.' But then I recalled how just last night he was hovering with tongs, almost counting the grains of rice I was eating, fussing over the radio, the music. Demanding that whatever was up, he be the one to fix it, stroke it, feed it, understand it. Yet never noticing I was freezing all night. Alex's domestic performance. All so fake. Designed to draw attention. She must have stopped wanting to be the audience.

'I wonder why she ever married him,' Yvonne said.

'It was unexpected.'

'I know that Helen was lonely, Alex was lonely. She needed to stay in Australia. He had this empty house. I suppose they were both misfits. And they thought that they'd both misfit nicely together.'

'Yvonne, Alex told me Helen and he . . . well . . .' Awkward. I'd only just met the woman.

'I met Helen at Fancy Nancy's,' she said.

Click. Fancy Nancy's. Diamante. V & V. Freddy's. Canberra was full of specialty bars, I hadn't forgotten that.

'She told me about the position here.' Yvonne gestured around the lab. 'And no, if you're wondering, we aren't on together, never have been.'

'None of my business.'

'Well, what is your business?'

'Alex just wants to talk to her. I said I'd help, as a friend, that's all. But now you say you're worried. Do you think she would have gone away just to get him off her back?'

'She's not that sort of person. You know what he's like.'

Over the years I had felt like killing him, and again just last night. But then I'd imagine going to confront Alex and being met with those silly short arms, that bespectacled puzzlement. Maybe Alex's real problem was that people didn't care enough one way or the other.

'I'm going to close up early here and go to Melba.'

'Melba?' Melba!

'Helen's flat's there.'

I gave Yvonne my card, in case. She tucked it into the back pocket of her jeans where it would probably remain until the next wash.

The door was locked. I checked the time again: Alex had said he was having a flexi afternoon and would be home. I knocked again, then again, louder. The aluminium screen door rattled noisily. A dog barked. The neighbour's head appeared from behind a lasiandra shrub.

'Sorry,' I said.

'I saw him come home, a few hours ago.' He waved his secateurs at the door. 'Don't think he went out again. I've been out here all afternoon working.' He waved them again and I noticed the garden bags bulging with clippings. A gust of wind sent a stray twig gliding down the otherwise bare driveway. His dog ran up. We both watched as it caught the twig and returned to him. I stared at the dog, a kelpie-something cross, who dropped the twig and stared back. A fine day to kill oneself. It struck me why, given Alex's prodigious memory, he hadn't responded to that line from *Uncle Vanya*.

'You might be worried?'

I looked up at the man. 'Yes. Excuse me.'

I turned to the front door again and placed my backpack down, opening the screen door, which had not been locked. I lifted my foot and applied an R.M.Williams hard next to the lock. It flew open. Cheap ex-government places. I walked inside.

'No point in coming now.' I was sitting on the front step, talking to Riley on the phone. The police were still inside, the ambos had left. The neighbour's dog had come to sit next to me, leaning hard against my side, as kelpies do.

'It looks like Alex set all this up just so someone would be here to find him.'

'I'm really sorry. I can get there first thing tomorrow if you really want.'

'It's okay. Listen, I've got to go.'

'Tas?' he said. 'Tas?' His voice was already distant.

'Ring you back soon.' I pressed end and looked at the phone.

Inside, a police officer was in the living room, another in the kitchen. Irrational pride flooded me, thinking of the great effort I had made with the washing-up the night before. I went to the bathroom, conscious of a sudden urge to pee. It seemed to go on forever. Washing my hands I jammed the Palmolive Gold back into the soap dish harder than necessary, then quickly dried them and walked out. The thought had just occurred that I probably had to find a way to contact Yvonne when my phone rang again.

'You are kidding.'

'I wish,' Yvonne said. 'She was in her bed, dressed. She looked peaceful.'

'So did Alex. Let me guess: morphine overdose?'

'Yeah, they think so.'

I sighed. For the second time that day I thought, How very Chekhovian.

SECOND

Festive Food for the Whole Family

YOUR CHRISTMAS LUNCH or dinner need not be constrained by those fussy and inflexible eaters within the family. A perfectly splendid meal can still be created with a broader range of ingredients than might normally be used for a festive occasion, along with some careful planning and preparation in the weeks before. Knowing well in advance the dietary requirements of your guests will assist considerably, so you are urged to approach them with a checklist before finalising your menu. Modern families typically comprise vegetarians, vegans, non-pork eaters, seafood allergics and coeliacs, meaning your pantry should be comprehensive enough to provide anything from gluten-free fruit cake to tasty alternatives to roast turkey.

Naturally you commence with the pudding, which is already sugar-free, as you have been making this for years, relying entirely on the natural sweetness of the dried fruit. It will be easy to replace the wheat flour with a healthier rice flour, or even with ground hazelnuts; however, do not forget your younger sister's nut allergy and while you shall warn her in advance, you should perhaps on the day also present her with her own sugar-, nut- and gluten-free little pudding, just to be on the safe side. This is what Christmas is for: thoughtfulness, selfless gifts, reconciliation, peace on earth and within families.

Do remember that some guests will not consume alcohol and this goes not only for the cake and pudding but also for the brandy butter, which of course will not be eaten by the vegans. However, a more than acceptable version may be made with vanilla pods and coconut cream, and fat-reduced options will be best for those watching their weight. Note that while it might be tempting for you to regard the festive season as a time for liberation from diet-consciousness, others may not agree.

A perfectly acceptable gluten-free and vegan version of Christmas cake may be made with fine polenta, macadamia or coconut oil, a good quality dried fruit mix pre-soaked in cold tea, and spices that you should grind yourself for better flavour. Adding black pepper will be your secret ingredient to enhance the piquancy, and while the lack of eggs will mean the cake is somewhat unbound, the final moist texture will more than make up for this.

A good cook – and thus a successful Christmas meal host – will remember all the small but crucial details. For example, that jelly is prohibited to vegans, so the witty jellied salad in festive colours (cherry tomatoes, lebanese cucumber) you had considered making will only be consumed by the vegetarians in your midst. Or that the fish sauce in the Vietnamese dressing for the papaya salad must be omitted. And that you must find a substitute for the sugar in it. That there will be at least one Jewish guest and though they may not be strictly kosher they will not be pleased if faced with meat from a cloven-hoofed beast that has not chewed its cud. For the overall meal you should strive to provide as much from your own garden as possible, however modest this may seem; simple homegrown parsley and spinach and lemons from the tree will have their freshness guaranteed, not to mention a quality of flavour that surpasses any organic grocery store certification.

The best host of all will be the one who accommodates every guest's preference or allergy, no matter how rare the condition or self-indulgent the food choice may appear, since Christmas is that time for peace, love and reconciliation, and so on. Your uncle who is allergic to seafood always expects to be seated far away from the offending food since even the merest brush with a discarded prawn tail or oyster shell could mean an emergency trip to the hospital. This has happened in previous years and it has meant that he has thereafter been exempted from the washing-up, so as not to risk contamination. Likewise, your Jewish uncle-in-law, who soon after his arrival will remind you that he also does not eat shellfish.

However, on the day you triumphantly announce that your pretty platter of prawns and smoked salmon is made entirely from a potato starch, soy and angelica – not gelatine – compound, and that you have used an organic vegetable dye to paint on the orange-red stripes. The seafood sauce contains neither egg nor dairy. You pickled your own capers from the garden nasturtiums.

As your vegan cousin has brought her new fruitarian girlfriend they must be seated closest to the fruit platter which you have sourced from the organic co-op and selected with imagination: three types of banana, along with star fruit, guava and mangosteens, all far more interesting than the cherries and grapes that anyone can provide at this time of the year. They have brought their dog, Vita, who is not only also a vegan, but has a gluten allergy and cannot eat conventional dog kibble. Vita shall be dining on raw carrot sticks, which apparently she enjoys to such an extent that she will even perform tricks for them.

The remaining vegetarian and vegan cousins, aunts and older nieces and nephews have wanted to be seated at the non-seafood and non-meat end, anticipating that there is probably no easy way to avoid the turkey and ham centrepieces. However, you proudly assure your guests that the former is made entirely from rice and soy, rolled and seasoned to resemble a boned and stuffed breast (gluten-free breadcrumbs for the stuffing), while the latter is actually a cunning mix of breadcrumbs (gluten-free), egg substitute, sweet potato and smoked paprika, tinted pink with beetroot juice. The cranberry sauce is innocent of everything but cranberries. The only person who should not eat that is your younger niece, who is allergic to red berries, in fact to anything red.

The bread in the bread sauce is organic, salt-reduced and gluten-free and the vegetable stock is all vegetable, also salt-reduced. Your grandmother has made the bread sauce for years but you have relieved her of this contribution to the festive meal in deference to her years. She tastes a tiny portion of this sauce with a certain look on her face but then she eats very little these days anyway.

Unexpectedly, the greatest challenge was not the seafood platter, but finding a healthy alternative to roast vegetables, seeing as so many of the guests are cutting down on carbs. Of course carbs cannot be avoided altogether, but you must be seen to have made some effort: your own husband is prone to patting his stomach and ruefully talking about how he has given up beer and now eats salads for lunch, not burgers. The roast vegetable platter you produce might look like roast potatoes and pumpkin but it is artfully not, and you are particularly proud of the way you have slightly burned the corners of the chopped smoked tofu to resemble the way pumpkin caramelises at high heat. This dish is garnished with fresh rosemary from the garden.

Beans are easy. Everyone loves French green beans and you have steamed then blanched them in iced water to retain their vivid colour, then finished them in a light garlic and lemon juice dressing (the lemons are from the garden). Therefore it is something of a surprise when one of the children begins coughing and choking, and your older sister turns and asks you why you didn't string these beans properly, before taking the child out to be sick in the garden.

This small setback notwithstanding, you smile and refuse anyone's offer – there are only two – to help clear the main course, and while you busy yourself in the kitchen your husband ensures that the glass of every drinker is refilled.

You re-enter the dining room to remind him that the cloudy unfiltered apple juice with no added sugar is in the garage fridge, and find him leaning very close over your younger sister, but when he stands upright it is clear that he has simply been careful not to spill a drop as he refills her glass. He tops up your aunt's rosé, and then approaches your grandfather with the bottle of port; however, you decide that he will want his cup of tea, which you make, adding two spoonfuls of real white sugar despite knowing your mother is monitoring his diabetic diet with the eye of an eagle. When you return to the dining room with this cup of tea your mother peers at it but you say, very quickly, that you have made it with real tea, not a teabag.

By this stage of the meal your husband is leaning back against the sideboard where you have been careful to place the bowl of dried nuts well out of reach of the children. He is cracking walnuts deftly in one palm. He is very good at this. It is something of a party trick and he smiles at you and winks, while the children gape in admiration from the quarantine of their mother's side. In front of him, Vita is begging prettily, and the vegan cousin and fruitarian girlfriend loudly and in unison instruct him not to give her so much as a crumb of walnut. You hurry to the kitchen for more carrot sticks. After this treat is administered Vita needs to be ushered outside to pee.

It surprises you at first to understand that washing up by hand rather than dishwasher is actually advised on this occasion, given the volume of dirty dishes and the rapidity with which they accumulate. You do this yourself, even if there are offers of help, for the sake of peace (it is tl you remember) and because there is at least or of the family whose rare skin condition means any contact with detergents or perfumes in detergents or perhaps both is catastrophic. You should know which member of the family this is but you are somewhat tired and have now decided to drink a second glass of champagne, which always makes your head fuzzy.

It is because of this, the head fuzziness, that when you go to the linen closet in the hall for fresh tea towels and you see your husband emerging from the bathroom, you imagine he looks furtive, and is wiping his mouth more thoroughly than he probably is.

Back in the kitchen your vegan cousin's fruitarian girlfriend is standing with the final dirty platters from the table and, fixing you with a gaze through her thick purple-framed glasses, she asks how the papaya in the green papaya salad has managed to fall from the tree naturally, if it is green. The perfect host would have a sound explanation for this; however, you are by now tired (and fuzzy) so you tell her it is from the neighbour's garden and that you shook the tree very, very gently. That it dropped straight into a bed of fresh straw in a basket. And that you covered it in a pure organic cotton cloth, brought it home and played Sufi music to it for three nights in a row then chanted a Buddhist prayer of forgiveness before you peeled it and put it through the mandoline grater.

Returning to the dining room, you place the pudding, the brandy- and butter-free brandy butter, the Christmas cake and, for the children, the dried-fruit–free White Christmas with reduced sugar on the table, only to notice some absences. You find Vita out in the back garden licking up the last of the green-bean vomit, as your vegan cousin and her fruitarian girlfriend appear and commence yelling and showing signs of taking their leave, such as coaxing Vita into her mauve diamante harness. You return to the kitchen and start thinking about the coffee situation. Vita's owners would probably not have wanted coffee anyway, and she certainly does not, and if they do all return next year you shall have had plenty of time to consider appropriate hot drinks.

Your younger sister reappears and, despite looking flushed, reaches for another glass of wine. Your older sister has already packed up her two children's presents and toys, holding the green-bean choker close and lightly smacking away the hand of the other as he reaches for the White Christmas. No sugar, she explains to you, not even reduced sugar, otherwise I'll never get him to sleep tonight. You decide not to tell her about the candy canes he took off the tree earlier.

Despite the exertions and frustrations of the day you do not forget you are still the host. You are by now making coffee for those who are not asleep in armchairs (grandmother, uncle) or have decided to move onto exotic liqueurs (sister, husband, two remaining cousins), and this involves, firstly, an espresso for your older sister to scull quickly before heading out the door. You have already ensured you have various combinations of milks and coffees in order to make a long black with a dash of soy milk for your mother, a decaf almond-milk latte for your other aunt, three espresso martinis, and finally a Moccona instant with a dash of rum for your father. After making this last you decide on one for yourself, not holding back on the rum.

With so much thought, care and planning there should not be a single hiccup let alone catastrophe (beyond the bean/vomit incident), but as you are stacking away the best plates a distinct screaming comes from the dining room. Then your younger sister appears, extremely red in the face with visible swelling, and asks what nuts you put into the cake, and when you explain none, she demands to know the full list of ingredients. Handing her a glass of water, which she knocks flying from rage or distress, you list them. The swelling around her lips increases by the second and just before they meet permanently she manages to cry out that coconut oil is from coconuts you idiot which are nuts you fucking idiot and that you have deliberately sabotaged her Christmas you total fucking idiot and this is so typical you think you are so clever that you can not only shame her with her lack of culinary skills but now actually try to kill her, on Christmas Day.

Admittedly, you did consider adding Frangelico to her espresso martini instead of Tia Maria, but as it happened there was no need since you knew it was not the coconut oil but the fact she was in the bathroom kissing your husband, not long after he ate all those walnuts.

At this point you also realise that of everyone's culinary requirements for this special meal, you have neglected to consider your own. It has been a long and tiring day in the kitchen but a freshness and imagination and indeed keenness for culinary endeavour may be still summoned despite all your earlier fatigue. So much so that when your husband comes in to help your sister administer her EpiPen you commence smacking one hand clean across his handsome face. What you imagine doing next is easy: grabbing that part of his body which has caused so much damage to your festive occasion, and slicing it off with a cook's knife. Allowing the blood to drain into the sink, you would sear the fresh cut in olive oil in a cast iron pan until browned, then finish off in a hot oven (220 deg) for ten minutes. After resting for a further ten minutes, you could slice this into rounds: the number of slices would very much depend on the length of this cut of meat. You could serve this over a bed of any wilted greens, but a bitter leaf such as endive or rocket would definitely be best. Finish it with a chopped parsley garnish, cracked black pepper, a squeeze of lemon, and smear of hot English mustard. The correct wine would be pinot noir.

How to Mend a Broken Heart

WHAT WAS NEVER going to happen again does. You are thirty, you are forty, you are forty-five, and you still don't learn. You are an index of feelings from the deep end of the dictionary. Regret and remorse. Sadness and sorrow. All the feelings that weigh your disappointed heart down. Even aware that you are at risk of becoming a stereotype, you cannot stop the leaden, numbing pain of the oldest story in the book, which you need, for some god-only-knows reason, to tell again, this hackneyed story, this exhausted, dried-up narrative, for which there are no new words, no fresh images, no original metaphors. But there is still this compulsion to find them when you know they cannot be found. You have gone over and over this in your head in the early hours, when sleep remains a stranger outside the door, sniggering just loud enough for you to hear but refusing to enter the room.

Oh, but you said numbing pain, and that is far from true, in fact you wish it were true, for if so your heart really would be numb and then you would not suffer this story to be told. For it may be your heart, your love, your trust, your everything involved here but it is only a story, which means it had a beginning, a middle and will have an end. More than that, it will recede into the narrative of your life, your wry, comical, rather dysfunctional life, the one you unwrap at dinner parties and pass around for light entertainment and laughs in between the sashimi and the salad. Your friends appreciate this. You are such good company. At dinner.

But meanwhile there is the problem of this badly damaged organ, which needs to keep functioning though you wish it were tougher and more durable, to see you through the rest of your loving days. Your broken heart is so very sore. Open, exposed. And while a cold wind blows through it, your heart remains too hot, burning with pain. How could you have been so careless and profligate, to devote so much of yourself to one person? You have squandered yourself. Devotion and loyalty, you assumed, would be repaid in kind. You should have been more restrained. You should have remembered the only rule, the one constant, the thing you can rely on absolutely, even if everything else is a shifting, elusive, phantom set of rules: it will always end in tears.

The problem, as ever, is language. The c word again. No, not the word you think (they love that), but the other one, the one they hate. It's like a mouthful of sour wine, a bite into a rotten apple. They won't have it on their tongue. They think it means something else; they shrivel at its sound. They think it means *noun:* 1. end of fun, or 2. lack of freedom.

But get the dictionary, the definition is clear: all it offers are words like trust, consign, preserve, pledge. Commit is a verb. Definition 6. To consign, especially for safekeeping, *to commit one's soul to God*. You did exactly this, you consigned something for safekeeping, you handed over your heart, and look at it now, torn and bleeding like the prey of a fox. No safekeeping at all.

Yet now, as you examine your wounded heart (yes, wounded, you are that trite) you find it is not here that it hurts at all, but lower in your body. Your chest, in fact, feels remarkably whole. It is your stomach that registers all this pain. Eat? Not for days. It is part of the script, is it not? You can't eat. Of course you can't. Your stomach is a whirlpool. Your bowels feel either too tight or too loose. The idea of eating summons the taste of bile. But it's not so much the nutrition as the necessary ritual. And, in that, the necessary preparation, all of which adds up to time, concentration, activity. Three vital aspects of the healing process.

So you should eat. You shall eat. But just peering into the pantry, opening the refrigerator, depresses you. There are only so many instant noodles and no-brand cereals that you can live on. And the milk has run out. No, what you need is fresh food, prepared by your own hands. You will need to stock that fridge. It's empty, lonely. Its cold light reveals nothing but jars of pickles and olives, bottles of water, the tail ends of processed foods, salamis and cheese, dried, hard. Like his heart must be (you will cling to these clichés . . .). Vodka, on ice. The stainless-steel shaker that you keep – kept – in the door to make the cocktails you both love. Loved.

Shut the door swiftly again, for its contents, abject as they are, remind you of meals and drinks made for two.

You must shop. And no cheating with on-line shopping, but out there up at the supermarket, along with the elderly and the young mothers and all the other people you have felt you were so far above. With a wonky trolley. A form of punishment but one you need. The frozen vegetable aisle. The meat counter. The hot roast chickens, date *and* time stamped, cheaper as the day wears on. This is what you need.

But, oh, the ordinariness of it is so hard to bear. The ordinariness rises up like a demon, taunting you as you select a brand of curry paste, a form of pasta. The risible nature of this prosaic activity. Even doing the shopping cannot prevent your eyes flooding again. You reach for a two-pack of paper towels and have to replace them to find a tissue and blot your eyes again. Just the corners of your eyes, discreetly, so the people around you do not know that you are really soaking up that oozing part of you that is the byproduct of your dying heart, again. So that they think you are just watery-eyed from the cold air. You still need to get on with it, for you need to return home with the right ingredients to make a chicken curry or a spinach pie, and start the ritual of peeling, slicing, frying and stirring that will help keep you going.

And there's yet more ritual. You still need it. The tedium of the checkout queue must be endured. More punishment for your wayward soul. That elderly couple with tiny portions of every loose product being individually weighed and priced. The jar of sauce that has to be sent back for checking. The woman who insists the two-for-ten-dollars offer on the chocolate ice cream hasn't appeared on her docket. People who laboriously count out coins from tiny purses. Whose last dollar falls in between the counter and the cash register. The old couple with a trolley full of no-brand dog food on special, which you hope really is for a dog. The kicking toddler behind you, perhaps the same one who was screaming in aisle four, and his mother, whose trolley keeps nudging yours as if it's your responsibility, this long, frustrating queue, and yours to fix. Good for you. You need this form of everyday suffering. After it is over you can take your groceries and depart. Past the staffie cross (a relief to see it) tied up out the front, through the hazards of parking-spot Nazis and parents racing the end-of-school clock. Finally, home to stock the fridge and what about, seeing as it's so empty, cleaning it up first? How long since you've done that? Same with the oven. And then the ritual of preparing a meal.

See how much time has passed. See how the hours have ticked over and in some of those hundreds of minutes there have been a few – more than a few – when you have not thought of him, or felt the pain in your belly. And while you're waiting for this meal to cook you may as well write. Lose yourself in the process. Just open a notebook, take a pen and write anything at all. Let the words drag you along and out into the light. Let them be oars that carry you across the water. Where you might be rowing to is of no consequence, it is the action that is required. And the fact that on the water there are things to see that you did not know existed until you stepped into the boat. The way the surface, which seems so solid from the shore, breaks apart, like pieces of stained glass, a moving mosaic that is remade every second. The curious objects that float past. A child's dummy. An old biscuit tin, the lid rusted on tight, the parrot on the top still visible. A piece of timber, a miniature raft, bearing a lone gull. As well as all the usual stuff, the weeds, the plastic bottles, the bald tennis balls. Fishing lines, goon sacks, umbrella carcases, scraps of styrofoam. Abject as they are, all parts of a story somewhere.

You swore you would never write this story because you have contempt for writing as therapy and because, of course, you were never going to have your heart broken again. But there it is, broken, and the wound isn't even a clean one. It's ragged and infected, and with that you commence this story about how to mend a broken heart, as if you know, as if you've learned anything, as if you've found one fresh word or new image with which to express your anguish and the torment of rejected love. And in the end as you write there is a momentary sense of relief, a brief lapse when the pain becomes more of an ache, something approaching healing, for a while. And the oven timer pings. Your spinach pie is ready.

Migraine for Beginners

Migraine and the Wall

You're sitting on your bed. It's twilight, nearly the end of the second or third day. In your room, your little room upstairs that overlooks the street. You're upstairs in your room on your bed, holding your head in your hands and then what happens? Your head is being beaten against the wall beside your bed. The brick and concrete wall, the one with the badly patched crack in the top right-hand corner, the wall you painted off-white because someone gave you a tin of it. Your head is going *bang bang bang* against this wall, not long painted. Who is banging your head against the wall, making that dull *thud thud thud*? Careful, your head might crack open.

It's you. You're banging your own head against your own wall and if it cracks open it couldn't be any worse than it feels now, than it felt before it started *thud thud thud*ding. Besides, if it cracks open, it might all spill out, and you're convinced now that the reason your head feels fit to burst is that it needs to burst, there's something inside that's straining to get out, been straining for years and years. If it cracks open, whatever it is – and you don't have a clue except it feels malignant, like some bubbling caustic fluid, a black evil smoking poison, which might all explode – then your head will be released, be empty, will float away in peace forever and free of pain.

Close to your bed is the window; the window is open. You're near enough to lean out, near enough to do it. Just take one step, go on, one more step and you'll be there, you could just float out that window and away. It would be so easy, the window's open, no bars, no mesh, go on, do it do it do it do it.

But you're wearing your old Chinese silk dressing-gown which is ripped up the side and you can't go out looking like that. It's comfortable, but it's not the sort of thing you can be seen in floating off into the twilight. You'd have to change and while you believe you have the energy to slip over the windowsill and sail out, you know you don't have the energy to go over to the wardrobe and change into something more respectable.

Oh, it's so tempting, though; you're so tempted to break open your head and let the poison pain fluid explode away forever and yourself float off to pain-free land, when there's a rap at the door. *Rap rap rap*, like the one in your head, only this one isn't hurting. Your friend comes and looks at you with as much sympathy as he can for one who has never had a migraine and never will. He holds your hand and rubs your back slowly and says, Dinner, you need some food. No, I'll be sick, I can't eat, I've had nothing for two days. But he pushes you back onto the pillows and goes to the kitchen. I've brought steak, he says, and fresh vegetables, which you're going to eat.

And soon there it is, a dear little round of fillet steak, some potatoes and yellow zucchinis in butter, a mound of peas and slices of tomato. Plain, humble, perfect, unadorned food. You smell the smell of grilled meat, taste the sharp sweetness of tomato and nearly faint with desire. You eat it all up, you can't believe how hungry you are, how receptive your stomach is to his simple meal cooked with concern. And afterwards, coffee and sugar. Coffee? No coffee! All the doctors have insisted on that. All the herbalists, nutritionists, iridologists, trick cyclists, ists ists ists, naturopaths, vitamin experts, doctors doctors doctors. They've all said no coffee. Death to caffeine.

Caffeine, says your friend, helps constrict the blood vessels, thus easing the pain. After dinner, after coffee, you relax, and sleep an hour or two, the first real sleep for days, and when you wake and it's dark and your friend has watched the late movie on the old black and white set, you say, You're not going are you? My migraine's gone. Food and coffee and sugar. That's one to remember, you try to remember and sometimes it works.

Migraine and the Journey

Every journey seems to end in pain, though at this stage of your life the correct name is yet to be given. You will be perhaps thirteen. After a car trip to your aunty's place, you will receive a strong painkiller that makes you quite drowsy but fails to kill the pain. Your mother and siblings will have gone out to examine the garden, which on this glorious holiday afternoon is quite beautiful. Seated at the kitchen table, your drowsy thudding head in your hands, you will become aware of the presence of your aunty's husband. Within swift seconds or long minutes – time is something you entirely lose grip of when in pain – he will be close beside you, groping your still-developing breasts and trying to kiss you hard on the mouth. Resistance will be impossible for two reasons: he is your aunty's husband, and this shouldn't be happening, and so to reject him outright would be a monstrous acknowledgement of his transgression; and because you are already a victim, of pain. The scene shall dissolve when the family troops in the back door, he melts into the inner rooms of the house, and you will tell yourself you imagined it all.

Except for years afterwards you shall be confused, ashamed and guilty. And forever unsure if you could have resisted had you not been so ill, or if at awkward and unconfident thirteen you would never have had the power. Or if – being so convinced of your profound undesirability – you desired it all along.

The years after that will be punctuated by a series of patronising doctors who are always male, who will make you cry when you don't want to, who will decide you are the nervy type, who will tell you that you have tension headaches, stress headaches, tension and stress, stress and tension, you need to learn to relax and this won't happen, will reprimand you for your hefty doses of painkillers, hesitate to use the word migraine, as if saving that for the genuinely afflicted, not for frauds such as you. Until finally one of them will dismiss all such nonsense, tell you it is quite plainly a migraine, and administer your first dose of pethidine. You will have heard of this drug and so welcome it, and shall be amazed to feel its soft warm effect wearing away all too quickly, with the migraine still firmly in its place.

Migraine and Specialists

And how are we today, he says. We? We? You look around the surgery, there's only one of you, maybe he means both you and him, the patient and the doctor. Well, I don't know about you, doctor, but I'm not real good otherwise I'd hardly be coming along to see you, would I? Sit down, he says, then he calls you by your first name, shortening it like you never do. Well, doctor, or should I say, well, Nevvie, and g'day to you too. Like hell you do; you do not say a word, you can't, it hurts to think, let alone speak and as for getting in here today, it's only the third Mersyndol you took right after the first two that's almost taking the edge off it. So you can come in here and pay his one hundred and fifty-something bucks, and be asked all jolly and fatherly how are we today and have your name turned into a little girl's.

You don't give him the letter the other one wrote. You already read it – it said you were upset and weepy because of severe headaches, suspected migraine. Suspected migraine, that was a nice touch. It didn't matter when she said how long had you had them. You replied, Ever since I can remember, because it's true. And you're weepy because every time you blink your skull fractures. If you have a backache you can stay still and it won't hurt unless you move, but with this, just to *be* means you're in pain. So, Ever since I can remember, you said and she said, What about when you were a child, and you said, Yes. She wrote something on her card while saying, Migraines rarely manifest themselves before adolescence.

(But remember when your mother said, What's wrong? And you said, I've got a headache in my tummy, and they all laughed but you meant it. You never had tummy pain before but had headaches plenty of times and thought that was it, that was what it was like when you hurt, when you had a pain. It made sense to have a headache in your tummy, but Don't be silly, they told you, Don't be so silly.)

So you don't give him the letter. Do you have the referral? he wants to know, holding out a nice clean hand. Well manicured it is, soft. He probably spends a lot of time scrubbing his hands and clipping his nails; he'd have to, wouldn't he, what with all those important operations he does, all that surgery. All those brains to fix up, will he fix up yours, you doubt it.

Sorry, doctor, I mislaid it. Mislaid it. You screwed it up and chucked it into the bin, you were that angry when you saw what she'd written. Then you got it out of the bin and tore it up into tiny pieces, then threw it away again. Sorry, doctor, I mislaid it, very good. But she's spoken to him on the phone already, told him about you anyway, about your *condition*.

And you've already paid his receptionist, one hundred and fifty dollars out of your purse into her till, *slip slip*, just like that, and a receipt back in your hand before you know it. Of course, you can claim some of it on Medicare, she said, implying if you were in a private fund you'd get it all back.

So you're in here with tears sneaking down your face though you're willing them away, tears so he can say like all the others, Nerves, yes, a bit neurotic . . .

I'm crying, you yell, because it hurts.

But that's only in your head (the one that hurts). No, you don't yell, you say nothing at all, you can't speak for the pain. You just listen to his gentle father's voice saying in several hundred roundabout words that there's nothing he can do for you, nothing at all, but to take this or that drug when the migraines start, and he scribbles something on a pad, quickly. You've been in here just on five minutes, obviously your one hundred and fifty dollars' worth is up, but you don't know what the hurry is, there weren't any other patients out there in his grey-pink waiting room, more grey than pink, mood colours, nice calming mood colours . . . Maybe he's got to go off and operate on someone's brain over at the hospital, the private hospital, maybe he's dying to try out his new sports car, he could be overdue for his game of squash or golf or sailing for all you know, but that's it. You've had all the advice you can buy, he pushes over the prescription and says, There, two when you feel it coming on.

Brilliant, you say, very sarcastic. That's a lot of use to me when I wake up with them. You've just explained all that. What do you think I should do, doctor, never go to sleep?

Or set myself an alarm. *Brr brrr*, wake up now, you've had five hours sleep, do you feel a migraine coming on, oh good, well, pop the little pills now. Or maybe there's a special alarm you can buy, a sort of migraine detector. You could put it up there on the wall next to the smoke detector beside the mirror, stick a long-life battery in it. *Beep beep beep*, migraine alert, migraine alert. Wake up and take the magic pills. Ta da!

You say none of this, of course; instead you mumble, Thank you, thank you, doctor, they love all this humility, this gratitude, and you shuffle out. He's so pleased to see the back of you, you can tell, they just don't like these neurotic types, and who would, hey, who would?

Migraine and Pregnancy

He was such a busy specialist doctor and you were so lucky to get in to see him at short notice, most people had to wait months, but the receptionist made a special exception for you, due to your condition. You had a GP referral and you explained over the phone how acute the pain was, how often, how while you've had these migraines for so long they've never, ever had such frequency and intensity and . . . Yes, well, she said, and informed you that she had found you a spot – lucky you! – and you were to get there fifteen minutes in advance. In fact he kept you waiting an hour and a half, but then he was a very busy specialist and you were not a specialist, indeed no one special.

That particular migraine slunk away and hid but the next day returned savagely, snarling in your ears, so you got the prescription made up, the very special strong one that he produced with a very special wave of his very special pen, and took the pills, even though it was probably too late, but worth a try, you thought, anything was worth a try.

And it went. Those pills were amazing, they beat that snarling monster around the head and sent it back to hell where it belonged and you had peace. Peace! Until the stomach cramps began. Oh no, you thought, it was just like a bad period pain, tight cramps pulling down, dragging you off to a world of torture again though this time it was your abdomen not your head. So you took more pills, different ones, not the special ones he gave you, and lay down with a hot water bottle and waited and waited, and soon the pain went.

You felt all right, you felt good. The next day you felt good too. Empty, a bit weak, but good. No pain. You walked outside into the bright beautiful painless day. No pain, you told the seagulls and the waves and the wind and the entire world, you called out, It's good to be alive with no pain. How good it was to be well!

When he rang, you were astonished, what could be wrong? A special specialist doctor like that, people like that, didn't ring you at home. Yes? you said, wondering. He said, Those pills, they shouldn't be taken in pregnancy, you understand, you'd better not take them after all, then mumbled something about slight complications from ergotamine, a something in twenty risk of miscarriage . . .

Slight what? Oh, thank you very much, Doctor You Kept Me Waiting for an Hour and a Half. Thank you and praise you for all your great skill. Those pains last night? They were, in fact, your baby nearly miscarrying. Thank you, doctor, you paid this time one hundred and thirty dollars cash only nearly to lose your baby, thank you thank you thank you indeed, oh, your stomach, your head, your baby.

Migraine and Dogs

Another neurologist. Another referral. You go to a doctor in the new shopping strip behind you, a pleasant young man who has set up shop while you have been away for a few months. You are alone, your head swells and pounds for two days until you can take it no longer. All you have done in those two days is creep out the door twice a day and down the stairs to wait, your head pressed against the foyer door, while the poor dog relieves himself in the garden. You have managed to give him food, none for yourself. You put on a dress and take the dog to hold on to his leash and creep out of your flat again and around the corner. You are the only patient; he seems fresh out of medical school, he's never seen you before. Migraine, you say, migraine, two days, please give me something for the pain before I go mad, I can't stand the pain any longer.

But they get drug addicts all the time, these doctors. People who do the rounds of the surgeries for injections of anything, hopefully pethidine, and it's worse in an inner-city suburb. It takes a long time to convince him, and he is so young, straight out of medical school, where they have probably been cautioning him only the week before. Drug addicts, now, they will try to put it all over you . . . Please believe me, you say, do I look like a drug addict?

Do I? Don't give me pethidine, then, you add, give me anything else, is there something else, some new potion or treatment or a well-aimed tap behind the ear or *something*? Anything, it doesn't have to be pethidine, just anything to stop the pain?

You say all this but of course there is only pethidine, and even that only works as a blanket, covering the pain for a few hours to make it bearable, never eliminating it. He believes you finally, then insists he should drive you home. No, you say, I only live over there. But he is still doubtful. You go outside the surgery and point, There's my place, you can see it, I'll wave when I get to the front door, and look, here's my dog. The dog is waiting where you have tied him to a rail. It is the presence of your dog – and such a homely sort of dog too, with his appealing eye patch and revolving tail – that convinces him, proves your moral worth. So you creep off again, you and your dog, and you just make it home when the warm waves start caressing you from head to toe, whispering soothing things, and by the time you fall on the bed you are totally enveloped in a dense nimbus which holds you safe for hours until the pain goes. No wonder the drug addicts love it.

The next evening you return. Look, it's me, you tell the doctor, a normal me, a pain-free person, someone who can walk and talk and laugh like anyone else, not a creeping shameful crippled bundle of agony, not a drug addict trying to con you. And here's my dog again, his name is Douggie, by the way, did I tell you that? As if the owner of a dog called Douggie could be suspect in any possible way.

The young doctor is glad you have come back, to show him you are bona fide. I'd like you to see a neurologist, he says, if you've been getting these migraines for so long . . . Sure, doctor, I'll go. He trusts you, doesn't he, it's the least you can do and, besides, you do want a cure, you want not to have another migraine ever again. If the new neurologist or anyone comes up to you and says, Look, a million dollars or no migraines for the rest of your life, take your pick, it's not a competition, is it? It just doesn't take any thinking. You'd laugh and push the money away and take the gift and go off laughing, the rest of your life. A gift. What a holiday that'd be.

Migraine and Madness

There is no stranger offering you a lucky choice, no cures, no doctors who can give you a speck of hope. This neurologist, you go to her, it takes ages, she's way across the other side of the city. Yes, she knows how you feel, she gets a migraine herself, every Friday; it's tension, fatigue, the strain of the working week, a let-down effect, she can tell you all about it, can't she. But she can't tell you about your migraines and when you try to tell her yours aren't like that, neat Friday-night migraines, she doesn't listen. And to be fair you don't listen either, you never do, because all you want is to know how to stop them. Perhaps, then, she says, you could consider going to a psychiatrist?

Perhaps you could. You'd never thought you might be going nutty, though you feel that way sometimes with the pain. Never thought you might even be imagining all these migraines, or bringing them on unconsciously, willing them on yourself, your wilful sneaky little mind creating them and forcing them on you, and for what? Some kind of punishment? So that's what happens, is it?

You've paid this neurologist how much this time – only eighty-something dollars: cheap, really – to be told you should toddle off to another doctor, who will say, Tell me about your dreams, or whatever they say, laying you back on the couch there. Or maybe he could hypnotise you out of them, like making you give up smoking or chewing your nails or something. Now you feel a little drowsy and when you wake up you'll never have a migraine again, you'll feel relaxed and refreshed and alert . . .

Good one, Doctor I Have Migraines Too. Now you've forked out money to have a near miscarriage, money to be told you're mad, what else can you fork out for? What else can they get you on? You've been told before that you need to loosen up, relax, that there's too much tension in you, that you're stressed out. This is by the new agers, you've forked out money there too. Herbalists, naturopaths, acupuncturists, iridologists, go on, name it, you've seen them, you've heard them all. Too stressed out, too much tension.

Of course you're stressed out, of course you're tense. You're like a coiled spring trying to be watchful for those migraines which are so cunning, so sneaky. They wait until you're not looking then they move, leaping out from behind corners, closed doors, grabbing you and holding your head in thrall for two, three, four days. Of course you're under stress. It's a very stressful business, waiting and wondering when the next one is going to leap on you like that. Wouldn't you be stressed not knowing when the next one was coming, you say, knowing how much it's going to hurt, how much time you're going to waste lying on the bed in your darkened room grinding your teeth and thrashing about and moaning and thinking how many more days, how many more hours. All the wasted, wasted days and weeks of your life. All the books you could have written in that wasted time, all the jumpers you could have knitted, the floors you could have polished, the artworks you could have painted, the gardens you could have weeded, the toilets you could have cleaned: anything, anything, to be doing anything at all, anything but this lying down, a foetal ball of pain and frustration and anger moaning hating and hating yourself most of all.

Stress. Tension. Madness. What a laugh. That's not what I mean, says one of these practitioners. But you don't want to hear what she means, let her have one of these migraines, just once in her life, just for a couple of minutes even, just to let her know what it's like and see if she talks about being stressed out and having to come to terms with unresolved tension and all that bullshit.

Migraines and Real Headaches

It is commonly thought by those who do not suffer the condition that it is like having a headache. When you are in your late twenties you have one of these, for the first time in your life. You find the pain quite amazing, worthy of analysis and reflection, which it is possible to do given the very mild level of pain you are experiencing. During one of these headaches you discover you can still walk around and watch the television and even read. You can say hello to people coming into the room, and make a cup of tea and drink it with them. You take two Panadols and the headache goes. It goes! This is after two hours, with a couple of little Panadols. Then you understand that this is what people mean when they say, Oh dear, I have a headache, I might leave work early today, or, No, I won't join you for a beer, I might have a little sherry instead, my head's aching a bit.

This is vastly different to what you have until this point known. This does not involve having to crawl off, to slink away like an animal and hole up in your cave of a room. There is no need to take every drug you can lay your hands on just to take the edge off the pain, just to make it faintly bearable, just so you can whisper to people, Don't worry about me, there's nothing you can do, thanks.

This headache makes you realise that this is what people think, then, when you whisper that you have a migraine, a headache. All these years when you have been feeling like *this*, they have been feeling like *that*, with their headaches. Theirs are these sweet little headaches which perch neatly on the front of their heads ready to fly off soon after being given just a cup of tea and an Aspro.

They think you feel like that, so they have no sympathy. They think you have felt like that all these years, these long decades, and so it is not surprising that they have also been saying to you all along, Why don't you go and lie down, I'll bring you a Panadol? Or, Can I get you a bit of soup or something? Meanwhile inside they have been thinking, Why don't you snap out of it, you whinger? Why are you malingering like this, it's only a headache, for god's sake, only a headache.

Oh, please, you'd take one of those sorts of headaches any day. You'd take two. No worries, you would be laughing. Oh, you would say, only a headache, don't worry about me. I shall take my cup of tea and have that lie-down and be right as rain in half an hour, you'll see, right as rain. Oh, give me one of those headaches, give me one, give me, give me, please please please.

Migraine and Medicine

You go to the university for an interview. The old university, the one on the hill. You meet five old men; they fit with the university. They're in a huge room with sunlight pointing down from high thin windows, the furniture is dark, the five old men have enough glasses and beards and pipes between them to convince you they are important. You are a special case they must consider.

Now, just why do you want to study medicine, can you tell us? You certainly can tell them. You intend, you say in a clear voice, to find a cure for migraines. That's why you must first study medicine. They don't laugh, but the beards twitch a little. Well, young lady, what makes you think you can do what doctors in research have been trying to do for at least a century? Young lady. Why don't they just come out with it and say, girlie or kiddie, like they really mean. You're twenty-four or twenty-eight – you can't remember but twenty-something – and they want you to stick to what you're best at, what you got honours for, not try to change to medicine at this stage. What was that gentlemen, professors? What am I good at, what should I stick to? Playdough modelling? Lego construction? Scones and ribbon sandwiches? Leave the important things like breakthrough cures to the beards and the pipes?

Besides, they're now saying, this sort of research attracts a low priority in terms of funding, I mean, it's not like cancer research or heart disease now, is it? Migraine, really just glorified headaches, *heh heh chortle chortle*, cough in the beards. Assuming you could get through the course, I mean, my dear. Then there'd be years in practice before you could even think about turning your hand to research. Have you any idea of the commitment required, you'd be thirty or thereabouts before you even left the university, then you're looking at two, three years' registrar work, say ten years in practice, and you'd be going off to have kiddies at some stage, eh? They look at you over the glasses, meaning, but not quite saying, Nice-looking sheila like you, should find a bloke, settle down, want to bake a few buns in the oven, that sort of thing *ha ha ha*.

Forget all about it. That's their advice.

Migraine and Malingering

You take the advice. Because it is, in the end, all too hard. And also, in the end, there is more than a glimmer of hope that something might work. You have, you think, exhausted all the possibilities. By now no painkillers ever work: the pethidine makes it bearable for several hours, and nothing else touches it, while the brief and two-edged miracle of the ergotamine is never repeated. Every migraine is like you have embarked on a speeding train that does not stop at any station you expect it to, but instead must hurtle through a dense and lonely darkness until the line eventually and quite mysteriously ends. You, of course, are the only passenger, and there does not seem to be a driver.

By now you are no longer pregnant, and your babies were born perfectly healthy and unharmed by the tsunamis of pain that have regularly crashed through your system in the first trimesters. The few doses of pethidine you've been given during these months are viewed with the greatest horror by all except the most wise health professionals, and you are easily the worst mother-to-be, exposing her foetuses to such powerful drugs. All the chambers of your heart and all the fibres of your instinct and all the vast rooms of your soul that protect the babies you nurture with a raw fury that surprises you with its force – all this cannot stop your submission to the offer of pethidine, even though the warm kiss of its effect lingers for no more than a few hours, muffling the pain.

Thus you are: a liar, a malingerer, a drug abuser, a hysteric. A gross exaggerator of pain and suffering. An attention-seeker. An avoider of the realities of life. You want to get a day or two off work, escape your domestic duties, hide from the demands of your children, convince the world you are somehow special due to the exquisite torturous nature of your suffering.

Migraine and Memory

One of the reasons each migraine is so spectacular in its pain is the simple fact that every migraine is so spectacularly painful that when it is over you lapse into a state of forgetting. More than repressed, more like a quite conscious decision of your mind to eliminate all cellular memory of the pain associated with this condition. Every time you recover you not only never want to think about that pain again, you simply cannot contemplate the prospect of it ever happening again. This deliberate denial via memory no doubt means that some prophylactic remedies are unavailable to you, or that you try them but discontinue them, or that you can never imagine that you would need to take them.

Even when Imigran becomes available and you discover it works – you still call it the magic pill – and when it becomes cheap enough to have at least a packet on hand – two precious pills, in one tiny box – you do not carry it with you wherever you go or keep a stock in the medicine cabinet.

So profound is this denial that you find yourself in extreme circumstances again and again: for example, away visiting a friend interstate when a migraine strikes, and she drives you to a local doctor whose waiting room is so full you could have died right there. Kindly, he promotes you to the top of the queue, and kindly he gives you an injection of tramadol, and even though deep down inside you know this will not work, and know you need Imigran, somehow you forget to ask him for a prescription. You go home and the migraine becomes bearable for the rest of the day. You have already been denied a flight home due to this migraine: when your friend had run into the airport the day before, explaining that you were late for your flight and just making your way from the car now, due to a migraine, the desk clerk insisted you were not permitted to travel and instructed you instead get a doctor's certificate before she would reschedule your flight. Fury and frustration made the pain more intense, but in between bouts of vomiting into a polystyrene cup and holding on to your friend, you could imagine what the airline thought might happen. Perhaps your head would explode mid-flight. Perhaps you would die from the added pressure.

The next morning you lie to your friend and tell her you are well enough to fly. The hour's flight home is one of the more painful ordeals of your life. When you land you ring your daughter to ask her to run up to the chemist for the blessed drug, and tell her that you will be home in a taxi within the half-hour. And an hour after falling into your own bed you begin to feel that unique and distinct sensation that every migraine sufferer knows: that hard welcome empty space in your head that might be nothing at all but is the very palpable absence of pain.

When people phone you saying they can't do this or that, or email you, which means they are sitting at their computers, you are astonished that they can claim they have a migraine and perform these simple tasks. The prospect of making a phone call while in the grip of such pain, the possibility of climbing out of bed, of getting into a car and driving, of uttering anything more than a groan, is as mysterious to you as quantum physics.

Migraine and Love

This is the time when you are taken to hospital yet again, and no one looks at you sideways or interrogates you about your drug use or demands a whole family history of allergies. This is when this doctor simply walks up to your bed in EU and briskly says, Migraine, right, let's get you hooked up to the intravenous aspirin. Which actually works, good old aspirin.

Another doctor, a few years later, says, We don't give pethidine or aspirin any more, we're using intravenous largactyl. Largactyl? The drug used to control mental health patients back in the day? Absolutely, yes. And it works. And, although it leaves you feeling mind-numbed for a week afterwards, it's worth it to escape the pain.

These are the doctors you could clasp to your breast and kiss. The ones who don't think you are neurotic/psychotic/drug-addicted/playing games/just having a stressful time at the moment. The ones who know. Who roll their sleeves up and jump in just as if you'd been in a car crash and needed emergency surgery.

My god, how you love these doctors.

Migraine and Irony

There is no bruising. There are no red marks. And inside the head, in between the skin and the cranial bones, where the dilated blood vessels have recently pulsed until the sufferer felt their head might burst, there is not the faintest sign of injury. While gripped by the pain, the victim has felt that veins and blood vessels have surely exploded with pressure (in fact, they have felt their entire head would explode) but there is not even a trace of discolouration. Nothing is pinker or redder or purpler than it is meant to be. No membrane is inflamed, red or swollen. There is no blood clot, nor any shrivelled and dried-out veins or vessels. To an outsider, even a sympathetic one, it appears that the pain is all in the mind. As indeed, in the most insidious way, it is.

The migraine sufferer has no tumour or growth, no abnormality. When the pain goes, everything vanishes, leaving nothing but the nightmarish feeling of gross, distorted reality, the belief that this horrific experience never really happened, and the desperate hope that it will never happen again.

A migraine victim might regularly vomit, be dizzy or even faint, be unable to bear strong light, feel numbness down one side of the body. But for every person who experiences some or even all of these symptoms, there are those who experience none. There is no visible outward sign of their suffering. There is no evidence. It is hard to believe that a pain as overwhelming as that of a migraine is actually not doing the sufferer any damage. The extraordinary intensity of pain, when it recedes, leaves not the faintest trace of its passing. After an attack, any residual effects, such as weakness, dizziness or fatigue, will be the result of the treatment or the drugs taken, not of the migraine itself.

Hence the sense of helplessness. You are suffering, but you are not bleeding, ruptured, torn, bruised, shattered. This is the silent scream of the migraine victim who nurses their pain in complete and total secrecy. A monstrous joke is being perpetrated. Only the most intense pain a body can experience, with not a single sign that the patient is suffering.

Migraine for Beginners

It is stunningly creative: every time it's the same but different. Thus never able to be anticipated, contained, controlled, cured. In your pain-free moments you admire this migraine, how clever it is, how elusive and how resistant to definition, which none of the many books on the topic you have read manages to capture. Every migraine represents a brand-new challenge, where the old and learned approaches have to be discarded. Where once strong coffee with lots of sugar helped, now it no longer does. Where a combination of paracetamol and aspirin worked, now it won't. Where pressure-point massage and heat packs provided relief, now they do not. Hot baths, ice-cold showers, or a combination of both, like in a Nordic noir story, now have no effect. Where the bed with cool fresh sheets made up by your mother provided solace, now it is just an irritant. Once dim lights or no lights made a difference, but now you may as well be parked under the interrogatory glare of fluorescence, as indeed you have been many times in the emergency ward.

Every single time it is as if you are a child taking its first precarious steps in a new world, except there is no nervous thrill, no expectation of developing power, no skill to explore, no sense that these steps will ever become stronger and firmer.

The Master Shavers' Association of Paradise

EARLY ON THE morning of the final day, you are ready to leave. You have already packed your belongings into the government-issue striped carryall. One for each person but one is too much. You could have fitted your cousin's and your uncle's possessions in your carryall alone, but it is too late for that. As it is, the fat blue-and-red stripes sag somewhere around the middle, whereas those of others who have already left seemed to have contained enough to make a firm, proud rectangle. You look around the room. You could take the blanket off the camp stretcher, or the stretcher itself, which dismantles and folds into a package. But these items belong to the camp, to the contractors, or to the government. You compromise by taking the towel. Grey-blue, the colour of marine paint, it is still damp. It will not dry before you leave. You fold the towel and place it on top of the carryall, and then turn to face the open doorway. The little sign – a piece of cardboard with chalked lettering that you propped up every day next to the doorway – has already been taken down.

You sit on the step and look across the quadrangle, empty apart from puddles gleaming in the early light, to the huts in the row opposite. Their doors are held open with cabin hooks to comply with the regulation airing, their windows already shuttered with plywood. Beyond is a line of palms – you can just see the tops of them brushing against the morning sky – and beyond that is the hill that slopes down to the water and although the beach is bounded by a wall of rocks and barbed wire and you have never once felt these waves lap at your bare feet or even seen the colour of the water or the sand, you have heard the sea, day and night, and you hear it now, slapping at the shore. They cannot stop you hearing.

A good hour previously, you had gone outside and stepped down the long muddy pathway between the tents, careful to avoid the potholes from the rain, to the shower block at the end of the row. At that hour it was still dark, but it was better to wash alone in the dark than jostle at first light with the other men. The men were fewer, as it was the last day, but the showers had never been sufficient, as if two or three years back the camp were expecting a dozen men, not hundreds.

But the water was very clean. There were plastic rain barrels at each end of the larger sheds. These were bright blue, stamped MAUSER BIOFUEL, which some of the men said meant toxic but you'd never been sure. All the tents had buckets parked at the corners to catch the drips. And when you moved into your uncle's hut you took your bucket with you in case the men were right about BIOFUEL – not that it would have made any difference, not after all this time. Unfortunately your bucket was bright pink, but then so were many others so you could tolerate the joking, though you would have preferred grey, or blue. Even yellow would have been preferable. Nevertheless in your pink bucket you still collected Paradise's purest, even up to today, the very last day, for it rained frequently.

You took this bucket to the shower block. There were meant to be plastic bowls set all along the wooden bench that ran opposite the latrines, but most had gone missing, which was a shame. A bowl would have been so much better for your business, these past few months. The conveniences were not very convenient. Men crouched there unconcernedly in the stalls, separated by a flimsy plywood panel not even waist height, and no doors. They stared back at you from the far end of the block, rising and hitching their trousers afterwards without so much as a glance back at their mess, barely breaking eye contact with you, the flies descending greedily the second they left. They were the kind of men who never came to you as clients, never spoke to you, never glanced at you except those times in the shower block, when they would stare so hard you would understand, without the need for words, the precise nature of your status in the camp. These were the men who would do nothing day after day but lie on their camp stretcher beds and smoke. From time to time one of these men would, as if on a roster system, throw himself at the fence screaming obscenities about the guards' mothers or sisters, and then be taken off to solitary detention with a look on his face as if he were an avenging angel who had stormed the gates of hell.

You did not shave, this last morning, as there were no more razors. Fortunately you had shaved cleanly a week before they were banned altogether and now you have produced a neat new stubble beard. You set your bucket on the bench and scooped some water out to rub over your face and neck. The day before there had been a sliver of soap like a cuttlefish bone, but in the dark you could not find it. You rubbed and rinsed with Paradise's purest, saving the last bit to clean your teeth and rinse your mouth. Your toothbrush was in the side pocket, velcroed, of your cargo pants. You were meant to hand this in every night but somehow yours had gone unnoticed despite the extra vigilance. Or maybe the guards no longer cared, now that it was the final day. As you examined it, holding it out in the growing light, you saw how the bristles were all flattened. Over the months you had so chewed and worn it down that how it could ever be turned into a weapon puzzled you. But then you had seen a man slash himself with one carefully cultivated thumbnail, slicing across his other wrist as if he were cutting through banana skin. You had seen men tattoo each other with iron nails filed back to fine points. You once saw a man stitch his lips with plastic thread teased from a rope and a needle made from a chicken bone.

You dried your face and neck with the grey-blue towel and scraped your damp hair back with your fingers, pressing the curls as flat as you could. Now that there was only you, the last member of the Association, you did your best with what you were left.

The day you arrived your uncle took you around the camp and ate his evening meal with you and sat on a stool in front of your tent until the other men had gone to sleep, when he left for his hut in the second row, across the quadrangle. And the next morning he appeared again to stand with you so you would not be confused or bullied. Before breakfast he took you to the shower block, where the guard distributed plastic disposable razors. Like lollipops, they were handed out one at a time, each recorded in a book with a pencil tick. Your uncle grabbed you by the arm and took you to the bench inside.

Ten minutes, he said, they will collect them again in ten minutes. You have to be quick.

How will we know? you said. No one here had a watch.

They'll ring a bell. And if we're not done a guard will take it off us, mid-stroke if necessary.

You laughed. But maybe he was right. You looked around. The showers were a long, open-sided building with a low tin roof and blue plastic sheeting attached to one side, to protect from rain, you assumed. A long wooden bench contained a stack of plastic basins. Two stainless steel sinks were covered in plywood, the taps above them wrapped in plastic bags.

They've never worked since I've been here, your uncle said. Instead of a mirror, a polished steel sheet was screwed onto the timber walls above the bench. Opposite were the doorless stalls with low dividers and lower toilets with no seats, also steel, but not stainless; rather they were very stained. There were two men in the cubicles staring at you as if shitting were an act of aggression. The three standing at the trough next to them were pissing at the one spot on the wall as if in competition. Come on. Your uncle grabbed your face, then after staring a few seconds laughed and thrust your chin away, slapping your cheek.

Puppy, he said. You are just a fuzzy pup.

You felt your face. It was true. Your struggling beard still shamed you. It was like baby's hair.

That's what Mr Kondappan used to say, you said to your uncle. He would not believe I was fifteen already.

And then the mention of Mr Kondappan made your words clog somewhere in your throat. You stood very still, willing your face to remain immobile. Your mouth threatened to become too loose. Your uncle opened wide his arms and embraced you.

My boy, he whispered, my boy. We must be only grateful that you are safe.

Over his shoulder you squeezed your eyes so hard to stop the tears it hurt. When you opened them one of the shitting men was staring right at you. He brought his cigarette to his mouth and inhaled and exhaled slowly then let out a long loud fart into the bowl he was squatting over.

You do me then, your uncle said. Let's be quick.

That you could do. This is where you were skilled, where you could take charge. You would never see him again but you would make Mr Kondappan proud. You placed your uncle's towel over his chest and, standing there beside the wooden bench, rinsed the razor in the cold pure water then rubbed the soap into your palms.

No lather, you said.

It's all we have, he said. You'll get used to it.

You soaped his face then applied the razor. It was white, with an orange head. It said Bic. The blade was spotted with rust. You scraped down one cheek then the next.

Careful of my moustache, he said.

It needs a trim, old man, you told him. He nudged you. Later, he said. I think I can find some scissors.

He rinsed and dried while you washed your face and as you were both combing your hair the shitting man pushed past you. His beard was rough and tangled. The guard appeared with his box and book just in time, and your uncle handed the razor back and had his name ticked again. The box was tin, with a lid and a lock. Inside were about a dozen disposable razors. The guard snapped the lid shut and took it away.

You began to notice the number of men walking around badly or half-shaven, or scraped all over their faces. Some men were like Janus, with a beard on one side of the face, a stubbly but clean face on the other. Conversing with these men was improbable, like talking to a circus freak. Shaving was permitted every five days. Your uncle joined you most of those mornings, to line up, be checked on then off, and you shaved him, and it was always a scrappy soapy mess but you did your best. Sometimes the Bic disposable was too rusted. There were also some blue Gillette Double Blades in the locked tin and once or twice you were lucky enough to get these. As you shaved him your uncle stared at you and you at him. You were his mirror. You tried not to notice how like your mother's were his eyes, how the eyebrows arched then tapered past the eyes towards his hairline in the same way. Soon you began using your own bucket, and the grey-blue towel that was finally issued two weeks after your arrival in Paradise.

After a month you stopped asking what there was to do. The first time your uncle laughed at you and then, uncharacteristically savage in a low voice so Mani could not hear, told you, Stay sane. And shut up. Just shut up. He was afraid of the guards but also of the shitting men, the ones who would hurl themselves at the fence screaming. The same men who refused food, for weeks if they could. They would still line up in the mess hall but then, not breaking eye contact with the orderly, would tip the contents of their plates onto the floor and then the plates, before turning and walking out. But you ate the breakfast – porridge, bread, margarine and jam – and washed your plastic plate along with the others and returned it to its place in the mess hall, and walked around the quadrangle, like the others. Like all the others you sat in the opening of your tent and stared at the others sitting at the opening of their tents. When you moved to the hut you sat with your uncle and Mani in the doorway, and stared at the other men sitting in their doorways. When it rained you sat and watched the rain. If it was not raining you walked around the quadrangle in the mud. Your pair of running shoes were soon filthy, but like all the others you set them aside and went barefoot. You sat and waited for lunch – ham in perfect squares, sometimes sausages, and bread – walked some more and waited for dinner. Rice, pasta, sloppy mince in gravy. Potatoes, boiled, mashed and often in their skins and still gritty. Once a week you had an orange, or a banana.

Sometimes you and your cousin would sit in a corner of the quadrangle, or behind the kitchen shed, or up by the gate. Mani was twelve, large for his age, unlike you – still growing at sixteen, still sporting a laughable beard at seventeen – otherwise he might have been sent with the other children to the mainland. We are the lucky ones, your uncle said again and again, you and me and Maniyarasan, we are lucky, we must be grateful. Mani would stare at his father. You knew how much he hated hearing these things, though he did not contradict him.

Mani and you would speak in whispers. The water, the hunger, the parching heat and of course the thirst when there was water all around. He'd been in the water, along with your uncle and seven other men, rescued after a night and most of the following day. They were lucky, your uncle says, because they had a lifebuoy to share. Mani did not care that the beach on Paradise was forbidden. He would be happy never to see the ocean again. Sometimes sitting at dusk by the gate a quietness descended, as if the whole island was asleep, and then you were aware of the slap of waves down on the forbidden beach. Mani sometimes clamped his hands over his ears and walked back to his hut.

He spent a lot of time on his camp stretcher bed with the blanket over his head.

After your first three months you had walked the perimeter so thoroughly you knew every rut in the path, every puddle after rain, every rock, every weed. You couldn't lie and smoke and stare like the others. After the tenth or hundredth game of playing cards you thought you would die of boredom. Your uncle would patiently deal the cards, so worn they were barely readable, sitting on the stool in front of his hut, using your upturned pink bucket for a table.

For six months the Red Cross ran a weekly afternoon discussion group. They served Cheezels while men practised the new language. *Cheezels are made from cheese. Cheese is made from milk. Milk comes from a cow.* There was also orange cordial from a large orange plastic barrel with a big M on the top. You pronounced the words, *orange*, *drink*, *thank you*, *thirsty*, and held the Cheezels up to your eye before popping them in your mouth. They tasted good but not of cheese. You did not say you had been learning English since you commenced school, nor that your school had been closed down when you were eleven, when all the teachers disappeared and the buildings were shot up one night.

The Red Cross worker left a year ago. There was also a library, in a converted kombi van. Every Thursday afternoon, the library volunteer set out plastic crates with magazines, *National Geographic* and *Reader's Digest*, plus English-language primers and comics for beginners, and an entire set of Ian Fleming's James Bond books, *Casino Royale* to *Octopussy* and *The Living Daylights*, with clever covers: a bullet shooting a hole into the title page; playing cards fanned out against green cloth. One day your English would be good enough to read them, but before that time arrived, the volunteer stopped appearing.

The men began their own smoking club, down behind the mess hall late at night, where hidden packets of favourite cigarette brands or tobacco would be mysteriously produced and traded. Longbeach and Champion were the most prized brands, if they could be obtained. White Ox tobacco and Ventti papers, somctimes handed over, one at a time, in return for favours, information, documents, signatures, anything, even promises. One packet of cigarettes for a name that would give you a passage to freedom. You did not smoke, and your uncle never participated, retreating to his hut doorway and playing cards laid out on the upturned bucket. The Red Cross parcels that brought Champion and White Ox also brought essentials and other small indulgences: Lux and Palmolive soap, Cadbury's chocolate, dried fruit, socks, writing materials, sunscreen.

The camp rule forbade long beards. It was better to shave badly, or to use the scissors, than fight it. The guards were meant to supervise a proper trimming. All the scissors were aluminium bladed, with bright green plastic handles; however, if a man was lucky he would get a new pair and it would not tug as much, at least for the first few times.

You had no need for the scissor option. Your beard, what Mr Kondappan had kindly called incipient, straggled down the sides of your face like a delicate weed. You still trimmed it and rubbed oil down your cheeks to make it shine. Meanwhile you made yourself useful, for the men who wanted a shave but did not have your patience with the rusty Bics. The guard handing out the razors every few days got to know you and after several months the ten-minute rule was not quite so rigid.

In the shop Mr Kondappan had had a cutthroat razor and a leather strop and he had begun to teach you the art of proper barbering. You had long and steady fingers, he said. You were his best apprentice by far and although your job, when you were not sweeping the floor, was to whisk the badger-hair shaving brush in the cup of soap to make the creamy foam just as he liked it, you had already learned a great deal. It was when you were out the back rinsing the brushes and combs that you heard the van as its tyres squealed to a stop. You heard shouts, then shots, then the squeal of the van again, and in seconds it was over and you were left staring out into the street that had been busy five minutes before, empty now but for the smell of burnt rubber and a stray dog that shook its coat and turned away. And no one had seen a thing. It was not that people were unsympathetic. Just unwilling to get involved. When you left, bewildered, you were still holding the badger-hair brush so tight your knuckles were white. You took it with you when you fled. It was in the backpack along with everything else at the bottom of the Indian Ocean.

Once, lawyers came. At least your uncle thought they were lawyers, but on reflection no one was sure. They could have just been government officials, secretaries, bureaucrats, policy makers. They were driven up to the camp gate in four-wheel drives and set up an office in an empty shed, with their boxes of papers wheeled in on a trolley. You were called in one by one, five or ten minutes each. The men all waited, sitting at their doors as usual, and when your uncle filed back you saw there were tears in his eyes.

What happened? Will you be freed? you asked, but he pushed past you, shaking his head and gathering Mani inside, and shut the door to your hut. You waited your turn in the corner of the quadrangle where the queue lined the perimeter. When the guard called your name you were parched in the mouth, but not from the heat. The guard, like all the others, had AIDS emblazoned on his shirt and it had taken you weeks before someone explained it did not stand for the disease but for the immigration detention service of the country you yearned to go to.

The man two places before you in the queue began crying. I wanted my children to be free, he said. I only wanted them to go to school and learn as I had learned and not be frightened that the next lesson would come from the barrel of an automatic. He cried again, a sniffling noise that made the man in front of you turn around and snigger. And then they took my wife and daughters anyway, he said, and so I left with my sons. They have drowned.

The man in front stopped sniggering but now had a look of contempt on his face, as if to say to you, *Only drowned?* He should be so lucky. There was no room for compassion here in the camp.

When you went in, the looks on the faces of the three lawyers or officials were of profound boredom. In the corner behind them sat an oscillating fan. On the trestle-table desk, large pebbles held down folders of papers that protested in the breeze as the fan rotated back and forth, back and forth. The questions were fast. No, you had no papers, no passport, nothing that would prove who you are. They had all gone in your only backpack, lost when the boat capsized. You had even kept your indentured papers from Mr Kondappan.

Can I get another passport? you said. Can I get a visa? Can I leave this place? Please, sirs, when can I leave?

They looked at each other. The fan's rotating head caught a flurry of papers in its wake. One of them, loosening his tie, said, Steady on, mate, where do you think you are?

Where? Somewhere that gave you a bed to sleep in, and shelter from the rain and the sun. Where there were beautiful meals, white bread and gravy mince, three times a day and bananas on Tuesdays. Where you could drink the water, which never ran out. Where men walked around rubbing their hands over their clean chins, wearing clothes that no longer stank of diesel fuel and rotting fish and salt water. Where there were no corpses of your mother, your sisters, your friends, to be hauled out and tossed away. Where the waves could not swallow you or worse: spit you out and let you live a little longer under the unblinking sun. Where there were no men to point their weapons at your groin, your head, your heart, simply because someone somewhere once decided that your corner of your country, your language, your religion were subordinate to theirs.

You did not care that this was the place where men threw themselves at the chain-link fence screaming, where men stitched their lips and were taken away for refusing food for more than a week; this to you was a place that had saved you from hell, and you told them so. Paradise, you said. I am in Paradise.

Parcels would come. From Red Cross, from Amnesty International, from the Coalition of Christians for Refugees. Allowed to help unpack and distribute them, you examined the labels, sounding out the strange names of so many worthy groups. The Asylum Seekers' Action Group, Lions clubs, the Salvation Army, the Women's Peace and Greens parties. An organisation called the Young Matrons' Welfare Association of Ginninderra ACT, which you later learned was in the political heart of the country that sent you here, if heart was the right word. The parcels contained toiletries, handkerchiefs, snack foods. Once there was an entire box of Lux soaps chipped and dented but still okay. The men laughed at scents like Supreme Cream and Exotic Aromas, but took them from you anyway, to hide under their clothes or in their beds. Sometimes the parcels brought clothing: trackpants all the same colour with sporting names on them. Your first winter in Paradise, dozens of men walked around wearing maroon pants with Junior Pro League printed down the side of one leg. Everyone fought over the Bondi Breakers baseball caps, though no one cared for the sport. You were happy to unpack and distribute these parcels to help the numbing boredom before it got to you like it seemed to have hollowed out so many of the men, including the shitters who stared at you as they crouched and smoked as if their lives depended on it, and maybe they did.

But a week or so after the lawyers/officials departed, men were still walking around talking of their new lives, as soon as they would leave. Even the shitters were seen talking in huddles, with a look of expectancy in their eyes. One of them almost smiled. Another charity box arrived and by now you knew that the AIDS guards were likely to keep these parcels from you as punishment or for fun, their fun. But this time you were called over to the guardhouse at the gate. The box was already ripped open and the contents tossed about, most of the items out of their packaging, but that was normal.

Toiletries, the guard said. You're the kid who likes shaving and that, aren't you?

Barber, sir. Third-year apprentice, you said.

You take this and see if you want any of it. I reckon no one else will be interested, not with your hairy lot.

There was more Lux, this time only Exotic Aromas, and tubes of Colgate toothpaste, and other products squashed and split and out of their boxes: shaving gel and foam cream, aftershave balm. Vaseline hair oil. Gillette and Palmolive and a brand you hadn't seen before – Fast, with a large signature across every tube. Fast Aloe Vera Shaving Gel, by Ross MacDowell, Master Shaver. Fast Shea Butter Face Balm, by Ross MacDowell, Master Shaver.

What is this master shaver? your uncle said when you showed him. He has some kind of award for it?

Don't laugh, uncle, you said.

Mr Kondappan had taken you on as a promise to your father, before he disappeared. He wore a pale blue buttoned tunic and had a red-and-white striped pole outside the shop. He favoured sticks of Palmolive shaving soap, and hair waxes that came in tins, ordered from America. Mr Kondappan, who could have been a master shaver if there were an award for it, was in his shop on the wrong day, along with tens of others when white vans with missing numberplates tore through the town. The soldiers trashed the barber shop, smashing the window with the red-and-white pole before dragging him out onto the street and into the van. When you crept home, much later under cover of night, your mother opened up the box where she kept her valuables – wedding certificate, birth notices, your grandfather's silver cigarette case, and your grandmother's rings. Enough, she said, we have had enough, controlling her sobs in front of your wide-eyed little sister. This will be enough for three fares, she said, handing you a large sapphire ring, and when you reached out for it you realised you still held tight the badger-hair shaving brush.

Afterwards, you had an idea. The guard shrugged, though later you would wonder at his calculated indifference. You put up your sign, chalk on cardboard, propped at the doorway to your uncle's hut. The Master Shavers' Association of Paradise. Free Life Membership. Shaves and Haircuts. No Appt Necessary. At the bottom of the box, under the litter of packaging from toothpaste tubes and plastic combs, was a torn pack of razors, Gillette ProGlide, a six-pack, one razor overlooked. Gillette, the best a man can get. Overlooked, or ignored. You took this to your tent and hid it in the bottom of your bedroll, then took it out to the dark gap behind the step and the hut, and then put it into the pocket of your cargo pants. You would be responsible for this razor, and you had the right to it, of all the men in Paradise.

Mani and you were sitting at the doorway under your sign when your uncle appeared from mess hall duty, panting from having run across the quadrangle.

Are you crazy?

Maybe, you said, but at least I will not be bored.

Listen, he said, six men have just been taken away. It is said they had ropes, shaped as nooses, in their tents. There will be an inspection, he said, looking over his shoulder. Soon, before dark. Take down your sign.

No, you said. But you hid your razor, this time under the cement slab step.

The Master Shavers' Association flourished and you performed numerous excellent shaves and many beard trims until one morning your Gillette ProGlide was missing, and later that day a man was carted off with bleeding wrists.

And now it is the last day in Paradise. Your uncle and Mani were taken away some weeks before, and in all that time none of the remaining men have spoken a word to you. At least the men in their stalls no longer stared at you. There has been a report, it is said, several reports. The guards are doubled, and the clients are diminished. Clients, you are now called. You have not read these reports, naturally, but representatives of Red Cross have returned to discuss developments with you, part of your basic rights, you are told. You are now called clients and the Red Cross representatives report details. The clients are termed problematic. The clients do not cooperate with security personnel. Clients refuse to formalise their concerns in writing. Clients continue to be involved in voluntary starvation protests. Clients are being monitored. Termination of client services is imminent.

You, one of the last clients, wait at the doorway of your hut until a whistle will blow, after which you will be transported through the gates onto a truck and thence to the landing strip further into the island. After all this time, during which your beard has finally grown to something respectable, and you have attained your full height, or so your uncle claimed, you will leave still not having sighted the waves on the beach that you hear as you sit beside your carryall and wait, your cardboard sign in your hands.

THIRD

Carry Your Heart

THE GATHERING WAS on the opposite side of the river, just out of her line of sight. Marion turned her head far enough to see without slowing down. She always walked at a brisk pace, too quick for most of the people she knew, so she usually walked alone, and this didn't bother her. But this afternoon she had purpose. The 423 would be arriving soon and if she missed it there would be a forty-minute wait for the next bus. And then her Sunday afternoon would be gone, and then it would soon be dark and chilly, and then she may as well stay home and not bother treating herself at all.

Past the bridge over the river was a grassy section, recently landscaped, a new apron of lawn surrounded by a gravel path, a stand of callistemon protecting it from the wind that rose from the river. On the lawn were knots of people wearing bright clothes, lime green, aqua, orange, and more brightly coloured blankets or shawls – hard to tell at a distance – were pegged against the cyclone wire of the adjacent children's playground. There was music, soft and flute-like, and she caught the scent of incense. A hippie party. She saw women and men busy opening wicker baskets, and handing around plastic laundry buckets, more lime green, purple and yellow, and prising lids off Eskies. A trickle of people led from the car park past a clump of casuarinas, whole families, with children in strollers and on pushbikes crunching over the casuarina needles that were thick on the paths. Everywhere were vibrant colours; even the browns and dark blues on the women's skirts and men's shirts seemed to shimmer. A pair of miniature dachshunds sporting matching tie-dyed jackets were tethered to the fence next to an enormous shaggy dog. As she passed, the shaggy dog glanced her way and then at the ground, beseeching forgiveness for his cerise neckerchief. The dachshunds maintained an erect pose of contemptuous overconfidence: they could wear anything and need not look at anyone. One side of a marquee slowly rose from the ground as four people pulled on ropes. Balinese flags were already fluttering at the perimeters of the party. But she would not pause and watch; she would get that bus.

Five-thirty at the latest she'd be at the bookshop. A good half-hour for browsing, then she would make her purchases, giving herself plenty of time before the shop closed. Depending on how busy Newtown was, she might eat at the cheap Vietnamese place, or wander down to the Indian diner on Enmore Road. Then take the bus back again, before it became too late to walk home along the river path.

The council needed to install more lights to make people like her feel safe walking alone.

When Edward appeared at the doorway she was reaching up to replace a thick paperback on the top shelf. In an instant he took in her long hair under the LED downlight, the long neck, her long arms and legs, saw the whole lean length of her, dressed in black jeans and dove-grey shirt, something green knotted around her neck, and his heart, already racing from the quick scramble across the road against the traffic, skipped a beat.

Skipped a beat. He caught himself out before the cliché was fully formed. Still eyeing her under the downlight (she was looking at another title on the top shelf, the fingers of one long hand fanned out, brushing the shelf) he put a hand to his chest. Of course his heart had not skipped a beat. His heart was in excellent condition, confirmed at the doctor's only last week. And hearts only skipped beats in the worst kind of stories. So what was it?

He realised he was staring and turned to the shelf on the right. Non-fiction. Our Staff Picks. Sidestepping a man in a bushranger beard and cloth cap steering a baby in a pram towards the door, he squeezed against the display of hardbacks on sale to let them pass. The pram was black, massive, bearing three inflated wheels with deep treads. A Panzer of a pram, designed to destroy and vanquish. The father looked grim under the cap and beard, asserting a right to occupy bookshop territory as if Edward, the regular book buyer – the book-buying *nut*, in fact, as his sons always said – were the invader. It had been different when his boys were little. He never considered taking them into a bookshop, let alone ploughing through narrow aisles and busy shoppers in such bulk. The stroller he and Anne had for the boys was a lightweight thing, yellow and blue stripes. Even so, they had avoided shops and cafés. Inner city bars were unthinkable. The inner city unthinkable.

A drink in a bar would be good now. A quiet bar, where he could read and sip a martini. It was on the cusp of martini season, in Edward's view. Another few weeks and it would be too cold for martinis – it would be red wine and Irish whiskey season – but now, when the afternoon had been warm, and the cool of the evening was just laying itself down, it would be perfect. He glanced across at the woman. She was peering through gold-rimmed glasses, which were not even fashionably unfashionable, at two books in her hands, glancing from right to left as if she would buy only one. As he eased out of the wake left by the father and pram on his way towards Travel, he allowed his head to swivel right to take her in again in full. She was so tall. Her hair was long and thick, falling past her shoulders. She looked to be anywhere between forty and sixty. She struck him as a possible martini drinker. Anne had hated martinis. She had only drunk white wine, the fruity kind.

He would never know if it was a sudden stab of pain (or anger) at the thought of Anne, or something else, something the poets might have explained for him, but he dropped his hand from the Patrick Leigh Fermor title he was considering buying, turned away from Travel altogether and walked as directly as he could, stepping around Crime and Thrillers and past another pram, this time with two babies, to the shelf in front of her. He was so close he could have tapped her on the shoulder, said something unoriginal like, Don't I know you? Followed by a laugh, and an apology, and then he could have initiated a short chat about the books she was buying, then suggested a drink. Possibly. He did not suppose she drank martinis after all.

Standing beside her, he glanced up to check the fat paperback she had been replacing when he walked through the door two minutes before, when dark was already settling on the street and throwing into soft relief the yellow warmth of the bookshop's nooks and corners. When he first saw her and his heart skipped a beat, or appeared to. *The Luminaries.* He had heard of it. It had won the Booker. He rarely read fiction so probably wouldn't bother, but he reached up and took it down anyway, trying to watch her without appearing to, hoping his glasses would disguise the effort his eyeballs were making to take her in sideways.

Marion stepped away but only slightly, the gesture intended as politeness, to allow the man more room. She registered the bulk of him, solid and tall in a black t-shirt, charcoal jeans, sensible shoes, black-framed glasses, curly brown hair. He looked like a poet. For a second she felt disorientated, Poetry being way down the back of the shop, past Children's and Drama, on the way to the second-hand collection that lined the passage to the back door.

Or maybe he was in the wrong section? But poets were entitled to browse Recent Fiction, surely? In fact poets probably never looked at the poetry section; they probably found it too depressing. These thoughts presented themselves so engagingly that she involuntarily turned her head to look down the shop towards Poetry – as if to check for herself that no poets were there, that no one at all was there – and in doing so saw him full in the face, staring at her, *The Luminaries* in hand, his mouth slightly open as if he had been caught out doing something wrong.

She glanced down at the book, then back into his face. His mouth pressed shut. Behind the glasses he had beautiful almond-shaped green eyes. She registered that his beard needed a trim before looking away again so as not to appear rude. But then they'd made eye contact, so it would be ruder not to say something, surely? But what would she say? She realised the most conversation she'd had with anyone all day was when she'd got on the bus and said good afternoon as she tapped her card, and even so the driver had merely grunted in acknowledgement and then ignored her when she had called out thank you before she alighted. Feeling too warm, trying to unknot her scarf with one hand, she fumbled with the two books and, as if some B-grade screenplay now dictated all her movements, the scarf slipped to the floor while she was still considering what to say. He bent and retrieved it and handed it over.

'Lovely scarf.'

'Oh. Thanks. It was a present.' Holding her hair aside, she looped the scarf back around her neck, considering how to return the courtesy. The book, of course, the one he held. 'Are you buying that?'

'Maybe. It's very long, though.'

'Yes, that's what I thought. Not sure I'd have time to read it. God, I've only just finished *War and Peace*. Took me two whole months.'

Was she an idiot? What ridiculous pretentiousness possessed her to mention *War and Peace*, even if it was true she'd read it recently? More precisely, re-read it. She had first read it when she was twenty and ignorant but had assumed that reading the Russians made one literary. Now, aged fifty, she realised she should actually read it properly, and the effort had literally strained her wrists. Only when she was towards the end had she realised she should have simply taken a Stanley knife and sliced the volume into four or five sections. That way she could at least have taken it on the bus and into the bath with ease.

She could say none of this to him, of course. He was probably thinking she was a total nerd. Then again, they were in a bookshop.

The scarf was a present. Not from a lover, he found himself hoping (what the fuck was wrong with him?), but a nano-second later felt grateful that it had provided the perfect excuse for a gesture of chivalry. When he handed it back, noting its fine green weave with a pattern of small zebras, he also observed the length of her hands and delicate tapering fingers. No ring. Not that he was looking, especially. It was when she held out the books she was still clutching awkwardly – he accepted them without taking his eyes off her face – then with her hands free reached around and scooped her hair out of the way with one and slid the scarf across her neck with the other, that his heart definitely skipped a beat, no mistaking. He felt something deep inside his chest, like a miniature prisoner was trapped there, hammering to get out. Without intending to, he clapped the books to his chest, and breathed audibly.

'Are you okay?' Frowning, she took back the books.

'Yeah. Yes, fine. Occasionally, I just get this . . .' He patted his chest again, thinking.

'Heartburn?'

'Yes,' he said. 'But nothing a decent martini can't fix.'

Her daughter would have warned her about this. Kelly would have applied her twenty-something scrutiny to the scenario and exhorted her to turn around, walk back to the cheap Vietnamese in the opposite direction, have the dinner alone that she planned, and return home unscathed. The thought almost made Marion reach for her phone, but of course her daughter was in Japan, and had been since last year when she'd acquired a teaching position. It was Kelly who had given her the green zebra scarf. She touched it now, stroking it all the way down as she walked along the busy street beside the man, whose name she didn't even know. Oh, yes, what Kelly would have to say on the matter. Well, she was only having one drink, and nowhere was safer than a Sunday autumn evening in Newtown with hundreds of people around.

Afterwards she could still have her dinner for one and be home by nine.

The man walked slower than Marion. She had got a little ahead of him and then a safety bollard at a side-street crossing – would they never finish repairing the footpath? – caused them to break and pause and she saw a look of anxiety pass across his face. So she held her left hand back and up, and he took it and they raised their arms over the bollard as they walked past it, then dropped them in tandem as if they both did this every day of their lives. Another obstacle appeared straightaway, in the form of a homeless person and his dog squatting on the footpath, raspily demanding a gold coin. The dog, like all dogs belonging to homeless people, seemed both calm and indifferent.

She stopped, realising she had no change in her purse. The homeless person called out again. 'Two dollars, luv, just two dollars?' The dog lay down with its nose on its paws as if denying all responsibility. The street was so noisy she leaned closer to the man, who with his free hand started patting his pockets for change.

'Listen, where are we going?'

'It's just up here,' he said, nodding towards a sign she couldn't make out.

'And I don't know your name. You don't know mine.'

'Two fuckin dollars. Anyone got two dollars?'

He turned and faced her, looking at their clasped hands. He brought hers up then drew it towards his chest. 'Edward,' he said. 'Or just Ed, if you like.' He pushed her hand back towards her and then released it.

'I like Edward,' she said. 'I'm Marion.'

'Two dollars?' barked the homeless person again. Edward tossed him the coin he'd finally found in his pocket.

The ache, the pain, the skipping, the stab, the whatever. He felt it in his chest once more. He put the martini down and lifted his hand towards his heart when he realised what he was doing, and reached for the glass again, gazing at her as he sipped. The light in the bar was weak but warm, making her face look like toasted gold. Her hair gleamed. Finally he recognised the sensation – even though he also knew he was feeling it for the first time in his life – the sensation that was bearing down on him with the force of a bullet train threatening to carry him along at thrilling speed, or obliterate every trace of him. He was dizzy. If he closed his eyes he might just keel over sideways.

'Are you all right?'

There was a crease between her eyebrows. It was the second time she'd had to ask that, and they'd only met fifteen minutes ago. He watched her hand reach around to sweep her hair to one side of her neck, the gesture already achingly familiar. And they'd only met fifteen minutes ago. He glanced at his watch. Seventeen.

He recognised it, he understood. He needed to act quickly if he had any hope. This was not a condition any doctor could fix. Only one person could help. He stood up.

'What's wrong?' Alarm now in her voice.

'I'll be back.' He raced out the door.

*

Her mouth fell open. She stared at the table, avoiding the glances of anyone else who might have witnessed the last few moments and been curious, or worse: pitied her. Abandoned barely fifteen minutes into the first date in years. She put the glass to her lips and refused to let them tremble when she sensed a movement and glanced up to see him dart back through the door.

'And whatever, whatever you do, please don't ever cut your hair.' He raced off again.

Marion pulled out the two books she had bought. *The Marriage Plot* and *The Time Traveler's Wife*. Her mouth twisted. Was her subconscious telling her something? Or maybe the literary industry, the universe? The light in the bar was too dim for reading and the noise level was escalating quickly. She sighed and opened the first. She could pretend to be reading, which would ameliorate the humiliation, but within minutes she was conscious that the narrow corridor of the place was filling with young bodies, and that a group perched on stools at the bar was almost pressing into her back. She edged the chair around the dot of a table until she sat sideways to them and faced directly away from the door. She would finish her martini, and not rush it. His martini too, fuck it. Plus the olives. Then she would arise with dignity. She would put on her jacket, pack her books into her bag and, with her back very straight, walk out of the bar and into the evening. Thank god she would return to an empty house, because telling Kelly about this was unimaginable.

*

Before leaving, she went to the bathroom to stare herself down in the mirror. When she squeezed her way out the door Edward was standing in the street, looking forlorn and guilty. He butted a cigarette and handed her a thin volume.

'Had to run down to the other bookshop. The first was closed already.'

'What is it?' She couldn't believe how glad she was to see him again.

'Just the *Selected Poems*.'

She took it and held it close under the streetlight. e. e. cummings. He had marked a page with a card.

'Read it later,' he said.

'Can I just read this?' She extracted the card. Its cover featured three martini glasses, blue, red and green, with a printed recipe inside. '"Classic Martini",' she read out before staring at him. His forehead creased, his mouth twitched on one side. 'Well,' she finally said, 'we'd better have another one then.'

Still holding the slim book of poetry in one hand, she wobbled down the aisle, the second-last passenger, and alighted at the stop before crossing the river. This late at night she should have continued to the better lit stop and walked home along the street. But instead she picked her way down the cracked steps, and followed the path beside the river. She walked warily, glad she was wearing flat shoes as her only meal for the night had ended up consisting of five Sicilian olives. Before they farewelled and she got on the bus, she had inspected the book of poems, and the page where she had reinserted the martini card.

'"i carry your heart",' she had read, then closed the book and looked up at him. She was tall, but he was taller. 'How is your heart, by the way?'

'Oh, good, now. Poetry and gin are excellent for it.' His smile was so full she could see a dimple on his right cheek, under the beard.

The hippie party was still in progress, though evidently winding down. Candles had been placed everywhere, small tea lights in glass jars on the grass, tucked into branches of trees, set along the shoreline amongst the stubs of mangroves in the low tide, placed here and there around the seated guests. And at the centre of the gathering tall candles surrounded a couple seated on cushions. As she walked closer the music dwindled to a quiet hum and a man wearing a striped caftan stood up, picking slowly around the seated people to arrive beside the couple. He held a candle in one hand and a book in the other. Marion paused and leaned against a casuarina. It was not really stickybeaking, not in the circumstances. Besides, everyone but he and the couple was looking away from her.

'I am now going to read Skye and Ben a poem.' His voice was clear, declamatory, as if he were an actor. He placed the candle on the ground while he leafed through the book to find his place, then picked it up again and held it over the page. 'Or part of a poem, as it's too long. It's an epithalamium, by Edmund Spenser.'

Her mouth fell open and her breath caught. The trained

voice had projected each syllable across the darkness as if meant for her ears alone. She lived in a world where knowing long Greek words for certain forms of poetry was useless. But it was a good word, she thought. She had learned it as an undergraduate English major, and still loved the way it engaged every muscle of the tongue and lips to pronounce. She said it now, quietly, as she listened. Epithalamium. It sounded like a rare medical condition, or a drug for an acute form of psychosis, not the name of something celebrating one of life's best occasions.

After several verses of the familiar lines, she smiled, then smiled wider, then laughed and commenced walking away before anyone could hear her. They had their epithalamium and she had something else, something in her chest that quickened as she walked faster, holding tight the book in one hand, her zebra scarf in the other, calling out as she went, 'I carry your heart, I carry your heart,' louder and louder as she ran, enunciating the words perfectly. There, she was not so drunk after all! Fleet with joy, she ran towards home, laughing, her mouth wide open to drink in the remainder of the night.

I am at Home Now

HE WANTED SOME stockings and shoes, two pairs of each. And some handkerchiefs.

She stands by the window, re-reading the letter. It is well creased, no longer crisp, and the seal has crumbled away. There is no stamp. It is twenty-seven years before the first Penny Black, with the image of the queen, twenty-four years before there is a queen. For all these years her husband kept the letter in a drawer in his desk. Now it is amongst the last of his things, which she will keep in a box: the curls of hair, coloured amber and corn silk, tied in scraps of once-white ribbons, now yellowed, and the silver locket containing her portrait only – he never did have the other one painted. The letter is not dated, and it is addressed to her husband. She recalls him reading it to her, and then after that everything is a blur – of the coldest February she had known, of their first infant dying from influenza, of them all being so ill it was many months before she returned to the world.

Hope you remember me madam. She does indeed remember the two men who came from the bottom of the world to live with them, in the house of Edward Kent, where they worked. One was already ill, dying only weeks after they arrived at Eltham, despite the doctor's recommendation of fresh air away from the city. The other enchanted her, once she overcame her surprise. She had never seen a black man before, let alone one with missing teeth, and scars on his face. This was just before the spring of 1794, and the men had become sick, quite literally, of London.

His hut on the point has now been demolished. After all this time he mostly prefers to be on his own but when the desire for company takes him, he moves from place to place in the town. Some days it is as if his own family spurns him. Other days he may saunter into the governor's house when he pleases and eat at his table, or sleep in the servant's room provided for him. But he knows the men of property despise him. Scoundrel, wastrel, drunkard, savage.

His hut faced the water, glittering by day, shot with shrieking gulls and dotted with ships groaning and creaking in the wind. Now he stands at the point where it stood, gazing at all that has changed since he has been away. No more canoes ferrying families from cove to cove. No more fishing. Yes, he prefers to be on his own but does not want the loneliness. *I have not my wife; another black man took her away.* He expects he will not have another wife now. At night the peace is almost terrifying: on the opposite shore there is such stillness, with few fires any more. The cold starry world above him seems wider than ever.

It has been too long. She will take the shirts, finish embroidering the handkerchiefs. She sets to work, sitting by the upstairs front window to catch the best light. The last time she did this was when Mr Phillips was already too weak to stand. She had intended to measure the length of him one last time, but rather than fuss around him, she took apart one of his old frayed shirts and used that as a pattern. She would sit here in the same spot by the window, with the door across the landing ajar so that she would hear him if he called. He rarely called out, but if she heard the cough she would drop her sewing and rush in, in case he needed a damp cloth across his face, or a fresh handkerchief.

You nurse me madam when I sick. He knew what this was like, had nursed his first wife, who'd caught the serpent dust disease. He shivers now, remembering the suffering of that time. How he brought water to his wife yet could never quench her thirst. How she cried and cried for relief, until her throat almost closed over with the pustules that had crawled inside her mouth. The terrible heat of her body, then the sudden clammy cold. And how he expected every day to develop the same trembling chills and pain in his back that signalled the start of that disease. Why he was spared when so many others were not, he has never known. He cremated his wife's body close to where she died, wrapped in her possum-skin blanket, a stone on her forehead.

Mr Phillips never wore these shirts. By the time she was hemming the cuffs he was barely able to move in his bed. She sat right beside him then, urging him to drink some beef broth or take bread soaked in warm milk. She took to sleeping in the armchair rather than risk the distance of her own room. The day after the funeral she put away the unfinished shirts with her fabrics and patterns in the box at the foot of the bed. All she has kept aside is a small basket with essentials, threads and needles, a few notions, just for repairs.

When he thinks about it, he realises he has always needed to live near the water, sometimes right by it. Once he lived *on* the water, in ships that sailed for months and months, taking him and his companion to see the King and back home again. *Not me go to England no more.* In London it was such cheerless weather, they always felt cold, even in summer. He enjoyed the company of so many interesting people, enjoyed the attention, even enjoyed the qualified respect. They thought he was ignorant and insensitive, but he knew when he was being paraded, mocked. He kept this knowledge to himself, sharing it only with Mrs Phillips, who looked after him towards the end. Together they made their fun, and her merry charm eased the pain in his heart, when Yemmerrawanne died.

*

He was always so polite. When she first met him, when he and Yemmerrawanne were brought to Mr Kent's house, he took her hand in an educated style and bowed deeply as he pronounced the words, Good day, Mrs Phillips. I am very pleased to meet you. He impressed her with his instant regard for her little spaniel, who licked his hand when he held it out. Later she invited him to call her Betsy, but he would refuse. And so in turn she insisted she would call him Mr Bennelong and that is how they spoke to each other, with exaggerated courtesy, each colluding in the part that had been written for them. Oh, Mr Bennelong, she would say of a morning, Would you care for a boiled egg for breakfast? Or perhaps you might partake of a bowl of porridge? He would always reply by asking for bread, toasted if it were no trouble, and they would eat at the little breakfast table in the parlour, like genteel folk.

She never called Yemmerrawanne Mr Yemmerrawanne, though he always called her Mrs Phillips. He was so shy, barely speaking to anyone, except his companion. It was Mr Bennelong who came to the kitchen asking for a cup of sweet tea for him, or a slice of bread and butter. His friend was far too diffident to have her tend to him but when she realised how ill he had become she could not stay away, and brought him cooling cloths when his brow sweated, and more blankets when he shivered. She made sure the fire in the grate never went out, even though the weather was turning warm. When Mr Bennelong went out on his excursions with her husband or Mr Kent, she fetched her knitting and sat with him, Penny on a cushion at her feet, watching as he slept and dreamed.

I live at the governor's. It amuses him to satisfy his hosts when he perches his cutlery directly above the food, spears a piece of corned beef or a round of potato, and brings it to his mouth. Equally it amuses him to see the glint in their eyes when he brushes the silver knife and fork aside and takes a joint in his hands, tearing the meat from the bone and licking the fat off his lips with exaggerated sweeps of his tongue. And when he applies the linen napkin to his fingertips and mouth, dabbing gently as he has been shown, before half-folding the napkin to one side of his plate, as he has also been shown, he can barely keep from erupting in laughter, such is the consummate joy of watching their reaction. Once he sprinkled salt from the cellar daintily over his soup using thumb and fingertips, gazed serenely around the table to evident approval, then plunged his face into the bowl and slurped the broth with gusto. He stood up, bowed, then ran from the table that day, laughing so hard he was almost doubled over.

It was her job to make their meals and tend to their other domestic needs, her husband's job to accompany them out, take and send messages, make introductions and meet with important men. Once Mr Phillips came home with new frockcoats, breeches and shirts for them and she helped tie their neck scarves, standing first behind Mr Bennelong and then Yemmerrawanne, seated in a chair before the cheval mirror, tying and retying the white silk until they took over for themselves. They would rarely look directly at her, but that day she held the gaze of Yemmerrawanne in the mirror and noted the flat dullness of his eyes. She knew then that he would not recover.

Scoundrel. Savage. Traitor. This is what the men of the town call him. He has read what they write about him, heard the talk. He understands now the mighty price of that long voyage to England and back, with its banquets and parties. The outings to the theatre, the galleries. The audience with the King. He will not repay all that with his clan's land, life, blood. He will not. *All my friends alive and well.* He welcomes the company of sailors and ex-convicts, with their demijohns of rum and their pipe tobacco. Mr Squire comes to him one day and persuades him to return home to Wangal country. You need your clan, not all this, Mr Squire tells him, waving his arm around at his drunken companions in the tavern. And they need you. He understands this, that he will die without them, as he nearly did in England.

Back up the river, embraced by his people again, he finds his tastebuds sharpened, his eyesight clearer. He hears so much more: the call of magpie geese, the sly plop of burra at the riverbank, leaves talking in the breeze.

They buried Yemmerrawanne in the Eltham church-yard, in a plot reserved by Mr Kent next to the wife and baby he had lost years before. Mr Bennelong would not be comforted, wailing and crying for days and nights to follow. He scraped a knife against his head, he scratched his fingernails down his face until his cheeks bled. Penny whined and trembled and ran away from him to hide under the bed and, even when he became calm again, regarded him with caution. He lost weight and his face became dry and dull, and when Mrs Phillips heard the first gurgling in his cough she went and spoke to her husband and then to Mr Kent. He would die soon if he did not return to his own home, she knew it. There, she had learned, it did not snow in winter, and for months and months on end people could walk around wearing little or no clothing, so mild was the weather.

You very good madam. She went to him one morning like this, some weeks after Yemmerrawanne died. He was sitting with his face upturned, eyes shut, his chest bared to the sun. Her shadow fell over him and he flinched before opening his eyes, and drew the cords of his shirt together. He knew she did not like to see his cicatrices. Mr Bennelong, she said to him, your cough worsens. I fear you will not recover, like your friend. By then he was eager to leave. By then there were no more excursions to the theatre, the galleries, the cathedral. Here on the edge of the city he toured gardens and went boating on the river with the men. The suits made for court, and not worn since a formal dinner some months back, now hung in the wardrobe. One morning when she took them out for airing, he stopped her and said, I will wear this when I return. I shall live at the governor's house.

Shall you, indeed, Mr Bennelong? she said with mock formality, and that was the first time he smiled in weeks.

He departed on the *Reliance*, on a cool bright day, the sky scrubbed clean of clouds. At the quay Mr Kent introduced him to a tall young man. Here is Mr Bass, he said. He will take pleasure in your company on the voyage. And he is the ship's doctor, he will look after you. He took his hand and shook it with the usual courtesy he applied in such circumstances, but Mr Bass took his hand in both and held it with warmth. This is a genuine pleasure, Mr Bennelong, he said. I hope you and I might find much to talk about over the next few months. Then he introduced his friend the midshipman. Mr Flinders is to chart the coast of your country, he said.

Country, he repeated. My country. The words tasted like lilly pilly, sour and sweet.

Something has shifted in her. It is the tide of grief, receding. Whole days at a time pass when she does not think of the little ones, all five of them dead before the age of three. And she is able to walk to the churchyard and lay flowers on their graves, her husband's only a year old, and feel that her grief is slowly being laid to rest too, underneath the same soft grass that waves in a breeze and in spring produces tiny daisies. She is able to rise and drink her morning tea and go about her day as if there is something approaching purpose in it. She has resumed attending church and on other days will venture out, visiting the Wednesday markets, or just walking in the parkland beside the river. One day a week she attends the poorhouse with knitted socks or mittens, or bowls of puddings and soup.

But even as his senses seem to sharpen and gain focus, his bones and joints begin to soften. He is not an old man but has the body of one. After yet another fall from a leg that buckles without warning, he is persuaded to move into the room set up for him in Mr Squire's house on the river. With its feather mattress bed and bowl of flowers on the pine dresser, it is more than comfortable, but he insists the French windows to the verandah remain open day and night. Now he comes and goes as he likes, resting alone when he needs to. Often the orchard workers arrive in the morning to see him sitting on the verandah, wrapped in the white counterpane from the bed, a blue wisp rising from his pipe.

Mr Bennelong never asked for shirts, rather for shoes and stockings and handkerchiefs, but she takes the shirts from the oakwood chest anyway. They only need their cords inserted and some final hemming on the neckline. There is no one else to give them to and besides she is glad to send them to him: she enjoyed helping her visitors with their attire, correcting the tilt of their hats and adjusting their neckties. It intrigued her that Mr Bennelong still had trouble with his buttons, and yet had such deft fingers he could conjure lengths of string from out of a few strands of hair or wisps of rag, or fashion a musical instrument from a leaf pressed to his lips. Once he took dough in the kitchen and with a clean stick made tiny faces on each scone, every one amusing and different. Her husband's shoes are still fine, they should fit him well.

Three days into the new year, Mr Squire is aroused before dawn by a sound he knows and dreads – voices joined in such deep and penetrating song it seems the very sky itself should crack apart. He finds Bennelong lying on the verandah, one hand still curled around his pipe. The singing reaches a height, now accompanied by the slow clap of stick against stick and the beginning of a ritual wailing that is so powerful it creates a long shiver up and down his back. In the stillness of the early morning the river catches the anthem, throwing it back from the opposite shore. He turns, embraced in an amphitheatre of sound, an opera of grief. As the light grows he sees row upon row of people standing at the garden fence, the song now melding with their cries, the dogs howling with their throats exposed, their snouts pointing to the grey sky. He reaches down and lifts up the body of his friend and turns and slowly walks towards them. *I am at home now.*

It has been eighteen years since he sailed away, back to his home. The journey still takes eight months. She wraps the shoes and clothing in a piece of calico and then in brown paper, two layers, tying it with string. Tomorrow she will take it to the carrier who comes daily for parcels, and can be trusted to ensure it reaches the depot, to be forwarded to Portsmouth. She has checked the weekly shipping report and knows that the convict transport *Archduke Charles* is leaving for Cork in two weeks, en route to Port Jackson. She addresses the parcel to Mr Bennelong, care of the governor's house.

Note: In about 1796 Woollarawarre Bennelong wrote a letter to Mr Phillips, with whom he had stayed in England; in this letter he thanked Mrs Phillips for caring for him, and asked for some items of clothing.

No Hot Drinks in the Ward

By the end of the second day she decided there was perhaps no need to appear to be so pathetically grateful. She had been saying thank you an awful lot. We will come again in another hour. Thank you. Don't hesitate to ask if you have any more questions. Thank you. Let the ward manager know if you need anything else. Thank you. You can sleep here in the pull-out bed. Thank you, thank you, thank you.

She had stepped through too many sets of electronic glass doors. She was in a spaceship, a Tardis. Time collapsed and space expanded. Had a day passed, or a week? A purple bubble-shaped monster lurked in a corner somewhere. All the children looked like freaks, moon-faced, trailing machines on wheels that beeped and flashed. Perhaps she had landed on another planet. The language was alien, the lights eerie, fed along the corridors from the floor. Even her son noticed it, the one who was ill. All the kids here are bald, he said, suspiciously, tugging on her arm when they first entered.

A lifetime of crying, down there in the emergency ward. A crying child slows down time, and there was a dozen of them downstairs, children, babies, watching TV in between their wails, arching their backs and thumping their grim-faced parents. They had a private examination room, where a series of doctors and nurses trailed in and out, asking the same questions over and over, which she answered again and again, between tears, and with thanks. Thank you, thank you, thank you. And I'm sorry for crying so much. A nurse handed her son a handlebar thing attached by wires to a box and a TV screen.

PlayStation! he cried. I've always wanted one.

She would buy him one, just as soon as they got out of here. Already she was making elaborate deals in an economy of illness and recovery. If he makes it, she would buy not only the PlayStation but every other toy, she would forsake every principle that was opposed to mindless electronic games, if it meant he would survive.

More doctors trailed in and out. More questions. Forms. Tears. The weariness. She could sleep for a year. She would never sleep again. She answered questions and ticked boxes on forms. Is your child lactose intolerant? No. Is your child prone to nosebleeds? No. Does your child bruise easily? No. Is your child asthmatic? No, no, no, no, he is the healthiest child I have ever had, she wanted to scream.

Maybe she did scream it, and the warm mellow surfaces of the hospital absorbed those words along with all the other bacteria floating around. Maybe an orderly with a mop and bucket of antiseptic took those words and flushed them away in a scrubbing room. As she answered questions the child played on, his thumbs and fingers instantly aligning with the buttons of the console as if he had been doing this since the womb.

Oh, that, the womb. The wicked, wicked womb. Maybe it was her fault. Wasn't it always the mother's fault? Between doctors and their questions she raked through her pregnancy. Did she scrape lead paint off walls? Visit nuclear power stations, live near a waste dump, breathe in toxic fumes, eat soft French cheese? Maybe it was the freeway nearby, the weedkiller she sprayed on the path, the microwaves. That was it. She must have used the microwave oven too much, pressing her belly close to the bench as she heated her other kids' noodles, oatmeal, warmed milk for her coffee. She would never forgive herself. The coffee, that must have been it. She should have bought organic. Fair-trade. Given it up altogether. Now that she thought about it she recalled reading an article about carcinogens and caffeine. It was definitely the coffee.

That didn't stop her drinking endless cups of it, that first day, night, weekend, week. Instant, from the patient kitchen, where ripped sachets and packets of sugar littered the bench amid a sticky sprinkling of brown, where there were never enough cups but a fridge full of milk.

And the tears, how much could she weep! Would that she would dry up, but no, it was the reverse, as if inside all her cells were bailing water, preparatory to jumping ship themselves. Tears and drinks of water and visits to the toilet, twice, five times in the hours that passed, she lost count. All the tissues in her pocket turned to crumpled sog, and still she kept them in her hand. A handful of her tears that flowed for hours, like summer rain, unpredictable, violent, that stopped as suddenly as they began, and then commenced again, flowing into her hands, through her fingers, down her shirt. There were plenty of tissues, plain boxes parked on the desk. Nurses and doctors silently handing them over; at least she supposed they were all medical professionals, though it occurred to her at some point she could have been weeping to the cleaner. An army of doctors and nurses. She didn't know who was who. Whom, whom, she repeated to herself, don't let your grip of language slip as well.

In their democratic outfits, casual, monochrome, even ungendered, they all looked the same. They could all have been orderlies and cleaners. She did not know which of these doctors were more senior, she did not know there was even a hierarchy, until the final appearance late into the first night, a short man in normal clothes, with a gentle voice and a loud tie.

The first thing you need to know is that your son has every chance of a full recovery, he said. Now we won't know yet what type of leukaemia it is – there were varieties? – that will be determined through a biopsy. But it's more than likely it is acute lymphoblastic leukaemia.

His voice was like a balm, even as he uttered the words that announced disease of such grave proportions. His demeanour was reassuring.

We have an eighty per cent success rate of curing ALL here, he said.

She began crying again. But then there wasn't time for crying; he was telling her it was called acute for a good reason: the cancer cells were multiplying as they spoke. They were wasting time down here off the emergency department. The cancer cells were, right this second, huddling in corridors having meetings on the run, hitting the phones and securing support. Within an hour they would have consolidated their numbers, by midnight doubled in size. Tripled. Before they counted the ballot and announced victory, the team had to get her son up to the ward and initiate tests, start treatment.

Could she not even take him home for the weekend? Think it through? They looked at her, pitying but resolute. Once, if she had ever thought about it – as if you ever did, oh, I wonder what it would be like if my six-year-old got leukaemia, and what's the fare to Bali this time of year – she would have thought they'd get a second opinion. It would have gone something like this: Yes, he does seem rather tired and listless, and that's certainly an odd bruise. Keep him quiet and rested for the next few days, and we'll run a few tests after the long weekend. Make sure you keep his fluids up and, yes, cordial is okay. Now the blood does seem abnormal. Let's send you off to the McDonald Clinic, they have a lot of facilities there. And then we'll get Dr Spry in, he's a specialist in paediatric haematology, and then we might have a chat to Dr Kind. And/or Dr Queen.

But there was no time for second opinions, not with those cancer cells caucusing in corners and calling in favours right now. Besides, this doctor, their new doctor, emanated calm. From the moment he spoke she trusted him. He'd been at his family dinner when called by the hospital to return and assess her son, his new patient. A paper napkin was still tucked into his pocket. She would do whatever he said.

This doctor was a kind of deity, a king amongst deities. Zeus, surrounded by Hera, Poseidon and Gaia, in this whole new panoply of divine medical staff. He reappeared the next morning, and that afternoon, and again on the Sunday morning. On the Monday morning when he appeared again, she asked him if he didn't have any time off. He explained that the doctors worked four weeks straight, to ensure continuity for the patients and their families. She felt guilty for this, as if she'd overused her quota of care, swallowed over the weekend in one greedy gulp. The whole family should never come to hospital again, never present at an emergency ward with a broken limb. None of them, ever, have appendicitis, or incur a burn, or be injured in a road accident. She could not afford that; she would fry chips and slice beans with extra care, or not at all. She should give up driving.

Meanwhile, each visit he had remained calm, patient. It was as if her son was his only patient, as if his only concern in the world was the care and recovery of this child. She wanted to embrace him, but she would stop saying thank you.

By then she must have met fifty people. Information, reassurance, kindness, help. She was overloaded with it, each morsel of information, each new piece of advice, representing a little wrapped gift on the way to her son's recovery. The treatment was delivered via a team, so she met systematically every doctor, resident, registrar, nurse, social worker, play therapist on the oncology ward.

The day after the boy was admitted came further blood tests, a biopsy, yet more blood tests – were there actually enough litres in that little body? – and a steroid drug that was already starting to flush cancer cells from his system like a benign dose of Drano. One of the oncology nurses took her on a tour of the ward. She showed her the parents' room and balcony, the bathroom, the laundry, the kitchen, explained about the roast dinner offered every Saturday, the protocol for use of the fridge and the freezer. She could keep food for herself and her son here in a marked container; she could wash and dry their clothes there. She was shown the children's playroom, for mobile patients and their siblings and friends. She learned about the hospital school, the play therapists, the music therapists, the volunteers. The otherworldliness of it all was enhanced by the eerie lighting of the green and purple decor, and that alien game machine that lurked in every ward, which the kids all begged to play. She politely inspected it all, somewhat bemused. Why all the showing-off of these facilities? She had been told that her son would be in hospital for a few days to commence treatment, to have a portacath implanted in his chest, for the giving of chemotherapy and the taking of blood. What possible use might a laundry be for her, what interest might she have in keeping food in their fridge? Her son was to be treated as an outpatient; she was not going to need all these facilities.

Perhaps at some point someone had told her that despite that he still could get sick and need to stay for more than a day, and perhaps she'd even registered it, but not consciously. She toured the ward like a mere visitor, as if inspecting a property with an idea to rent, humouring the nurse, taking note of sagging window blinds and peeling paint, avoiding saying thank you but nodding and smiling.

Within twenty-four hours she was familiar enough with the cramped kitchen routine: expertly juggling styrofoam cups and teabags, sidestepping other parents, opening the fridge door only so much, recognising when not to look another parent in the eye. Too soon it was as familiar as home. Within days she was an old hand, and by the time her son went home she had the kitchen dance down smoothly. Within weeks the need for that tour became clear.

And the children, the other patients, their parents. The parents especially. She rapidly discovered that every parent had a story, many of them too willing to share it. In those first days and weeks she did not want to hear stories of treatments that had failed or stalled, about children who proved to be allergic to certain types of chemotherapy, children who had relapsed, children in or awaiting transplant. Children whose temperatures soared, whose skin burned up, who rejected their medication, whose coughs racked their chests, who were resistant to antibiotics, who had not left the hospital ward for three whole months, three and a week, to be exact. There were parents who were experts, frighteningly well informed, in a way she did not want to be. Experts eager, over-eager, to pass on the wealth of their experience, to welcome her into the strange fraternity that hunched in the ward corridors, speaking in hushed voices, nursing illicit cups of coffee away from the signs on every wall saying NO HOT DRINKS IN THE WARD!, apparently the very worst hazard of all.

She resisted their embraces, their empathetic smiles. She was suspicious, like a potential recruit to a special cult. She would not be approached on the subway walk by people in skivvies urging pamphlets on her. But as she became accustomed to the ward, she could see it was a secret society, a sorority of trackpants and takeaway dinners, dressing-gowns and cup noodles. Members of this cult huddled in the dimly lit corridors pretending they hadn't just returned from a quick cigarette on the fire stairs. Membership did not seem optional. She never wanted to belong. One night a father passed her a beer from a stash under his daughter's bed, and she thrilled with complicit joy. Unlike HOT DRINKS, alcohol was never expressly forbidden, but there was the deep sense that someone called Matron would spring them and turf them out. As the weeks passed she tried not to be so cold, but still, she could not roam the wards with jolly purpose like other mothers, paying visits here and there and organising hairdressing and massages. *Put your name on the list below, Janelle will come on Wednesday afternoons to do Mum's nails!!* It smacked too much of a cruise ship somewhere. One of the fathers, to whom initiating conversations and cheerily exchanging information was second nature, organised weekend barbecues on the service balcony off the parents' room. She said she would go but then did not. She wanted to do what her son did and lie in bed with the sheets pulled up over her face. Her son refused to be the prime audience for the clown doctors, the Wiggles, the footy stars. He remained aloof and unresponsive to the play therapists and the volunteer teachers, the music therapists and the Rent-a-Grandmas. It was not fun, having cancer, and he would not pretend to make it so. The isolation ward was the worst, the ultimate punishment, when his temperature was so high he had to be kept away from everyone but his parent. The bonus was his own bathroom, the downside was that by the time the meals arrived in Isolation, a floor higher, they were even more grey and limp.

But here in Isolation was a small miracle: one day a dog appeared, led by a pet-therapy volunteer, both wearing red bandannas. No hot drinks allowed, but a dog? And what a beautiful dog: Pansy was sleek and black and licked her son on the forearm then snuggled in for a nap. He patted the dog and smiled, and she thought it was the first smile of his she'd seen in weeks, and then when another parent down the hall was yelling about health risks and dogs, and a nurse explained that these dogs couldn't transmit any disease, he cuddled Pansy closer, and shut his eyes and breathed in her normal doggy scent.

And then she cried, because that was when, for the first time in months, she allowed herself to imagine that he might recover.

She learned to count her blessings, to accept clichés, to not be so bothered by the split infinitive. You count your blessings.

The logistics of managing a job and the needs of the older children were eye-crossing at times, but she could see that the alternative was worse. In the day ward, Daffodil North, she met mothers who had no job and only one child. And that child had cancer. Frustrated and exhausted with work that she could take home, or rather to the hospital, reports and spreadsheets, she felt that these things were also a blessing. Entire hours at a time could disappear while filling fields in Excel documents or ensuring objectives were met in prose that was thrillingly peppered with acronyms. Which she was also learning to use in the ward. ALL. AML. The other mothers were able only to focus on their child and that illness. Their emotions were hogtied, their need for the child to recover undiluted by any other demands.

All through the first few months people commented on how well she was coping, but there was no mysterious art to it, no great show of maternal courage: she coped because she had to. There were the other children requiring attention, there was no question of not coping. She absolutely had to cook their dinners, supervise homework, and get them to school on time. She saved her tears for the private times. Mostly.

Sure, they need to nearly kill them in order to cure them. That was an Irish mother doing the kitchen dance, flicking the door of the microwave and opening the fridge and stirring something on the pot as she minced around trying not to be in the way. She was awed by the Irish mother's composure, the practised ease with which she prepared food at all hours of the day and night for her ravenous child on steroids. Her child was entering maintenance – what was that again? she knew she'd been told, just couldn't remember – while her son was only a few months into treatment. You'll get used to it, the Irish mother said.

There was a vast part of her as spongy as jelly when she heard that voice. Any Irish nurse inspired her with a total belief in their powers of healing. This matter-of-fact mother assured her that her own son would practically die, yet survive. It was strangely comforting.

Fuck this, said another mother, who then disappeared for two weeks, leaving her bewildered husband to sleep by the cot of their baby daughter. The child cried when her father left her to go to the bathroom, cried when he headed out for a cup of coffee – which he never brought back to the ward – cried for no reason at all or every reason. Even when Pet Therapy Pansy appeared, she cried, standing wailing in her cot with her fist knuckling her mouth, while her father remained calm and smiling.

She watched from the bedside of her own son across the ward. She wanted to rush over and grab the phone whenever his wife rang and yell at her to come back here at once, while at the same time wishing she could be that woman. Fuck this, she now thought a lot, and realised that finally she had stopped saying thank you.

Nourishment

SHE WAS IN aisle nine – sauces, condiments, seasonings – and had her hand on the packet of star anise when he rang.

'I've googled another recipe,' he said. 'This one says cinnamon stick and cardamom pods and palm sugar.'

She tossed the star anise in the trolley and looked along the rows of tiny bottles. Cardamom, ground. Cayenne pepper. Chilli flakes. Chilli powder. Cinnamon, ground. No cardamom pods. 'Ground cardamom will have to do.'

'No, it says pods. And cinnamon sticks. Can you get cinnamon sticks?'

'Seeds or ground, it won't matter.'

'Not seeds. Pods. Cardamom pods.'

'Seeds, pods, same thing. Anyway, the ground will have to do.' She spotted the cinnamon sticks in the next rack and tossed them in.

'Are you sure? This recipe sounds a lot better than the

other one.' His voice had crept up in pitch, like when he was angry, uncertain, fearful.

'Trust me. It will work the same.' Mary wedged the phone close to her ear, keeping her voice low. She despised shoppers who did this. Especially the men, standing blankly before the stacks of nappies, saying did you want infants' or toddlers' size. Asking what was the difference between skim and Lite White. There weren't any chicken necks and would the dog eat hearts. She could always see the women at the other end of the phone sighing.

'It also says to wash the meat.'

'What? Oh, and I'll get more fish sauce. Wash meat?'

'I don't know. You skim it then strain it then wash it. That's what it says.'

'Okay, I'll look at it when I get home.' She spoke even lower, as if they were conspiring in a robbery. 'I'm just grabbing the last few things then I'll be out of here.'

'Palm sugar,' he said again before she said goodbye and pressed the button. She put the phone into the trolley too but before she rounded the corner into dairy it clattered through to the floor.

Andy watched as she lifted it with the chicken-patterned potholders. It was the biggest stockpot, too big for him to hold and pour the steaming liquid into the bowl. The mush of meat plopped into the strainer, the bones sticking out grey and bare. She wiped the scummy tidemark from around the inside of the pot, rinsed it under the hot tap, and placed it back on the stove.

'Get me the other strainer, can you?'

He fossicked in the drawer for the one with the wooden handle.

'The conical strainer is better,' she explained. 'See how the mesh is finer? You get a clearer soup that way. But the handle is broken.' It sat askew in the bowl. She took it out and placed the other one over the stockpot, poured the stock back in, and turned up the flame.

'Now what?'

'Now you taste it.' Mary held the serving spoon up to his lips.

'It'll be too hot.'

'No, it isn't.' She sipped from her side of the spoon. 'Tasting good.'

He pursed his lips, touched the spoon with them, then recoiled. 'How can you do that! It's boiling.'

She smiled. 'Asbestos lips.' She sipped again. 'Tastes beautiful to me.'

He finally tried it. 'Hey, that's just like the one in the noodle restaurant.'

'Wait until it's simmered another hour or so, it'll be perfect then. It needs a bit more fish sauce, though.'

She showed him how to skim the fat off the surface of the stock, spooning it into an empty yoghurt tub. He copied her movements with the smaller spoon, dribbling fat onto the kitchen bench as it wobbled from stockpot to tub. She leaned against the bench, holding in her impatience to do the job quickly and efficiently, watching the spoon move back and forth to the yoghurt tub until he'd scooped most of the fat out.

'Sometimes at school,' he said thoughtfully, 'I say yoggit. Yoggit. Just like that.'

'What, so kids think you're English?' She tore off a piece of paper towel and mopped up the bench under his spoon.

'Not really. Just for fun. Hey, what about the palm sugar?'

'I didn't get it.'

'You forgot it.' That pitch in his voice again.

'I didn't forget it, I just didn't get it. We can use brown sugar; it only needs a spoonful.'

'It won't taste the same.'

'Trust me.' She sealed the yoghurt tub and dropped it into the bin.

He poked at the meat and bones heaped into a bowl. 'Now it says we have to wash the meat.'

'Andy.' He looked at her. 'I refuse even to think about what that might mean. All we have to do is pick out the biggest bones and stuff. We can save the scraps for Tommy.'

Together, with a pair of tongs each, they picked off the loose bits of gristle and lifted out the largest bones and lumps of meat, placing it all back into the stockpot for the second boil. She had bought the beef bones and osso buco from the Vietnamese butcher, where the owner and his wife worked every day, seven days a week, in the cleanest overalls she had ever seen butchers wear. Mary hadn't consulted any recipe, but Andy had, researching it like a school project, bringing his laptop onto the bench, comparing sites and chewing his bottom lip as he read over the instructions. Palm sugar. Meat washing. It was why she disliked following recipes.

After she cleared up the curls of onion and garlic skins, put away the spices and rinsed the strainers and bowls, she went back to her bookcase. Ikea. Sixty-nine dollars. She timed it, and got it assembled in twenty minutes, no swearing. She was getting better at this, though to be fair it was probably the company's simplest item of furniture. She positioned it in the kitchen and began moving the books across from the stack on the floor that had been there too long, wiping the dust as she went.

'I don't even know why you want a bookcase for your recipe books,' he said, eyeing her from the doorway. 'You never use them.'

Then his phone chirped. He turned away, curling the entire upper half of his body into the phone just as his father did, as if they were spies.

The soup was boiling furiously by the time she finished the books, and she lifted the lid, turning off the gas. The broth was rich and fragrant, the heavy saltiness of the meat closing like a fist around the first delicate waft of the spices. She breathed it in, catching the smell of star anise before it floated off, the black pepper and the cardamom. Andy came over to sniff deeply too.

'All those bones, all that marrow and gristle,' she said. 'It'll be so nourishing, full of protein.'

It was true she never used her recipe books. Some she had never even looked at, let alone used. But it was the idea of the books. She collected them, glanced through them, then replaced them on the stacks of other books, returning to recipes in her memory or imagination. Once she had decided to collect the stray recipes, all the ones cut from magazines and newspapers, the ones on scraps of notepaper in her mother's or a neighbour's hand. She would write them neatly in a book and leave it for the children, for when she was older, or gone. It would contain their favourite dishes, the ones she had never written down nor even read, the ones she could have cooked in her sleep. They might have no idea how she made these dishes that had sustained them all through their childhood: the macaroni cheese, the spinach flan, the crumbed chicken, the jellies made with real fruit, not from a packet. She had even cooked her own baby rusks, way back when Frances was teething, tiny bagel-shaped ones enriched with malt, a touch of honey.

The book was almost blank, the recipes still in her head. Mary took it now and placed it next to *Classic American Recipes*. The last book she stacked was a vegetarian cookbook, bought when Frances was thirteen. She flipped it open. Spiced risotto cakes. Tabbouli. Lentil bolognese. She couldn't remember either of them ever using it. At that time, it seemed to her now, her daughter had lived entirely on a diet of soft white foods: cauliflower cheese and mashed potato, bread and bananas. Yoghurt and vanilla milkshakes.

By the time the broth was ready for its final straining the boy was bored, back in his bedroom hunched over his laptop. Mary glanced in. Facebook. She went back to the kitchen, threw away the bones and boiled onions, and took some of the cooled meat over to the dog's bowl. Tommy came sliding into the kitchen out of nowhere, swallowed the meal in a few gulps, and looked up with his tail wagging. He followed her hopefully and sat behind her at the sink while she washed the strainers and other utensils and wiped down the bench. When she was done she went back to the boy's room. He was on the phone again. She walked across to the other bedroom, pushed the door, and stepped inside.

The room was dark, close. She shut her eyes and breathed in the smell. Perfume – she had no idea which one; there were several brands neatly set out on the desk – stale sheets, leather shoes, hairspray, incense, musty clothes – the hamper was full – and under it all a smell of apples, fainter than faint. When she opened her eyes she saw that Tommy had quietly jumped onto the bed. She sat next to him, on the rumpled sheets, the only mess in the otherwise tidy room. There were several books next to the pillows, an empty shoulder bag gaping open, and an uncapped pen that had bled to death leaving a blue stain on the sheet. Next to it was a DVD in an unmarked cover, the disc blank except for the sticker of a professional photographer. Mary sighed, rose and went over to the wardrobe. Inside, every second or third hanger was empty. She leaned down to pick a hairpin off the carpet in front of the mirrored doors, then placed it in the glass dish on the desk. There was a mug next to the vase of incense sticks. It held a half-inch of black coffee with a film of scum. No sugar, of course.

Andy appeared at the doorway. 'We should go now.'

'Okay, okay. Come on, Tommy, out of there.' Holding the mug, she shut the door and leaned her forehead against it for a few moments, her eyes shut. Then she walked quickly along the hall and took the mug to the kitchen where she ran the hot water into it for a long time.

'And I said I'd take him some soup, but he's just rung and said he's nil by mouth because they're going to operate tonight.'

'I doubt that. Not on an evening, not on a weekend.' Mary locked the back door and went to her bedroom for her jacket.

Cooper was off his drip but still in bed. One hand was dark and swollen, with a cannula stub taped and bound tightly, as if it would run away otherwise.

'I'd kill for a coffee,' he said.

'But you can't eat or drink.'

'No.' There was silence as the boy tested the only chair. Experience had taught him they were all wobbly. Mary put her bag down and gazed around. The bed beside the window was empty but the sheets were flung back and a pair of sandals was beside it. The man in the opposite bed was dozing, his mouth an open hole in a skull of yellow skin so thin and stretched it looked like every breath would tear the hole wider and wider. He looked at least a hundred years old. In the fourth bed next to Cooper another man was sitting upright, his hair fuzzy around his pear of a head, his eyes bright, looking for an opportunity.

'Did you bring your notebook?' Cooper said in a low voice. 'It's like absurd theatre here. All day.'

'Hey, fella!' The boy looked up from his phone. 'Come over here, will you?'

He sauntered over, glancing back at his parents with a wry smile.

'What's ya name, fella?'

'Andy.'

'Sandy?' The man barked, cupping his ear.

'Andy,' the boy said, louder.

'Oh, Andy. Listen, Andy, are you good at English?'

He shrugged. 'Kind of.'

'Course you are, I can see you're a clever boy.' The man was almost shouting, though the boy stood right by his bed. 'Now I've got a question for you, Andy. Is it correct to say the yolk of the egg *are* white or the yolk of the egg *is* white?' Sensing resistance, he added quickly, 'Are or is, come on, now, what's correct?'

'Err . . . is,' Andy said, smiling at his father. 'Of course.'

'NO!' The man slapped his thigh. 'The yolk of the egg is YELLOW!' He laughed so deeply he started coughing.

'See,' Cooper said quietly from his bed. 'Every day, it's like a play.'

Andy came over. 'I *know* it's yellow,' he said to his mother. 'I just thought he was mad and didn't want to correct him.'

She held his arm and leaned over to his father. 'Can I get you something? A magazine?'

Cooper shook his head. Mary went with the boy down to the vending machine for a Coke and waited until he finished it all, so as not to be drinking in front of Cooper. When they returned the man in the bed opposite had reappeared and a nurse was writing in his chart. The wispy-haired man was again sitting upright, interrogating.

'Where do you come from?' he shouted, after the nurse left, eyeing frankly the long legs sticking out of the gown.

'Somalia.'

'Ay? Somalia? Where's that?'

'Somalia is in Africa.'

'AFRICA! Well, I never.' He paused, glanced round the room. An audience. 'Somalia. Is that a good country?'

'No, it is a very bad place.'

'Why's that?'

'There has been a war there for fifteen years.'

'What are you doing here, then?'

'I am a refugee.'

'A refugee!' This was gold. The man looked around again, trying to catch the eye of Cooper, or Mary, of anyone. He leaned further forward on his bed, his eyes brighter than ever with expectation.

'And a footballer.'

'No!' Now the man leaned back on his pillows, silent for a few moments, considering the patriotic implications of such conflicting roles. Then he said slowly, 'Footballer, ay? What, here, or in Somalia?'

'In Somalia I played professional football. Here I am semi-professional.' He then closed his eyes.

The man crossed his arms and blew loudly out his mouth, fluttering the white hairs fringing his dome forehead. After a moment he leaned forward again and said, 'What are you in this place for, then?'

The Somali man opened his eyes. 'Observation.' Then shut them again. When no more explanation came, the wispy-haired man turned to gaze at Cooper and the boy next to him, open-mouthed, shaking his head. The wonder. The rudeness. Mary saw the Somali man's lips twitch. His eyes opened again, and he added, 'Following a car accident. I am in for observation. My car was hit by a truck. We are all alive, but require observation.'

'All? How many of you?'

'Five. All members of my football team.'

Then an orderly arrived, followed by another nurse with a clipboard. They all stared as he was helped into a chair and wheeled out again, this time down to X-ray. The man turned to Cooper and said, 'Somalia, ay. D'you reckon he's making that up?' Then the ancient man in the opposite bed groaned in his sleep, his mouth still a wide hole, the noise so long and slow it was like a final exhalation. They all stared at the white mound in the bed until they could see the chest rising again, then falling, slowly but discernibly.

'Told you,' Cooper said to Mary. 'Beckett.'

Just then the nurse who had escorted the patient off to X-ray returned. 'Sorry to tell you this,' she said quite cheerfully, 'but theatre's rung again and they won't be doing you until later tonight.'

'It's after six-thirty.'

'I know.' She smiled, picking up his wrist for his pulse.

'So it's already later tonight. They won't do it tonight, surely.'

She shrugged.

'Do they even operate at night?'

'Of course. For emergencies.'

'Which I'm not.'

She shrugged again, scribbled on his chart.

'Weren't you meant to be done first thing this morning, Dad?'

'Yep.'

'You're waiting all day and you can't even have a sip of water?'

'That's right.'

The boy dug out his phone and resumed playing. Mary flipped through the colour supplement, then put it down in the litter of newspaper sections beside the bed.

'Have you heard from her at all?'

'Once,' said Cooper. 'Yesterday.' He looked her in the eye. 'You just need to give her some time.'

'Hey, fella,' barked the man next to him.

'I can't stand it any longer,' Mary said, jumping up. 'Come on, I'll get you a hamburger or something.'

Andy glanced up from his game. 'But aren't we having the soup for dinner?'

'It'll be too late by the time we get home.'

The hospital café was closing up. There were a few cellophane-wrapped sandwiches, hot pies, a slice of pizza. She bought him the last of the hot chips and a chicken sandwich, set him down at a table, and brought over a packet of tomato sauce. She went back to the cold food bar, inspected a bowl of fruit salad. Picked up a yoghurt, considering, then replaced it. Yoggit. Sometimes I say yoggit. Frances would always eat yoghurt. Her favourite was apple cinnamon, low fat.

She sat back at the table where Andy was squeezing the

rectangle of tomato sauce next to his chips. He dipped them one by one into the puddle. They would have the soup tomorrow. The stock needed some mint and noodles, beansprouts and lemon. No chilli for him, lots for her. And fresh fillet steak, sliced thin as wafers. She would half-freeze the meat before cutting it. If there were only the two of them, it would make several meals. Too many. She took her phone out, considered sending a message, then replaced it.

Back in the ward the boy took Cooper's hand, the one that was not bruised and swollen under the taped cannula. The other men were asleep, and the Somali man had still not returned from X-ray.

'We'll get going,' she said. 'He's got school tomorrow.'

The nurse walked in once more. 'Sorry about this, but your op's not happening until tomorrow now.'

'Tomorrow morning or tomorrow night?'

The nurse shrugged. 'We'll have to wait and see. But you can have something to eat if you like.'

'God, so much waiting,' Mary said. 'It's unbearable.' She dropped into the wobbly chair again, putting her face in her hands. The boy and his father looked at each other, then at her, then away. After a while Andy said, 'Maybe we could go out somewhere and get you a sandwich, Dad.'

He shook his head, drew the boy closer and held him with one arm.

Finally she lifted her head, drew a deep breath and blew it out again, then said, 'It's all right. I'm okay now.'

'You sure?' Cooper said.

'It's just all the waiting.'

'I know.'

As they left, the man in the next bed began calling out again but Cooper called out louder, waving his good hand.

'Stoppard,' he said. 'Definitely Stoppard.'

The Recovery Position

A DOG BITE. Cate slumped lower onto the bench, still shaking her head. The man had asked about venomous dog bites. If she still smoked she would have been reaching for the pack right now. She took another long swig of water. Fat bubbles volcanoed back into the bottle before the soft PET flattened, crackling noisily. She blotted her mouth with the back of her hand and hunched into the covert position she would have been in were she still able to light up.

Before she first gave up – Mara's insistence: she was threatening to go and live with her mother after the birth if she didn't – Cate had perfected a furtive crouch, with her back bent around to shield the cigarette from disapproval. By cupping her hand around it, turned inwards to the palm, she could often get away with pretending she was doing nothing at all, provided the wind was cooperative. Or thought she could. She wasn't stupid, but somehow smokers lost their brains when it came to giving up, or lying about giving up. How many times had she sworn outright she wasn't smoking when it was obvious Mara could smell it on her? She used to come home and ignore Bethany's outstretched arms to head straight for the bathroom, pretending she needed to wash her hands or something. After swilling her mouth out, she'd then emerge to embrace the toddling child. Mara would just stare at her from the kitchen. That was after they'd stopped kissing each other hello. Once, out at the barbecue, she'd pushed her hand into her pocket, still holding a lit cigarette, and then wondered why Mara had looked at her hip, the curl of smoke emerging like a question mark, rolled her eyes and walked off again.

She checked the time on her phone. There was not much shade from the sun but there were another three minutes before the session resumed, and the training room was stifling. She popped an Endone from the strip in her pocket, swallowing it with the last of her water, and pressed a paper towel from the medical kit onto her face. She was always thirsty these days, always sweating no matter what the weather was like.

Tall skinny pines stood all along the street side of the industrial estate and the section allocated to the training programs was behind a sand-coloured patch of grass. The estate was next to a new housing block, marked out but not yet developed. Across the street was a parking lot. The whole area had an unrelenting openness about it, so hot and dry that, with half-closed eyes, she could pretend she was back in Kandahar.

She opened her eyes and stood up. Why on earth would she want to do that. She walked back to the demountable. Training stages three and four to get through, then the lunch break. No chance that the idiot had decided to piss off. A lot of them did that by the mid-morning break, the ones who'd enrolled because they were told they had to, it being their only way to keep claiming their Centrelink benefits. She never knew what happened to these people, so frail and dysfunctional they couldn't focus on a one-day course, even one as dumbed-down as hers. You only had to have your basic senses to pass it. Maybe that was the problem.

She had been halfway through venomous bites, and the fucking idiot had asked about dogs. She'd been running through the obvious ones – funnel-web, red-back, tiger snake, brown snake – when the man's hand had shot up.

'What about dog bites?' he'd said. 'Do you use the same technique there?' Cate had just looked at him for a long theatrical pause. Waited three beats. Then replied as slowly as she dared without risking obvious contempt.

Now she flipped through the forms for the test, tapped them into a neat pile on the table and looked up. They were shuffling in and, yes, the dog-bite idiot was there up the back again. *Dogs are not venomous.* She'd actually had to spell that out to him. Were people really that dumb? Before the start of the session she'd looked at the list of participants and then, sitting outside in the break, mentally run through the possibilities. How likely was it that this man, here to qualify in order to stay in work as a security guard, community worker, certified volunteer, or – god help them – childcare worker, would actually ever need to use his First Aid Certificate? She sincerely hoped not at all.

Spider and snake bites, poisons, toxic plants, done. She handed round the test forms for them to complete their multiple-choice questions at the end of the day. If they all listened they'd realise she would be spoonfeeding them the answers. They could fill the forms in as she spoke, hand them up, and they'd all get out of here by five, certificates printed and laminated. All ridiculously simple. But they didn't listen. And there was always someone who'd learned first aid back whenever, probably in primary school, and kept asking was she sure you didn't suck out venom. Or nick the wound with your penknife and let the blood clean it. Did anyone even carry a penknife, for god's sake? Another idiot refused to believe that oleander was poisonous. 'That can't be true!' she'd said. 'We had them growing all round my place when I was a kid.'

'Then you're lucky to be alive,' Cate had shot back.

She moved on quickly, not caring now if she seemed rude. The pain in her back was no better despite the Endone. It helped if she stood up and moved around but the room was so cramped that was hard. Weaving between the inadequate desks to hand out the burns and fractures fact sheets, she tripped on someone's leg sticking out, and when she winced audibly they all stared at her. 'Army injury,' she said, limping back to the front of the room.

'It's why I'm now here teaching you guys.' There was a brief and what she thought respectful silence, but as she turned around from the DRSABCD Action Plan poster she saw three or four of the men staring at her. She knew what they were thinking.

Despite everything, Mara had kicked her out anyway. She'd accused her of duplicity, of letting her down once too often, of not being there enough. Then the smoking. It was true, she often went out saying she needed to go to the bank or fill the car with petrol, when instead she was buying a pack at the servo, then driving home via the cul-de-sac. She'd stand against the rear door of the Subaru, gazing across at the kids' playground in the park, have three or four in a row, then throw the rest of the pack away. How stupid that everything collapsed because of this. They went to counselling a few times, where she almost dared Mara to say it outright: our relationship has failed because of her smoking. How stupid it would sound. And yet Cate could see how much they both needed to focus on something specific. Grabbing hold of the entire truth about why they were breaking up was like trying to throw a net over a cloud and drag it close. Even she didn't want to think it all the way through, for what she might have to see.

There was no court case, not for the separation. It was the property settlement, the custody drama. Somehow her smoking always got a mention. Fucking Mara. Fucking cigarettes. Fucking whatever. She had never smoked until

Tarin Kowt. Fitness, a ten-k-a-day run on her days off, having to be able to jump up and pretty much stay awake for forty-eight hours if necessary, standing for the entire time during long shifts in the surgical unit. None of that went with smoking. Only after the accident. And now that Mara was gone, with Bethany – in the end she couldn't fight that, Mara was the birth mother after all, and Cate had always been the absent parent – she had given up smoking anyway.

Next to come were dressings, bandages and splints. As she handed out the dressings she could already see the worst. The stupid jokes about mummies. The ones who always got the stuff tangled, who had no idea how to unroll and dress in the same action. Cohesive bandage was foolproof but they somehow got it wrong, pulling out great lengths then wondering why it all clumped and stuck together. After she paired them up and got them to practise on each other there were two poor bastards to rescue before their toes turned purple. Some of them were using the kit laid out on the back table, and the class clown thought it hilarious when he tickled his partner's butt with a fake arm. Someone else had stuck an adhesive dressing across his mouth and was pretending to suffocate.

There was always a class clown, several if she was unlucky. Always the mummy jokes. Always the mucking around with syringes. Guaranteed, every time. She could pick them the minute she entered a training session: never a woman, always a guy in his thirties or forties. The banks sent them, the schools or childcare centres, if they were handymen or gardeners. The bigger bars and restaurant venues. They came to training full of resentment. As if they needed to know how to bandage a wound. Last thing they wanted was to give mouth-to-mouth to a drunk who'd collapsed. No matter how often she explained patiently the remote possibility of ever giving mouth-to-mouth to anyone, least of all a bloke suffering chest pains after a night out, they joked about it. 'Are we meant to be poofs or what? Germs, love, germs! What if their breath stinks, eh?' The guys from the security sector were less inclined to joke, more determined to direct their resentment at her, personally. They were the ones sitting back in their chairs with arms folded across their chests, singlets too tight, shaved heads held pugnaciously. The ones who'd ask, 'And how did a sheila like you get to be doing this? Training us in first aid?'

Even in a factory workers' lunch shop in an industrial estate, the menu featured shaved this and pulled that. When had sandwich-making succumbed to the language of the barber shop or the wrestling ring? She bit into her smoked turkey and cranberry panini with baby spinach. At least it featured mayonnaise, not a smear of something. The smear was the worst. Perhaps that was when things with Mara fell apart; perhaps it wasn't the smoking after all. Cate couldn't help it, her contempt was something she barely concealed, on the basis that she managed to conceal so much else. Mara had been attending workshops at the local deli slash picklery slash culinary emporium slash whatever. The fight they'd had when one evening she had produced a plate of meat so thinly sliced – shaved – beside a smear of something that might as well have been baby shit, it was the same colour and consistency. Pretty much what Cate said, of course. Along with the rest. Like what was the point of having a smear of mustard sauce if that's what it was, something that looked like a child's finger painting? Why have sauce if you couldn't actually load it onto your meat? Like how a smear was the perfect word for a medical test or for something you cleaned off the toilet, but was that what Mara was doing up there at the picklery eatery wankery? Wasting their money, her money, learning to turn decent food into artful displays. Of shit?

That night she'd locked herself in the car in the driveway, wondering why she couldn't tell Mara how she really felt. Why the nights were so long and the days even longer. Every time she shut her eyes she felt herself falling again out of that helicopter. Saw the white face of the soldier she was nursing.

Now, wiping her mouth – the panini was actually very good – she was struck with a sudden recollection of the look on Mara's face when she'd said all that. The terrible hurt and confusion, quickly followed by the smouldering hatred. That's what she always remembered, the hate, not what had come seconds before. What a bitch she had been. She threw her paper bag into the bin and walked back to the training room.

*

'The recovery position offers the best way for an unconscious victim to maintain their capacity to breathe.'

Then she asked for a volunteer. A woman from the middle of the room stood up, her name sticker announcing she was Jessica. There wasn't a great deal of space, but she got Jessica to lie on her left side on the front table so everyone could see. She asked her to bend her legs and tuck her top foot behind her other leg. Then Cate took her right arm and bent it, placing her hand across and over the other arm. Then she held her head.

'This is the tricky part. Keep the chin well up to ensure the epiglottis is open, but make sure the mouth is turned downward. Remember fluids need to drain from the airway.'

She went and stood behind to run through the main points again. Even brushing her limbs lightly Cate could feel how rigid she was. 'It's okay, Jessica, relax. Pretend you're asleep.' Jessica laughed self-consciously but closed her eyes anyway.

'We call this a lateral recumbent position. That just means lying on your side. The arms and legs are locked like this' – she touched the knee and elbow – 'to stabilise the victim. The less they're able to move the more chance of recovery. Another five seconds to study Jessica, then she can get up. We've got one last topic to do.'

She always taught CPR last. Everyone did: it was just the way things went in the course, for some reason. When everyone was bored and tired and even the few who had been trying hard and paying attention were thinking about the beers they'd be having as soon as they could get out of here, that for some reason was when she had to cover CPR. While they finished reading through CPR basics, Cate set everything up in the adjacent room. She thought of taking more Endone, but settled for Panadol combined with Nurofen instead, swallowing the pills down before the class trooped in. Sometimes even the effort of leaning over the dummy torso to demonstrate how the hands were placed, one over the other, was too much for her. If she could, she'd place the dummy on a table to minimise the pressure on her lower back. Today there was no table, so she set it out on the floor. She'd have to kneel and then get up carefully.

'There are five main steps we need to remember for most CPR situations. One: place the hands on the lower half of the breastbone. Two: the depth of compressions is a third of the chest depth of the victim. Three: perform thirty compressions followed by two breaths. Four: if you don't want to do mouth-to-mouth then keep the compressions up at the rate of one hundred per minute.' She turned around to face the class. 'That's pretty fast, okay?' They nodded and murmured. As she reached for a chair to help herself up, trying not to pull a face at the jag of pain, someone surprised her by calling out.

'That was four. You said five main steps.'

'I did. Thank you.' They were paying attention after all. 'Five: if you can't remember any of that, think of the song "Staying Alive".' They all laughed. 'I'm serious. Perform your compressions to the beat of "Staying Alive" and you'll have about the right rate.'

It was what she'd done in the helicopter for Trooper Brad Innes. After the explosion she was nursing him all the way back to base in Tarin Kowt and they were at least five minutes from landing when he closed his eyes, all colour in his face draining away faster than she had ever seen. Then it was five long minutes of singing 'Staying Alive' in her head while she pumped his chest with her hands, willing his heart to start circulating blood again and deliver oxygen to his brain until they landed.

'Cate?' She heard someone cough. Heard her name again. She opened her eyes to find them all staring at her. The room was very quiet. How long had she had her eyes closed?

'Sorry.' She reached for her bottle of water, took a swig then checked her phone. Twenty minutes to go.

'Sorry,' she said again. 'Such a long, hot day. You've all been great, so we'll just run through the final checklist for CPR, then you can go back to your desks and fill in those last few questions.'

She reminded them of clearing the airways, checking for obstructions in the mouth, only using one hand if performing on children, the procedures to follow once normal breathing had recommenced, and keeping them in the recovery position until professional medical help arrived.

She told them to return to their desks while she packed away the CPR kit. 'There are five more questions on your sheets, on the recovery position and CPR. It should only take you a few minutes.'

A man somewhere near the door turned around and called out. 'Can you just show us that once more? The recovery position?'

She sighed.

'Sorry,' he said. 'It's just that it's important. Obviously. I want to get it right.'

She looked at him. One of the singlet wearers. His arms were tattooed from the wrist up. His name sticker had come loose and he smoothed it flat across a prominent pectoral.

'Salim. Yes, you're right. It is important.'

Most of them were in the adjacent room, anxious to finish up their test sheets. Just five of them lingered.

'Of course I'll show you.'

She would have to get on the floor again. Gingerly, she lay down on her left side next to the CPR dummy. At least the lino was clean and cool. She tucked her foot around her leg and hooked her right hand over the other outstretched arm. She tilted her chin, opened her mouth slightly and shut her eyes. She lay there, just breathing, breathing, imagining her lungs were as soft and clear as Bethany's. They would be pink, dark pink, like watermelon. Breathing, that was what it was all about, simple, steady breathing.

Cate never knew what happened to Trooper Innes, but she remembered the pink flush that appeared in his face again after it seemed she'd sung 'Staying Alive' a hundred times over, compressing his chest. Her wrists ached and his breathing returned. That was just before the helicopter shuddered and tipped them both out. She remembered falling right on her coccyx then blacking out from the pain. Afterwards coming to consciousness back in the base hospital, and wishing she hadn't. Then the pain, the pain. Years of it.

She breathed slowly in and out, in and out. Perhaps she would stay in the recovery position, just stay like this for as long as she could.

Wipe Away Your Tears

It was a dawn landing. But as soon as she wrote the words in her diary she resiled from the phrase. It was far too apt. Forced. But it was dawn, and an especially picturesque one. She glanced out the window again, her stomach registering a dip as the aeroplane dropped another level in its descent. The sky was soft: thick misty bands of grey, dust pink, lavender. Dried lavender, she noted, a different shade to fresh. Beneath it the Sea of Marmara was dove grey, flat and smooth, the ships gliding across it like there was no effort involved, like they were floating towards the narrow straits as naturally as leaves on a pond. She peered closer, pressing her forehead against the tiny window pane. The water was so calm it looked viscous, the ships leaving barely any wake as they headed towards the Black Sea.

She shut her diary. Clearly she was reading far too much into this; she was too receptive, too keen to process all that she was about to experience. Yet she couldn't help herself, this was the fabled city she had heard so much about but had never once visited. The city of three different names, two mighty religions and their rulers. The city of minarets and great covered markets and *hamams* and wonderful fresh food – the best tomatoes ever, she had been told – and she *was* expectant and excited, she couldn't deny that. Even the names – the Sea of Marmara, the Bosphorus, the Golden Horn – were poetic.

Had Harry felt like this, the first time he ever visited Istanbul? She would have asked him but was unwilling to break the silence, could pretend she was arriving on her own. She barely slept on flights, and loved the times when the other passengers were asleep while the cabin lights remained dim and the crew moved in quiet unison in the galley. Discreet acolytes in the mysteries of air travel, they bowed over the few unsleeping passengers, offering fresh coffees or tumblers of spirits. The crew were always young and beautiful. They bore trays draped in white linen. They would bring her a drink, a blanket, the newspapers, and she would feel a sense of cosy privilege, that the flight was hers alone.

They were crossing the tramline towards the Blue Mosque when she noticed the first dog. Dirty light brown, indistinguishable as to breed. Then the next, similar. Indifferent dogs, trotting along with purpose, never approaching either of them, all with yellow tags in their left ears. By the time they had entered the park where the garbage collectors were raising enormous underground bins by chains to be emptied, she noticed there were perhaps six or eight dogs scattered around the square, all walking as if on errands. Two were standing near each other at an intersection, deciding whether to wait for the lights or make a run for it. Later in the day she would see the same dogs, or similar ones – it was impossible to tell – sitting on doorsteps or under café tables, or stretched out asleep on the grassy sections of the square, where tourists had to step over or around them, sometimes pausing to marvel or take photos. But for now, with Harry and Angela almost the only people around in the cool fresh early morning, it was clear that the dogs owned the streets of Istanbul.

She had found them a hotel in Sultanahmet knowing nothing about the area except that it was close to the most romantic of all the places, the mosques, the palaces, the markets and museums that she had read up on. But when they had arrived it was just past seven o'clock and far too early to check in, so they'd left their luggage with the sleepy receptionist and walked the streets.

After three days in the city, where they walked everywhere, she realised that although the dogs were clearly wild and ownerless they did not appear savage, arousing none of the vague primal fear she always felt when encountering any dogs, in particular large ones. Unleashed dogs, in the park nearby her home, were a source of apprehension: no matter how benign they were, how jolly and unselfconscious their names as their owners frolicked with them – Tickles, come here, Tickles! Good girl, Pom Pom! – she always shrank from them as much as possible, head down, shoulders hunched, as if they were hoodie-wearing youths and she the only other person in the park.

The coach down the peninsula took most of the day. Not that it was so far in distance, but the traffic was extraordinary. How was it possible that there were so many cars? Angela had never seen traffic like it. The route that took them from the depot followed Kennedy Caddesi, the same avenue that had brought them from the airport so quickly that cool morning just a few days before. Now it was blocked as far as they could see, and roads beside it filled with vehicles that seemed neither to sit still altogether nor to move but merely edged forward, as if teasing all the passengers inside. It took more than two hours before their coach was free of the southern suburbs of the city, but even on the freeway south they went slowly. The only thing slower was the occasional horse and cart they passed, at which they both laughed with rare, uncomplicated pleasure. They stopped for late lunch at a restaurant beside the water, a sprawling service centre with little service but, as everywhere, excellent food.

'And two Efes?' Harry said, holding up two fingers after he ordered his stuffed eggplant. But, no, like so many places it sold no liquor so Angela chose a pomegranate juice and they took their plates out to a table overlooking the water. The Dardanelles was like a huge canal, the water flat and dull, and the shore, as far as they could see, a bleak industrial yellow-brown, with barely a tree or anything green in sight.

*

It was a dawn landing. And that was just about all she knew. Apart from, of course, what everyone knew: the obscene numbers of men slaughtered and the ignominy of retreat eight months later. Now, as she stood on the thin strip of beach, she tried to picture it, without success. There, for instance, was the ridge these men and boys had been ordered to scale as gunfire rained down. It was almost vertical to her eyes. How had soldiers burdened with packs and bearing guns run up these ridges?

And, more importantly, why? Why had they run straight into the embrace of the enemy? It was impossible to imagine following orders of such blind stupidity. Water, sand, hills and then those bare perpendicular ridges with the enemy perched on the cliffs above: surely there had never been a more extreme collision of geography and men. Behind her was the calm Aegean Sea, where on ships young women with fear in their throats had listened to the thunderous noise of attack and watched the skies explode as they waited and waited for their first patients. And when they finally came, so long after they were first attacked, the screaming, the blood, the spectacular injuries that delivered endless possibilities of what a human body could endure. None of that could be imagined either.

Harry was walking towards her, holding out a fragment of pottery or something.

'Mark said you might still pick things up around here.' He had been halfway up one of the many paths leading over the first ridge before disappearing into the scrub with his map. The hotel proprietor – a war history buff who'd settled in Eceabat over twenty years ago – had told them that the place was very different to how it had been only a few years ago. More scrubby, less exposed. Now it was a lot harder to get around than it had been, though if you were lucky you could still find stuff. The hotel was decorated – if that was the right word – with all sorts of *stuff*: shell casings and broken demijohns, tin plates and brass buckles, glass marbles, knives, coins and little tin boxes blooming with rust. Stuff. Mark made it sound like a particular category of something.

Harry shook his map out and set off again. Angela did not want to find stuff. She could not even leave this little rubbly beach. They had walked along the main path and just past the cemetery, where everyone was looking for the mythical Simpson and his mythical donkey, had agreed that he would make his forays into the scrub and up the ridges, and she would continue along the beachfront. To be honest she had not wanted to tell him that she'd prefer to leave altogether, because they had only just arrived and were booked in for three days. But the sadness of the place engulfed her. She had been unprepared for this and was surprised to find herself so close to tears. It was as if the deaths of all those men in that senseless manner rose in a miasma from the ground to choke her. If she did not continue traipsing along the beach or the main path then she would only be able to sit down and weep. Around every turn of every path, down gullies, on the sides of hills, on the top of the most famous hill of all, where a solitary pine still stood – descendant, presumably, of the original – were cemeteries. The entire peninsula was a cemetery. And the thousands of graves were, she had learned, only for a fraction of those killed, the ones whose bodies had not disappeared altogether into the sodden earth, or been pulverised by mortar fire or wounded beyond recognition.

Harry could pay his tributes to his great-grandfather, find his grave: she would keep walking then find a shady place to sit on the beach and gaze out towards Lemnos and wait. It was far hotter than she had expected and she felt incapable of walking for hours up hills through the scrub. And there were flies, dust. It was windy. Whatever. She would stay down by the water and wait for him. She was also finding the tourists unbearable. They spoke too loudly, they laughed, they joked about finding souvenirs, they played awful music on their iPhones, and if they addressed her and found she was Australian too – well, who wasn't, here? – it was all she could do not to tell them to shut up and show some respect. She did not regard herself as a tourist. She was not making a pilgrimage or paying tribute. They were travelling, true, but she had not even wanted to come here and Harry said it was only the second, and would be the last, time in his life. The first had been when he was a hippie backpacker, only making the trek down the peninsula, away from the delights of the Pudding Shop and freely available hash, to oblige his mates.

At the memorial beside Ari Burnu cemetery she stopped behind a group of tourists and a guide who had just alighted from a small bus. She read the words slowly, repeating them to herself under her breath. *You, the mothers who sent their sons from faraway countries, wipe away your tears; your sons are now lying in our bosom and are in peace. After having lost their lives on this land they have become our sons as well.* The guidebook to Anzac Cove that Harry had brought had a paragraph on this memorial. It was from a letter written by Turkey's leader to console the people of the country he had so bitterly fought some decades before. The empathy of this, the generosity of spirit, the desire for reconciliation, not to mention the regard for the women in this whole bloody story that was always about men – all of this struck Angela as being far more manly and heroic than any deeds he or his men might have performed on the field, and again she felt the sting of tears.

The tour group clustered closer to their guide to hear him above the scrape of the wind. She heard him mention the name Mustafa Kemal Atatürk and the letter, before moving on to remind them of the hundreds who had died just below them, on the beach, that first day one hundred years ago. When he stopped speaking, without exception everyone in the tour group checked their phones before heading back onto the bus.

She looked down to the beach, so bare and clean. The sand here was greyish, the water a lively Mediterranean blue. Perhaps she should have been grateful for the presence of the tourists, for otherwise she might have given in to her own tears. She followed a short path onto the beach and sat down on a rock, drawing out the bottle of water she had bought back at the port. Though it was barely a port, just a small café with two dirty white plastic tables under an awning, and a jetty with no boats except for an old dinghy. As she and Harry had drunk their coffees, yet another dog had wandered towards them from out of nowhere, ignored them, and flopped down under the shade of the other table to sleep.

She took off her sandshoes and walked to the edge of the water, where timid wavelets ran back and forth. The water was clear and warm, and the day was so hot. There was no one around, even though she knew the cove was full of tourists. Would it be wrong to have a quick swim? But even as she thought it through she knew she couldn't, she couldn't enjoy a swim in a place that had once been awash with so much blood.

It was Harry who was weeping. She finally found him at yet another cemetery, seated under a small pine tree with his hands over his mouth, baseball cap pushed low over his face. Had anyone else noticed? She sat down and talked to him in a soft voice, brushing away the flies and eyeing the group of older tourists wearing proper walking shoes and sensible lightweight backpacks, willing them not to stop and chat. Harry took off his sunglasses, pressed the heels of his hands into his eyes.

'I know so little about all this,' he said. 'Nothing.'

He told her he felt ashamed that he had come here so ignorant. He had imagined there would be somewhere with all the names of the fallen listed on one great memorial, something hewn from white marble, polished and shining, a spotless testament to all those poor young men who fought and died here in those months of horror. He'd expected that he would be able to scroll down and find his great-grandfather's name, John Harold Cunningham, listed there alphabetically, and then walk over to his grave and place the sprig of wattle he had brought, pressed between the pages of his Lonely Planet guide to Turkey.

'How old was he again?' Though she felt she knew.

'Twenty-one.'

Of course. The same age as his brother had been. He would have been how old now? Forty-nine, fifty? Angela had met Harry many years after Johnny had died.

'He left a wife and baby. My grand-dad was just three months old when he was killed.'

That was right. He'd told her all this before. In fact over the years he'd told her a lot more about this distant relative than he had about Johnny, and she never understood that. Nor why a man would enlist in a distant war when his wife was barely an adult herself and his baby son still unborn. Or why his death apparently troubled Harry more.

She felt him shudder. A man's sob, hollow and dry, and somehow always more frightening to her. She put her arm around his shoulders. When men cried like that it felt alien, uncanny. When men let forth their great dry cries the world was wrenched from its axis. All four points of the compass swivelled wildly.

The tourists had wandered off and from their spot under the tree she could see the long unbroken rows of clean white gravestones, so uniform and orderly, as you would expect of soldiers. Not a single one sprouted weeds at its base or was blotted with mould. Overhead the sky was a cloudless, constant blue. The breeze brought a faint smell of wild-flowers, or herbs.

'I'm fine now.' Harry got up.

'You sure?' Though he did seem calm again.

'Yes, sure.'

They agreed he would keep exploring one more cemetery and she would walk back towards the main road and meet him there within the hour.

Dusk was falling when, supported by two other tourists, he hobbled towards her. There was a bandage around his ankle. She had waited at Ari Burnu cemetery as arranged. And waited, ringing his phone before remembering he had left it at the hotel. She had read the words on the memorial again and again; there was nothing else to read. *There is no difference between the Johnnies and the Mehmets to us where they lie side by side here in this country of ours . . . You, the mothers who sent their sons from faraway countries, wipe away your tears.* Then she had rung the hotel but Mark said he'd not returned, and she had just decided to start the long walk back alone when Harry appeared. Too relieved to be angry, she ran to him.

'I've been so worried!'

He was subdued. When she hugged him he remained stiff.

'Lucky for your fella we were on our way down the track,' said the man beside him. 'And lucky Sandra always carries a first aid kit.'

The woman had a backpack and a waist bag over a sleeveless jacket, which also featured what appeared to be well-stocked pockets.

'He slipped and twisted his ankle,' she said. 'I don't think it's broken.'

'Hi, I'm Grant.' He held out his hand to Angela. 'It's dangerous up there. Some of those tracks need safety fences, I reckon. You could fall to your death in a second, and no one would know. No one'd find you, if you were on your own.'

Harry eased himself onto the low wall beside her. He had dirt streaks on his clothes. His shoes were filthy. He had lost his cap and his wispy hair was sticking up as if electrified.

'Where was this, exactly?' Angela said.

'Up towards the Sphinx.' Grant turned and pointed up behind him, where the distinctive outcrop of rock now looked dark and sinister in the dusk.

'That's so high.'

'Yeah, like I said, bloody dangerous.'

Harry looked at his feet and kicked some clods of earth off his walking shoes, wincing when he knocked the bad ankle.

'Anyway, we've got to get going. You right now?'

'Yeah, thanks. Appreciate your help, mate.' Harry shook Grant's hand while Angela smiled and nodded.

She gazed up to the Sphinx again. Fuck, it was high up there. She wondered if the enemy had been positioned there shooting at those men arriving in boat after boat onto the beach. They could not have stood a chance.

'I'm sorry.' Beside her Harry was finally crying properly, great fat tears flowing over his dusty hands.

'You don't have to say sorry.'

'Yes, I do. You don't understand.'

She waited while he cried and cried, and said nothing. When she could sense the storm of tears was ending she took out her phone and spoke quietly to Mark.

'He's sending a taxi. Won't be more than ten or fifteen minutes.'

On the drive back to Eceabat she still did not speak, even though Harry was right that she did not understand. When they got out of the taxi and she gave him her shoulder to lean on he seemed calm, as if the incident had shaken something within him, some emotional cog or bolt, shaken it back into place and erased his anguish. He spoke in a matter-of-fact tone.

'I've never been able to deal with it. His death.' And of course she knew he was not talking about that afternoon or about John Harold Cunningham. 'I let him down.'

'Johnny's death wasn't your fault.' But she knew as soon as she said it that she had not been there and had never really known the truth.

He shook his head. 'I fucked up. And today I fucked up again.' He looked her in the eye for a moment then pushed past into the hotel foyer.

Mark had organised a late dinner for them. After he'd finished up in the kitchen, Angela ordered a second bottle of the excellent local red wine and indulged him as he talked about what he had done here over the years. She realised she had misjudged him, as he was clearly knowledgeable and had devoted himself to helping people like Harry rediscover lost ancestors, or just come to terms with their own ambivalent feelings about the place. He was not the sad trainspotter type at all. He brought out a book he had published, titled *Johnnies and Mehmets*, describing the relationship between the Anzacs and the Turks, the gifts and tokens thrown over the trenches, the tins of bully beef and tobacco shared when both sides had next to nothing. Some gifts from the Turks had come with notes, signed *Your friend, the enemy.*

In the morning they packed their things in silence. There was no point in staying since Harry was unable to walk unaided. They left the key at the desk and headed for the bus depot beside the waterfront. She knew Harry had more to tell her and that he might if she asked in the right way, but she would not ask. And she knew her silence was punishment though she didn't mean to punish him. All sorts of scenarios had played out in her mind, and in all of them there she was, with a busload of well-meaning tourists waiting for the police, the ambulance, the port authorities. The drama that this would have involved, the forms she would have had to complete, the difficulties with the language, the phone calls and emails home, the endless whys and hows.

Despite everything, Harry was an excellent sleeper. Whatever drama, tension, emotional turmoil, he always slept. He could sleep, they would joke, at postdoctoral level. He would be awarded an Olympic medal for it one day, a Nobel Prize.

Of course it could also have been the strong painkillers they'd got earlier in the day. Angela watched him from the foot of the bed. He was snoring so lightly it was really no more than strong breathing. She took her iPad and pushed the door to the balcony open wider and sat outside with a glass of ice and tonic water that soon became slick with condensation. Far below was the Bosphorus, still smooth but now the colour of blue-black ink under the sky, seemingly as busy with traffic as it was during the day, as all sorts of craft from container ships to tiny fishing boats made their way up and down. The lights on the Asian side stretched as far as she could see. Here in European Istanbul she was conscious of the muted night-time thrum of the city. It was quieter now than it had been when they were walking back to the hotel after dinner – Harry hobbling with a walking stick they'd got at the market – but it was still alive with people, most of them locals. It was as if the city's regular inhabitants stayed inside until the tourists returned home, before coming out in numbers. She had seen couples with small children way into the early hours, strolling around the parks between Hagia Sophia and the Blue Mosque, eating watermelon slices from the vendors, or sitting in the gardens of restaurants drinking apple tea while the dervishes danced. When it was especially hot some of these places sprayed a fine lemony mist over their patrons.

The streets would still be thick with humidity. Music reached her, seven storeys high. Smoky food scents. The salty tang of the water. There was a crescent moon, just to complement the skyline of rich midnight-blue above the minarets and flat-topped buildings where people like her in hotels and bars or private homes were sitting outside to breathe the cooler air.

Her hands were wet from the glass. She wiped them on her t-shirt then tapped at the iPad screen. Googling the memorial at Ari Burnu she found an article about the words inscribed on it, the ones attributed to Atatürk. Apparently he had not written these words, and they had not been contained in a letter he had sent to the Australian government, as the guidebook had said. There was no such letter. She skimmed through a few more articles but no one seemed to know how or why the myth had blossomed. She put the iPad down and stood up. Now she was profoundly tired, weary beyond sleep. She was nothing like Harry in this respect and it seemed to her that it was a good thing they would be leaving the next day; she realised she had barely slept since they'd arrived, and she imagined if she lived here any longer she never would. Istanbul was so rich and layered, so alive, it seemed a crime to sleep here.

Angela stood at the foot of the bed again, watching Harry's chest rise and fall. She had felt cheated that night at Anzac Cove, when they'd returned with Harry limping and crying and refusing to explain himself, and she felt cheated now, discovering the information about the memorial. All the points of the compass were still swivelling out of place. *Wipe away your tears.* She had been close to tears herself when she read those words: they had reached straight into her heart and now she felt used. Except she wanted to believe they were true; she wanted more than anything to know that Atatürk had assured the mothers of Australia that they could be at peace, that their sons had become Turkey's sons as well. And she should have felt more angry than she did.

Harry had no right to make of her an enemy too. If he had something to explain about the car accident, when he was with Johnny, then he should just tell her. And if he'd come all this way planning to throw himself off the Sphinx like it appeared – and then failed, like he said – she did not care to know.

She should despise him for his silence, his stupidity, his clumsiness, and despise him even more for his inability to tell her what was really burdening him, what clearly had been burdening him for more than half his life. And for ensuring that from now on, every day from here onwards, she would be on guard. Instead, she despised herself, for her emotional fortitude, for being the one who got over things quickly, who could move on. Who would cope.

'Harry. Harry.' But there was no point; she knew he wouldn't wake. She sat down on her side of the bed and put her head in her hands.

She had decided this was going to be their last holiday together and she was going to tell him that before they returned home, and maybe continue travelling by herself for a few more weeks. She had never been to Greece. She would visit Delphi, Mount Olympus, stay at the Hotel Grande Bretagne in Athens for just one glorious, lavish night. Or perhaps do an island tour. Then there was Spain. She could try out the Spanish she might remember, when she took a community college course years ago. Maybe she would return to him, maybe not.

Could anyone ever just wipe away their tears? Harry had cried for his dead great-grandfather, for his dead brother, both of whom were long at peace, and for his own yawning sense of failure. She supposed that meant he would never be at peace.

In the taxi early the next morning he took her hand. He smiled then squeezed it like he always used to, and said thank you. She looked out the window beside her. Again, the streets were deserted but for the dogs, masters of the city at this time of the day. When they pulled up at a set of traffic lights one of them was right next to the vehicle. It stared at her unblinking, its eyes golden brown, then turned its head and trotted quickly across the road.

Zebra

SPRING WAS LATE again. The day was never going to get hot, and long before nightfall it would be cold enough to have to pull on another layer. But for the moment the PM had laid aside her jacket – mushroom grey, part of the uniform of sorts she wore – and was enjoying the brief spell of warmth. She was seated at a garden table down under the port wine magnolia reviewing the draft report prepared by Health. Papers, folders, teacups, a roll of mints and several books covered the table. The jacket was folded over a lower branch of the magnolia, the telephone was back in the house. Or telephones: there were several office lines, along with the house's own numbers, including a personal one, as well as the official and her private mobile phones. She could never work with any of them shrilling beside her. As if on cue, right then Malcolm appeared on the back verandah, holding one of them up. Tucked under his other arm were several thick red folders.

She checked her watch, just after ten, and waved her hand at him, shaking her head. She wouldn't answer it, not yet.

A fat grub had dropped from the leaves of the magnolia onto page thirty-seven of the massive report. A complete overhaul of the national health budget was under consideration. She was up to chapter three, Health Industries Corporate Vision. *Key Strategic Objectives: Minimising Negative Client Outcomes.* She flicked the grub off then picked up her pen to mark a query in the margin. The grub left a brown stain, which might, she thought, pass as tea, though that would look unprofessional.

Half an hour on, and her lower back, right side, was aching. Deep in the buttock, but if she moved around it would ease. Leaving the report on the table, she rose. Her hip clenched. Perhaps she should have it seen to, except where should she go? The document she was reviewing, being a commissioned public service report, was woefully unclear. Actual patients did not rate a mention. Their specific health needs were smothered under bureaucratic jargon. Thick clods of managerese fell upon the subject as if it were already dead, shrouded, and six feet in the ground. She did not feel like a Health Service Stakeholder, and the report so far made her feel unenthusiastic about taking her right buttock, or any part of her anatomy, to medical facilities as they currently stood.

As she walked off she caught, in her peripheral vision, a glimpse of Malcolm at the side door again. She kept walking away. It was plausible that she would not have seen him. In any case she had already told him that she wanted to work alone and uninterrupted.

*

It was the PM's habit to rise early, after several hours of light dozing punctuated by intervals of wakefulness. This she had come to regard as a normal night's sleep after so many years of insomnia. Well into her middle years, she had begun to feel both diminished and constrained. It was something to do with her small body that was verging on metamorphosis, though into what she was not sure. It seemed that her skin was becoming looser at the same time that its contents were tightening up. She sensed there was a thickening at the back of her neck – not, she hoped, the start of one of those little old lady hunches, though twisting around in the bedroom mirror, she could never see enough to judge – and that stiffening in the hip was developing into a definite condition. Walking eased much of this. Plus it was a very pleasant property. Vast, varied. Always good for stimulation of the mind as well as the frame. She knew that in the years to come, retirement years, the post-leadership twilight world of sitting on boards and running consultancies and working for international charities – the quiet, morning-tea existence, as opposed to the nonstop sushi train that was life now – she could easily have regrets. She would look back on this time in her life and never wish she'd been to more briefings, overseen more committees, shaken hands with more delegations, attended more conferences, held more cabinet meetings. Especially not cabinet meetings. But she would regret it if she hadn't made the most of the garden.

Early, before full light, she would commence walking around the garden. The grounds were a mix of the landscaped and the semi-wild and offered variety every morning.

She had lived here for several years but always seemed to come across something new. And she felt – though she was not – the great advantage of being alone. In the half-light, often moist, sometimes foggy, she would roam the perimeter of the main house, then turn along one of several paths. To the north of the property, past the tennis court, and behind a hedge, was a wide-open patch that she wandered around, sometimes following the fence all the way along the boundary, until it curved back towards the house at the start of the driveway. Or she would follow the tennis court hedge back south, cross the gravel path, and walk around to the bottom of the garden. She would visit the gardening sheds, the nursery and the stables. She would avoid the gates and the booth at the front, likewise the staff quarters at the rear of the property towards the western fence. So early in the morning, she did not care to contact the security staff at the front gate, or encounter the housekeeper, who also rose early, or the head gardener, the only others who lived on the premises. It was not that she felt guilty or inhibited, just that she liked walking alone. She would be constrained if she had to share these times, have her burgeoning ideas squashed by the necessary polite hellos and good mornings and lovely days, which all came soon enough after the working day began.

Though she did feel a pang of guilt; she would admit that. In recent weeks a man had appeared to camp at the front gate, and she literally had no idea what to say to him. She could not turn him away, but neither could she invite him in. All she could do was maintain a polite distance. To be fair, he did the same, coolly ignoring her when she drove in and out, maintaining an erect cross-legged posture as he gazed somewhere into a distance she could not easily discern.

That morning, she had been out even earlier than usual. She was already fully dressed – black trousers, white t-shirt and the jacket she would remove thanks to the warmth – and had headed towards the south of the property. It was not yet six o'clock, and still dark down towards the fence line where the dogwood trees grew close and high. The leaves were dense underfoot and she kicked at them, raising a flurry that smelled pleasant. Earthy and damp. Almost wholesome. She reached the furthest perimeter of the fence, adjoining the neighbour's backyard, then turned to walk back towards the house.

'Piss off!'

A flock of noisy miners exploded from the trees behind her as if the words were shotgun pellets. The PM looked up, then around. The birds screeched and settled in the upper branches of a horse chestnut. Without them as evidence she might have thought she had imagined it.

'Pardon?' She walked right up to the fence.

There was a clattering and rustling from the other side, then again the unmistakable words, 'Piss off, why don't you?'

She had not come here on a whim. Several times recently on her morning walks she had thought she heard her neighbour on the other side: the scrape of a shovel, the creak of a ladder. He was evidently doing some kind of work in this part of the garden, but what, and why so close to her fence, she was unsure. Not to mention in the near dark.

Over the years she had been here she was aware of this presence, registered that activity was going on in the place behind hers, but they had never met. She had seen him often enough – he always wore an orange baseball cap – when up a ladder amongst the trees, trimming branches or tying ropes. She had seen him out the front of his place, securing gates or locking his letterbox. Always mysterious, furtive, almost as if he were intruding on his own property. A few times curiosity had overcome her usual early-morning desire for solitude, and she had even called out good morning. However there had never been a response, beyond a blank stare that hovered on the edge of hostility. Assuming he had no desire for the usual niceties of neighbourly life, she had left him alone.

This was the first time he had spoken. Imagine him telling her to piss off. She was almost amused by it. Intrigued – where should she piss off to, and why? – she called out again: 'Hello?' But there was no further noise. 'Hello? Are you there?' Nothing.

She walked back through the horse chestnut grove and into the light, crossed the park-like lower garden, then went up the sloping lawn and across the parking area behind the house. Underfoot, the gravel crunched agreeably. A fresh load had been spread only the week before.

The door to the kitchen was open, and the housekeeper was already at work, squeezing oranges.

'Therese, that man down the back,' she stopped in the doorway and jerked her head behind her. 'Have you ever had anything to do with him?'

'Never. Didn't know there was anyone there.'

'Oh. Maybe it's just me.' The PM took the glass that Therese handed out. Behind her the toaster pinged with a rusty-sounding squeak as two slices spat high. Her arm shook and a few drops of her orange juice spilled on the floor. Perhaps the man had upset her more than she realised. The toast landed on the bench, and they both wrinkled their noses.

'Burnt again,' said Therese.

'Frankly,' said the PM, 'I think those fancy retro appliances are overrated.'

Negative Client Outcomes. Patient Attrition Rates. She inked a large question mark in the margin. These sounded exactly like more euphemisms for death; however, she would seek clarification. The PM did not mind paperwork. She was a steady, focused reader and very capable of sifting through complete documents to extract their essence. Normally she did not require much in the way of summaries and briefing notes. The problem was, there did not seem to be any essence in this report. It was yielding very little. After several hundred pages she felt like she'd been squeezing oranges herself, except they were hard, dry ones. She did not expect that major deficiencies in the current health funding scheme would be solved, but she expected they would at least be addressed, or identified in something approaching ordinary prose.

She pushed the report aside. It would have to be sent back for redrafting. There was the large box, lower house green, stamped with the floral emblem of the Tasmanian blue gum, crammed with documents. Send me your submissions, she had told the people of the most southern state. I will consider them all. She felt bound to her word. She had much affection for the little triangle of land beyond the strait. It was just that she had not expected quite so many submissions. There were other matters nibbling away in her mind. The calls she would have to take. That man sitting at the front gate, who would not talk or otherwise communicate but who would also not leave. She had ordered things like hot tea and blankets, a camp chair and fresh fruit to be taken out to him. Sometimes they were accepted, sometimes not.

Malcolm appeared and placed the folders down in front of her.

'Just to review the afternoon's commitments.' His way of reminding her that the morning was nearly over.

'I already said I wanted to finish this. And I intend to go through all the files on the Tasmanian crisis.' She nodded towards the box, which contained reports, newspaper clippings, email printouts and handwritten letters and postcards, from the citizens of that state whose recent election had created an excess of independents – was there a collective noun for that? a nuisance of independents, a self-righteousness of independents? – and as a consequence a hung parliament, and government in limbo. There were allegations of fraud and electoral irregularities. The public was demanding a re-election.

'Let them go, I say. Place is only good for cheese and apple juice anyway.'

'Is that your most professional advice?'

'It's caused trouble for years. Ever since that Green fellow went into the senate.'

'You mean Brown.'

'Same thing. Then before him there was that lunatic, the one with a hundred children.'

'Harradine?'

'Yes. Just one extremist dictating to the rest of the country. It shouldn't be allowed. But if we cut them off, it won't.'

'Make the state secede?'

'Why not? What do we get out of the place? Really?'

She was not sure at what point, over the last couple of years, Malcolm had progressed beyond executive assistance to policy advice, strenuously opinionated if not downright prejudiced, and unsolicited advice at that. It had been subtle enough for her not to dismiss him, or even admonish him. Now she wondered if she should have been firmer with his tendency to overstep his role.

'Now, taking it from straight after lunch today, we have a good three hours of appointments back to back.'

'Not right now, please. Come back in a little while.'

Malcolm looked almost hurt. He produced the prime ministerial mobile phone from his pocket. 'Will you at least . . .?'

'Sorry. Later.'

As he turned to leave she sat back in her chair, wondering. The Apple Isle as a separate sovereign state. What a juicy idea. Then she remembered.

'Malcolm?' He turned around. 'That man who lives down the back. What do we know about him?'

'Kerr? Not a great deal. Seems an oddball. Very secretive. The Bobs have had a couple of run-ins with him over the years. He seems to be particularly fussy about fences. Always fiddling with them.'

She watched Malcolm walk back towards the house, then checked her watch. A short break, another stroll around, then back to work. But first she would visit the stables.

Despite having the best anti-spam filters available on her personal email account, the PM still received a number of letters that she presumed were hoaxes and was prepared to trash. These arrived along with the requests from Nigerian sources for her bank account details and offers to enlarge her sexual organs that still eluded the software. However, she noticed these letters were, first, all correctly spelled, and they were addressed to her personally not only as Prime Minister of the country, but also as custodian of the house. A Mr Austin Beamish of a place called Lincolnville, Arizona, USA, was the owner of a private zoo that had *lately fallen upon hard times* (the spelling might have been correct, but the PM noted the euphemistic and old-fashioned phrasing). Consequently and regrettably Mr Beamish was obliged to relocate all his animals, or risk confiscation by the local authorities, specifically the Feral and Introduced Species Board. Possible euthanasia of many animals would ensue, while others would be sent to different zoos already overcrowded and/or inexperienced with the care of many of the species in his collection. He had undertaken to write to specially targeted prominent citizens around the world to offer animals that he believed would be uniquely suited to them. Testimonials would follow, but already he could reveal that he had secured acceptances from the President of South Africa, who was generously taking three lion cubs whose mother was unfit to travel and who would be remaining as Mr Beamish's house companion; and the Queen of England herself, whose two new hyena pups would be excellent companions for the corgis. And, although they represented a priority on his list, he was not only approaching world leaders. Others included Madonna, for whom he had reserved an endangered spotted serval; Bill Gates, who was adopting a family of rare red rattlesnakes; Angelina Jolie, three black-faced chimpanzees from the lower Congo River, recently orphaned; Ben Elton, a breeding pair of King vultures; and for Richard Branson, two rare white bison.

Mr Austin Beamish somehow knew that the PM was improving the grounds of her property and extending the gardens, and he understood *her facility ticked all the right boxes*. The animal was available at a time convenient to them both, i.e. now. He would await instructions regarding shipping of the as yet unspecified animal, and the exact street address, at her earliest convenience.

She had ignored the first two emails, and responded with brief and polite refusals for the third and fourth time. All Mr Beamish's letters were similar. By the fifth email, in which he finally specified the animal earmarked for her special care, she was intrigued enough to make a few enquiries, and after the seventh she was prepared to consider the idea. And then the emails stopped. Two weeks passed and she was almost missing Mr Austin Beamish's quaint epistolary style. She contacted him, twice, but with no response. Clearly it was a hoax after all. Thank god she had not provided any of her personal details. Had she? Of course it was a hoax. Imagine the Queen of England accepting hyena pups from an oddly named man in an obscure American town. Imagine her even falling for the story of a private zoo forced to divest its animal assets around the world.

A month or so afterwards, she had been summoned early on a Friday morning. It was just after seven o'clock, and she was awake though not yet up, reading instead of walking for a change. Hazel, just winding up her evening shift at the front gates, phoned through to tell her a delivery was on its way. She went to the window to see a battered Toyota Hilux utility pulling up in the front driveway. It was towing a horse float.

'Special delivery for the PM,' the driver called up, walking around to the back of the vehicle to unfasten the tow bolt.

'What's this? What's going on?'

'As I said, special delivery.' He drew the bolt free and lowered the tow bar, releasing the float from the utility. From inside came the sound of thumping and skidding as the float settled at an angle.

'Careful! There must be a horse in there!'

The driver shrugged. 'Assume so. I'm just the driver. You are the PM, aren't you? Coming down to sign this or what?' He waved the paperwork up at her but she was already flying out the bedroom and down the stairs, flinging on a dressing-gown.

'Where's this from? And what is it?'

'Dunno. Subcontract job. I just took possession in Port Kembla. Sign here please.'

'Port Kembla!' She scribbled her name and handed the clipboard back.

'Yeah. Ship docked late last night, I collected it soon after. Made good time, didn't I?'

If that was a hint for a tip, she ignored it. More thumping noises were coming from the float. It was an old-fashioned one with a small window that revealed nothing.

'We'd better have a look, then.' She held the dressing-gown together more firmly at the front and tried the handle on the float, but the driver had already returned to the cab of the utility and started the engine. Several metres down the driveway he stopped, jumped out and reached into the back tray.

'Nearly forgot. They said you might need this.' He tossed out two bales of hay onto the gravel, jumped back in the cab and drove away.

They said. Who were they? And what was this?

But of course she knew.

The door to the float was heavy. The latch securing it was rusty and ill-fitting. By the time she opened it the PM wondered if she should have asked the driver to stay, rather than facing alone the animal that was both strange and familiar. But it was too late, she stood staring at it, *Equus grevyi*, a Grévy's zebra – if her strange correspondent had been correct – one of creation's more beautiful and ridiculous beasts. The animal snorted, tossed her head, then stepped forward. Mr Beamish had also said she was tame. The PM stretched out a hand. The black and white head extended, and as the zebra walked down the ramp and into the morning, her first in her new land, and a particularly bright morning as well, the PM realised that Mr Beamish was a marvel, a genius. A stranger, half a world, a continent, away and yet he knew that the zebra was exactly what she wanted and needed.

KERR'S SIDE OF the fence was crammed with foliage, a haven for birds, except that haven would not be the first word that sprang to her mind, now that she knew more about the man. She approached the fence from the opposite direction than she usually did. Something, she felt, was not quite right about it. She would have a good look before returning to her table under the magnolia. The fence was Colorbond, sturdy, opaque, but the ground at this point was uneven, dipping to leave large gaps beneath the bottom of the fence. She stood there, considering. It appeared that someone was digging a series of holes along the fence line, for what engineering purpose she could only imagine.

'Woman! Get out of here, woman!'

She jerked her head up so quickly her neck hurt. There was no other woman in sight. Evidently the woman in question was her, but the PM felt unworthy of the attention, even less deserving of the insult. How was it that some men managed to make the word *woman* sound so derogatory? And why today should it bother her? She barely knew the man, had only just learned his name. There was no reason she should feel the effect of the insult. Woman. She had been called that before, several times, been told to *get lost, woman*, or *leave me alone, woman*, and she had been called a lot worse. In the last week of parliament she had been denounced as a middle-aged virginal vulture, the implications of which had not bothered her since she found the prospect of vultures having sex lives impossible. She had also recently been called a feral vixen and a hibernating sloth, while her government had been likened to an entire pit of venomous snakes. For some reason parliamentary debate inspired animal imagery. Insults like these were the reason she sported metaphorical duck feathers on her back.

But today the insult hung in the air like the cloud of an atom bomb, slow moving and oppressive. Just two syllables, shouted loud and clear over the fence. How had he claimed that word? It was as if the word itself had opened up and swallowed all his fury then come mushrooming up and out with the intent to annihilate her. In her entire life, the PM could never recall using the word *man* in a similar way, nor anyone else doing so. *Man* was not an insult, and never could be. Even if she were capable of unneighbourly hostilities, she could not convincingly march up to a fence and yell, *Man! Get away from this property, man!*, any more than she could perform brain surgery on an elephant. The prospect was ludicrous. She imagined ticking off the kitchen hand or her driver in this way. *Man! Clean that grease off the floor! Man, you've taken the wrong road! Turn around, man!* Of course not. The man in question would be puzzled, not offended. Either that or she would simply be laughed at.

She was not the type to admonish anyone, or be rude or aggressive. Even so, the fact that she was letting him get away with the insult troubled her. Countless men got away with it, every day. She should respond. Why did she not act? She was aware now that she had seen hints of his behaviour for some time, and that she had allowed her default approach to operate, one of cheek-turning. Now she was feeling the effect of his insult. In her heart. In her stomach, in fact. She felt it like a physical blow. It hurt. Having *woman* aimed at her in this manner was painful. She remembered then, when she was a child, overhearing the teenage sons in a neighbouring family speak to their mother this way. She recalled her astonishment at hearing boys speaking to a parent so rudely, then the added surprise when the mother reacted so submissively, blinking and tightening her mouth and turning back to the kitchen to rectify whatever it was that had caused the outburst. Cook the chops longer, or trash the omelette that had provoked such anger in those unruly sons.

The word *woman*, she seemed to have to remind herself, was not an insulting one. Yet this man over the fence made it sound so. He made it sound as grubby as the soil he was apparently digging. And he was not by any means the first, she could admit that now. How many times had she copped the force of this, yet refused to allow it to insult her? *Get out of the way, woman!* (A man elbowing her in a crowded street.) *Give us a break, woman!* (A man remonstrating over a shop counter.) *Listen, woman, I was here first!* (A man in a queue, possibly at the bank, or at public transport ticket machines, a well-known site of customer hostilities.) And of course the ultimate, the commonest, the most familiar of all: *Woman driver!* She'd heard that a zillion times, despite the fact that she herself did not drive. She had considered reciprocating. She had called it aloud a few times to test its effect – *Man driver! Bloody man driver!*

When are you getting your licence, man! – but it just wasn't the same.

The PM's throat tightened, her usual response to stress. It was the same feeling she'd had when she was twelve and receiving a lecture in the school principal's office for being late to class. The feeling she could only undo by proper breathing, which did not come naturally. She stood still and pressed her lips, drawing in a long slow line of air through her nostrils, before parting her lips and expelling the air just as slowly. She performed this small exercise three times before moving again and in a few steps, when she was standing right beside the fence, she felt her heart rate slow down, her throat undo. She breathed deep again. This woman was calm. This woman was in control.

'What, man, are you doing to this fence?'

It was not necessarily a question that required an answer, but it marked an opening salvo. She hoped it would not be a long, drawn-out battle. But it was better to initiate it now rather than leave it to someone else to work through, like Billy, or one of the Bobs. Or the property maintenance crew, who would cheerfully take action if she asked them. They would harness themselves up and bring in cherry pickers to tackle his monstrous trees, for starters. From what she already knew of Kerr, he and crews were predestined for incompatibility.

And the question permitted her to gauge the temperature of the battle. It was in this spirit that she tossed the word *man* back over the fence. It was only a hand grenade compared with his comprehensive weaponry, but it was a good start.

His head popped up. Yes, his mouth was open in shock, but only for a moment. Loose, fleshy mouth, pale skin but reddened from the heat, the anger boiling within. His eyes hardened as from his lips erupted a tsunami of abuse so strong that she stepped back, as if the ocean really had risen up before her.

'Bloody interfering woman! You idiot, you fuckin' idiot, that's what you are, a complete fuckin' idiot . . .'

It was so unexpected that she stared in amazement and then, unable to help herself, began to laugh.

'You loser, you stupid idiot bloody fuckin' woman! Why don't you go back to the country where you belong . . .'

She stopped laughing, and looked around. Which country? she wondered. Or did he mean the outer western suburbs of Sydney, where she had spent her childhood, which then was semi-rural and so perhaps considered the country? Or was she visibly foreign in some way? She glanced down and surveyed her neutral shirt, trousers and shoes, inspected her torso, and arms. Her hair was light brown, cut in a straight bob, her eyes were blue, her spectacles inconspicuous. What country could she possibly be considered to have come from?

'Fuckin' upstart useless fuckin' woman comin' here and telling me what to do, fuckin' stupid idiot, let me tell ya, you know fuckin' nothing, ya hear me, fuckin' nothing . . .'

She tilted her head a little, considering. There was a trace of accent in there, eastern European, possibly. Was he projecting something of himself in that demand to go back to the country she came from? She knew about families that kept so close they maintained their language and accents. Families that were tight with an equal mix of suspicion and loyalty, whose children were often taught at home in order to keep them belonging to the family alone, and whose social activities were restricted to necessary shopping and church attendance, if these could be counted as social. It was possible that Kerr's entire life was spent in a ten-kilometre radius, its limits embracing the closest shopping centre (for he was clearly a hardware-store addict), but that he still spoke, ate, worked, dressed and even dreamed – when he slept, which she suspected was not often – like his forebears. Whoever they were.

The baseball cap designed to protect his head from the alien sun, so unkind to that complexion – European, she was sure of it – had now fallen off. His face was shiny and damp, his broad receding forehead (completely bald within the decade, she estimated) bubbling with sweat.

'. . . godless, evil, fornicating, fuckin' useless . . .'

A religious angle. That was bound to emerge in this one-sided argument, this dysfunctional debate, this mono-course. Apart from his swearing, it was sounding more and more like an afternoon in parliament. Religious men could be very passionate about some things, in a fierce and decidedly Old Testament way. Parliament still had its fair share of them. Generally backbenchers, generally from the extreme, often ragged, edges of the Country Alliance Party. Though one could always be surprised. The Leader of the Opposition had recently been outed as an unreconstructed creationist. He all but denied the existence of dinosaurs. Critics had drawn a direct line between this and his conservative life. It was true that his wife had been quoted in a recent magazine interview as saying her husband did not know how to use their washing machine. She had been photographed icing cupcakes. The PM had felt the ensuing media mockery of this was unfair. She wouldn't have minded an afternoon in the kitchen making cupcakes. It would be innocent and relaxing, she thought, amid a world of inescapable complexity.

'. . . drunken lying whore of a woman . . .'

And, yes, of course there would be strict wowserism in there as well, completing the picture. She frowned, recalling an incident back at the start of the year. At the time she had not registered it as significant. It was New Year's Day, midafternoon, and the remains of a house party, four others, had been strolling through the grounds while she caught up with the news bulletins in her office. It had been a hot day. Her neighbour was celebrating the new year with a spade and a wheelbarrow, and one of the guests had mentioned something about the strangeness of working on such a day, in such conditions. He had stuck his head above the fence then, her guests had reported. She wondered how he'd done it, just appeared like that, so quickly. She couldn't elevate herself like that, even if she had wanted to peer over the fence into his property. Perhaps he carried an empty milk crate with him, up and down the fence line, wherever he was working, in case of imminent disputes.

He'd accused her guests of a series of offences and character flaws ranging from violation of his property to communism and cultural pretentiousness, until one of them – fed up and mischievous – invited him over the fence, for a relaxing new year drink. That guest was then called an alcoholic.

But now he had also called her a lying whore. Coming from the back of his throat, the words sounded like they were on fire, ignited by outrage and disgust of her shameless disregard for decency. Drunken, lying whore . . . She shook her head. Still, he was an amateur compared to the member for Hancock, in the nation's midwest, the Shadow Minister for Primary Industries, who in yet another mulesing debate had likened her to a suppurating wound on the backside of the pastoral industry. It had been nasty but metaphorically apt, given the matter under discussion.

Anyway, she drank very little. Always had. Even the night before, she had not drunk. Her series of evening obligations had commenced with a five-thirty address to an invited media delegation, with the object of defusing the imminent launch of the Opposition's proposed Higher Education Paper. The audience of media and academics drank, she noted, quite a lot. Then she appeared at pre-dinner drinks with the Japanese Industry Association, drinking apple juice while they had Sapporo and Asahi, before moving to appearances at three separate functions within the capital where she was expected to converse on topics from concrete formwork and swamp preservation to dog training, all of which demanded sobriety. She celebrated the opening of the capital's first dedicated cattle dog trial stadium with a mineral water rather than champagne.

But *woman*. The word alone seemed weighted with more venom than the honourable member for Hancock could amass in a lifetime of political warfare. If she could move closer she might open up a proper conversation. The PM's conversational charm was famous. But she could not see how that might be done. The insults had been yelled rather than spoken, from a safe distance. She had seen his head sticking up over the fence. While previously she had spotted him halfway up one of his trees with a bush saw, they had never been within normal conversational range. She had never managed to look him in the eyes. She did not know what colour they were.

And he had still not answered her question. It appeared he had departed. She examined the ground around the fence more carefully. And then she noticed the chalky white of new concrete footings, the cuts deep into the lawn, and evidence of recently turned soil. She squatted down close to one of the fence joins and looked along the line down to the south of the property, until she spotted it, small but definitely there, a dogleg, where the line blurred back. She walked down to where the dogleg appeared, trailing her hand along the fence until she reached the join that represented the end – or more likely the temporary stay – of his endeavours. Then she turned around and stared back along the fence. It was not an optical illusion. Panel by panel, he was shifting the fence forward. He was encroaching on her property. Well, not hers, but the government's. No, the PM's residence belonged to the Commonwealth, not the government; it was owned by the entire nation.

He was stealing land from the citizens of this country – she crouched down and examined the last seam – by six, no, a good eight inches. He was slowly moving the fence eight inches across. Months, perhaps, had gone into these endeavours. She imagined the furtive digging, planting, uprooting, sawing, bricking and raking all along the fence. She had not the slightest idea why. The result of all his labours being a few extra inches of land, though the long fence line could yield extra square metres. Skinny ones, but significant all the same.

'Spy! Spying on me and my land.'

He had not left. He was almost right above her.

'Get away from me, woman! Stupid fuckin' loser drunken whore woman . . .'

She stood up, deliberately dusting off her dustless hands and smoothing her trousers. Breathe, breathe. In through the nose, out slowly through the mouth.

'Isn't there enough excitement up your end, woman, that you have to come down here to spy on me!'

It was the most coherent and the least abusive thing he'd said all morning, and yet it made no sense at all. Asking him to clarify what he meant was out of the question. As for excitement, did he imagine this was entertaining? True, it was more interesting than the current health report she had abandoned on the garden table. But did he honestly believe that she came roaming along the fence out of boredom and the desire to inject drama into her days? No, she could not, she would not respond to that, would not bat the question back with anything that constituted an answer.

First, that would be an acknowledgement of the existence of a scrap of logic in his assertion. Second, it would represent an admission of the general dullness of parliamentary life, a palpable untruth even now when parliament was in recess. And third, it would only provoke more abuse.

She stepped closer, though it meant risking the line of enraged spittle that was gathering, ready to shoot forth. It might be preferable to withdraw and let him vent his rage until its natural evaporation, like a kettle boiling dry. But apart from almost enjoying seeing his anger percolate, she decided that he was tossing her a gauntlet, perhaps several, that could not be ignored.

'And my family, woman! You come to spy on my family. Leave us alone!'

He had procreated? Now the PM was intrigued. What woman cohabited with a man who looked like Noddy but was more bad-tempered than Mr Squiggle's Blackboard? Who spent his days scrabbling in the dirt beside a seven-foot-high security fence. Whose loathing of women was as powerful as it was illogical. She looked around for a milk crate of her own; she had to get up there and look over the fence, she had to see this for herself. She opened her mouth to speak. And then he yelled again.

'Why don't you get a life! Why don't you get a real job!'

Malcolm had ambushed her. He was waiting at the table when she returned for morning tea. Therese had brought out a tray with Earl Grey and homemade biscuits.

'It's going cold,' he said, handing out her cup.

'Yes, I know I'm late. There was a bit of an altercation.' She took a cautious nibble. Therese's ginger nuts were exceptionally hard.

'What do you mean?' Security was not his responsibility. 'No one has come in, have they?'

'Oh, it's just that man.'

'What, the one out the front?'

'Oh no, not him.' Now that Malcolm had mentioned it, that man was the last person she expected to offer hostilities. He was aloof, yes, but serenely so. 'Kerr. The neighbour. Down at the back fence. Nothing, really, though I might have to get someone to look into it. He seems to be behaving oddly.'

'I'll call one of the Bobs.' He took out his phone, in which the front guards were listed under Favourites as Bob I and Bob II.

'No, really. Don't, please. It's nothing. I'll deal with it later.'

'Well, if you're sure. Because we do have a lot on.' He placed his iPad on the table in front of her. Her appointments diary for the week was open, time slots all filled in with different pastel colours according to type of event, like a geometric world map. 'Now there's the Treasurer at one on the dot, and he's only got fifteen minutes, so you can get to the Indonesian trade function over at Kingston where you're the after-lunch speaker. Your speech is here.' He tapped his top pocket. 'Nine minutes. Actually I've slotted you in between the main course and dessert. Better that way, so you can leave before questions.'

'Why would I want to do that? I like questions.'

'I don't think you'll like them today.' He placed an email printout marked Confidential on top of the diary. 'This came in this morning from DFAT. It's looking very bad for our Mr Song.'

She put down her cup and picked up the page. Mr Roland Song, an Australian national of Indonesian background, and chief executive of a large livestock business, had recently been arrested in Jakarta on charges of falsifying documents to pass off freshly slaughtered lamb as halal compliant, to maximise his profit margins.

She scanned the text. Roland Song had now been tried and found guilty, but an appeal would be mounted by his lawyers. Her government had so far resisted pleas to intervene, though the growing popularity of the meat in the country's closest neighbour had been considered a great success, lamb not being part of a traditional Asian cuisine.

'The export lamb industry is fragile at the moment. If Indonesia pulls out . . .'

Lamb. Not a meat she especially liked, though it would seem unpatriotic to admit it. 'What else?'

'A radio interview, scheduled at one-fifty, we can do that in the car. Then there's the address to the –'

'With whom?' He looked up from the appointments book. 'The interview. Tell me it's not that ghastly Peters again.'

Malcolm pulled his lips down.

She sighed. Howard Peters. Her bête noire. Everyone's bête noire. He hated all politicians and policy, wrote off any initiative as subversive, denounced everything creative, innovative or environmental as left-wing. She herself was regularly branded a communist, the Minister for Foreign Affairs a spy, the Arts Minister a manifestation of the devil himself. He was a media version of her neighbour.

'I suppose he'll be asking about Indonesian lamb too. Indonesian everything.' Peters had a history of just avoiding prosecution under the Racial Discrimination Act. He was in particular outspoken on the Islamic theme. Female Muslim dress was a favourite topic.

'Then what?'

'Address to the Local Government Association; their reps will be waiting for you at Parliament House.' He paused.

'Ah,' she said. 'Avoiding questions there too?'

'Might be an idea.' There had been enormous hostility to the proposed overhaul of the local government system. Demonstrations all over the nation. Violence had been reported in some boroughs. And, the week before, a small fleet of council garbage trucks, state unknown, but it was suspected Queensland, had arrived in the pre-dawn and tipped their loads onto the sandstone steps of Parliament House. The refuse was especially pungent, a result, it was thought, of the long hot drive from the north. There did seem to be a large number of brown banana skins amongst the rubbish.

'Then there is the Alliance of Independent Churches. Three pm.'

'What do they want?'

'Tax exemptions.'

'Churches already have them.'

'On all their business activities. Apparently the legislation is inconsistent on this. And they want approval for their proposed national educational program. You being the prime minister who has been so progressive. Decentralising and diversifying and so on.'

Yes, she was that. She gazed at the diary list for the day, the events blocked out in green, blue and pink. Even for her it was getting daunting. What was after the 3 pm meeting? Afternoon tea? She doubted it. And fifteen minutes with the Treasurer was barely enough. The Reserve Bank was planning to raise interest rates by the end of the day. That would require more than a quarter of an hour.

'You're down to review the Production and Incentivation Commission.' Malcolm had chosen lemon yellow for that one. The Indonesian trade lunch was coloured in what appeared to be Commonwealth pink.

She slapped her hand down onto the iPad, covering the diary.

'I'll review it right now. It can be dissolved. There. Reviewed. Stupid name anyway. What on earth is incentivation?'

'A term minted by a former PM. Cross between motivation and incentive.'

'It sounds like something you do to a sick rabbit.'

Malcolm sighed now. 'Afraid I agree. But there are protocols . . .'

She drained her tea. 'Too many. Cancel all this, please. Apart from the Treasurer. I'd better see him. But the rest can be taken care of by someone else, surely. Isn't that what I have ministers for? I've more important work.'

*

What was a real job? On the first day of her prime ministership she had indeed wondered if it were real. If *job* were quite the right word for it. Position? Appointment? Incumbency? *Job* did not seem to encompass it. It suggested manual work, in a laundry or bakery, or on a building site. The sort of work almost revered when she was young. Honest work. Good, honest, sweat-creating work. Toiling in the fields, the vineyards. The sort of work you never had to feel guilty about performing. People may have despised you or regarded you with contempt if you were a sewerage worker or a hotel housemaid, but they did so with a curious mixture of respect as well, the sort of respect reserved for people willing to undertake menial labour without complaint.

Like many of her generation, the PM had felt guilty for living a life of the mind. In her youth, as a student, she heard people talking defensively about the real world, as if so long as she was sitting in classes or studying for exams she was indulging herself in a dreamlike existence entirely empty of work or cares or responsibilities or commitments. And some of this had rubbed off on her, so that she felt uneasy when she thought about the real world of other people, those who had to drive buses or collect rents or run sandwich bars. This guilt sat on her like a lead collar. Why should she enjoy the benefits, however modest, of a cultured life? How come she could sit down on the weekends to immerse herself in novels, go to art show openings, listen to opera, when the vast majority of the population could not? Or did not? The fact that there was a choice here, one that only people like her exercised, still did not explain all this satisfactorily.

Then she entered the most unreal world of all. All the accusations people levelled at elites being out of touch reached a crescendo when it came to parliamentarians. But she was probably the first prime minister of the country who knew the price of a litre of milk. At both the supermarket and corner store. Previous prime ministers had been crucified for less than that. Entire governments had been criticised for their arrogance, for being indifferent to everyday economic concerns. She would never be that sort of politician. Consumer shows posing as current affairs were fond of exposing politicians' ignorance. Reporters shepherding hapless ministers around supermarket aisles. Senior ministers, cabinet ministers, if possible, ministers for health or defence – any lofty portfolio to make the humiliation worse – who all expressed surprise when told the price of sliced bread. Who had no idea if a dozen eggs cost two dollars or twenty. Along with the rest of the nation, she had cringed when seeing these sorts fumbling through the self-serve fruit and vegetables section, dropping avocadoes and not knowing the difference between new and old potatoes, or – the ultimate shame – revealing at the checkouts that they were without wallets. Only a small and elite section of the community could afford the luxury of not carrying a wallet or purse, of conducting themselves as if they were royalty. She, on the other hand, was the only prime minister to do her own grocery shopping. Let her political opponents say what they liked about her unmarried state, her failure to produce children, her unfashionable hairstyle, her refusal to wear high heels: she knew the cost of a box of laundry powder or a packet of Weet-Bix. She knew when the prices of lemons or parsnips would soar. And why.

And as for getting a real job, she doubted the man down the back had one himself. He was no more in the real world than she. At least she had her cabinet papers, her reports and her policies. She made decisions, she acted on them. In the few years she had been in government she had achieved a great deal. He could not boast about making company tax more equitable, about simplifying the paperwork for small business, about establishing a non-profit national telecommunications provider. He had not implemented the quiet triumph of her entire term: people answering the phones again in government departments. He hadn't found a way to keep manufacturers onshore and small schools open in small towns. Nor had he ever got all six state premiers together without a single fight. More than once.

And she was sure her garden was in better shape than his. She had devoted a lot of thought to its improvements and had personally overseen most of the work. In the space of three years, the garden had developed into something spectacular, magical. There was her peony bed, a showcase for the territory, rivalling – no, complementing – the annual floral festival. And her native animal sanctuary. Real kangaroos amongst the kangaroo paw beds all along the south lawn. A family of frisky Tasmanian devils in a pen nearby. A spot set aside for the bandicoots, which Billy once cursed for tunnelling up his lawn. And frogs back in the lily pond again, frogs where there had been none for years. Apparently they had disappeared after the Keatings left.

She was proud of what she had done in the garden. All that had been hard work, as well as the other job, the real job, of running the country. The property was her responsibility too. It was *work*. She had every right to roam around and inspect it, whatever her advisers thought.

Nevertheless she drew the Tasmanian box closer, and began rummaging through the submissions. Amongst the letters and reports were what seemed to be gifts and tokens, hopefully not bribes. Ribbons, rosettes, pressed flowers, dried leaves. Poppies, flat and agreeably crumpled, but not faded. Apple butter in a small jar topped with a red checked cover. A handful of something fragrant and earthy. She sniffed. Hops, she thought. The beer brewing industry was an important one down south. And in an envelope some star-shaped leaves between pages ripped from an old exercise book. She sniffed them deeply, sniffed again. Really. She tossed them back. If the citizens of Tasmania were hoping to get her intoxicated, or stoned, or softened up with local produce, they were wrong. Perhaps Malcolm had a point. Not that she would concede that, especially at the moment. It was probably about time for him to reappear, threatening her with his iPad.

A breeze had developed. She anchored the papers on the table with her cup. She gazed over at the garden beds behind the house. A stand of native pines clustered in the slight rise that marked the place where the more formal grounds ended and the wilder, park-like space began. Just beyond that was her neighbour, her other neighbours, whom she had never met. Not so far away was an entire neighbourhood. They would have names for their houses. They did have names. Even the man behind her had called his property something. Jorobali. The gilt plaque was fixed on his front fence, above the locked letterbox. She passed it all the time. Though most unneighbourly, he at least had bestowed on his property a better name than hers. Jorobali was a curious name, suggestive of an exotic place: say, a lake in central Africa. Or perhaps it was a cognomen, so beloved of Australian householders in decades past. Not one she would have wanted for her house, but it imparted something approaching personality to the place. Curious, given he had none himself, or one limited to aggression and abuse. She supposed that was still personality.

She had never been happy with the name of this house. The Lodge was an ugly, masculine name suggestive of shotguns and game keeping, hunting dogs and tankards of dark ale drunk by log fires, and all sorts of things she was sure had never taken place here. But she had not known what to change it to. Names were something the PM had never been confident about. For years she felt like she herself had had no real claim to one. It was as if the narrative of her life did not require one. Her first name was as ordinary as the dust on her shoes. Her surname was worse. Altogether it was a dull, muffled name that sat thick on the tongue. Not a thrilling, literary or musical kind of name, one that could be uttered endearingly or called out in passion, but a coming-to-the-dinner-table one, as uninspired as a meal of chops and mashed potato. It was almost a relief to be called Prime Minister, or even ma'am, though she still stiffened at the surprising formality of that, occasionally looked around for some more important person. As if one were the Queen. Or her representative.

Only after the PM was installed in the house had she come to understand that her long-dead mother's personality was more influential than she thought. She had discovered an interest in the garden that she could only assume came from her early years, as much as she had disdained her mother's utilitarian regard for the land on which they lived. Perhaps this was why she found her early mornings in the capital so beguiling. She never tired of strolling around, inspecting the flowerbeds and the shrubs. It seemed only proper to approach work in this way. There was no hurry, at least not in her mind, though occasionally she was conscious of some murmuring and shuffling of feet from inside the hallway on mornings when she walked past her office downstairs and out the door. And the security staff would exchange looks behind their dark glasses, she knew that. She smiled at them from a distance. The Bobs had already begun to take turns in patrolling the front gate and tidying the front gardens. It was boring for them, and wasteful for the nation anyway, having two of them just standing on guard either side of the gate. She would encircle the house slowly, stray off the gravel, go right up to the fence line, then meet the driveway on the other side of the house before returning to enter, usually via the kitchen door. The detour would be long, on some days. Sometimes she felt she should spend as much of the day outside as possible. Not to do so would be somehow disrespectful, though to what exactly she wasn't sure. The weather? Nature itself? And now her morning walks had a distinct purpose.

The day after the zebra had arrived, the PM had walked down to the garden sheds where, in an empty section between the stacked wheelbarrows and a pile of bagged mushroom compost, the zebra had spent her first night. Billy had already provided her with water in a plastic bucket. She was waiting outside, flicking her tail and lifting her nose to sample the air. The tenderness with which the PM regarded this creature surprised her. It was not something she remembered feeling for any animal before this.

Late the night before, in her pyjamas and slippers, she had walked across the dewy lawn and down to the sheds to check the animal was all right. She was almost expecting there would be no zebra, that she had conjured it out of her imagination. That it had all been a folly, a result of hard work and the end of the week. A dream. But no, she was there in the shed, breathing audibly and blinking at the PM from out of the gloom. And she was there again that morning, smelling agreeably of something earthy, like warm dust and fresh mown grass, and looking as mythological as ever, despite appearing quite at home.

What was so wonderful about the zebra was her silence. The PM could spend a few minutes in the animal's stable, if she were there (for she loved to roam the rear grounds of the property) and silently commune. She loved just breathing in the horsey smells – the manure, the hay, the grassy, dusty richness of it all – and listen to the sound of nothing more than the animal breathing. The zebra would stare at her, blinking calmly. After a while she would lower her head and nudge the PM's pockets. She would think that she should have brought a treat. Then she would pat the zebra's neck, put her hands back in her pockets and keep walking.

The day the zebra arrived Malcolm had sent an assistant out for every relevant zoological book obtainable from the national library, exerting the privilege of the prime ministerial office to check out books, since the library was not a lending one. While she waited, the PM combed through internet sites, and within a few days felt extremely well informed about the animal. There were three main species of zebra. Hers did indeed appear to be, as Mr Austin Beamish had said, a Grévy's zebra. Studying the full-page illustrations in *The Complete Zebra* by Colonel Arthur Waygrove (Retd), published in Cape Town in 1932, she could see quite marked distinctions between the species. The more common plains zebra, like the mountain zebra, *Equus zebra*, resembled a horse, while the *Equus grevyi* had a narrower, more mule-like head.

But, to be sure, she had taken the books with their illustrations out to the zebra, who was by now nibbling the back lawn. The PM had learned that zebras were adaptable eaters, preferring grass but settling for shrubs, herbs, twigs, leaves and even bark if necessary. The garden might have to be protected, or the zebra provided with enough fodder. She had displayed no signs of wanting to run away, but each time the PM approached she had remained aloof. Twice she consented to having her neck patted and seemed content when the PM brushed a hand down her side. But she hadn't returned any signs of affection. There was none of the usual nuzzling and snuffling, the nosing near pockets in hopes of apple or sugar treats, which the PM remembered from her encounters with horses as a child.

Comparing the illustrations in Colonel Waygrove's compendium, she could see now very clearly the differences. It was Waygrove's opinion, and she quickly agreed with him, that George Stubbs's famous subject, a specimen taken to England as a gift for the Royal Family and displayed at the Windsor Great Park, was an *Equus grevyi*. Stubbs's beast – Malcolm's assistant had thoughtfully provided a print that the gallery shop had in stock – compared with Waygrove's photographic evidence, featured a much smaller head and ears, while its neck and forelegs looked very much like a base of black had been overcoated with thin white stripes.

The plains and mountain zebras, on the other hand, had a different pattern stretching almost horizontally across from the rump to the middle with thick, even stripes as if its maker had wielded a brush dipped in black and white paint in either hand. Around the middle of the belly the pattern shifted, tilting vertically, and the stripes, though still even, were thinner. Although the underside of the zebra's stomach was predominantly white, as the black stripes tapered while the white remained the same, the PM knew, having checked Waygrove against two other titles – J. B. Pearson's *Guide to Hoofed African Mammals* (1956; 1986) and Hayes and Barnes's *Illustrated History of Equine Art* (1990) – along with the Wikipedia pages she had printed out, that the zebra was essentially a black animal, patterned in white stripes. The Grévy's zebra seemed to confirm it. To exist, perhaps, just to pose the age-old question: was the zebra a black animal with white stripes or a white animal with black stripes? The plains and mountains zebra suggested the latter, teasingly displaying black and white stripes in equal proportion until the belly region. But then the Grévy's dragged the argument back in the opposite direction.

One source cited embryological evidence, proving that in the womb the animals were entirely black until a certain stage of development. Others theorised that the stripes, well known to assist camouflage, also served the purpose of resisting the tsetse fly, which could be visually confused and therefore deterred from alighting. Lions, known to be colour blind, were apparently confounded when the zebra stood still. Entirely black and white, the zebra would blend in perfectly with the landscape. All of them agreed that the patterns were unique to each animal, who recognised each other by their stripes.

Extraordinary, thought the PM. It was like glancing at a collection of barcodes and instantly seeing the differences. All three of the species, the plains, the mountain and the Grévy's, could interbreed, apparently, though they never did in the wild and rarely in captivity. Plains and mountain zebras were most similar but the latter was now vulnerable, restricted to highland reserves, and generally failing to thrive in captivity.

In captivity. These were herding creatures. Was it fair to keep just one? The Grévy's zebra was the least sociable, living in small family groups for a few months, while the males generally lived alone. But it was arguable that her zebra was in captivity. She showed no signs of fear or apprehension, and hadn't, even on the first day, strayed any further from the lawns. As dignified as it was possible to be, given those amazing stripes, she emanated a clear sense of independence. It was almost as if she had chosen to be here. When the PM had encountered her grazing in the native garden the day she arrived, raising her head to nibble at an early blooming callistemon, she had asked Billy to drag around the bales of hay dumped by the driver. The zebra calmly transferred her attention from the natives to the hay.

The PM had never been able to take zebras seriously. Maybe it was because her experience of them until now had always been manipulated by art. She had once embarrassed herself by laughing out loud at the original of Stubbs's painting on show at the national gallery. The sheer incongruity of the zebra standing still before the English forest background. Yet the wild creature looking so calm and contemplative. Thousands of miles from the vast open grasslands, and seemingly resigned to a fate of pinched cold winters, damp hay and shrivelled root vegetables. Now there was this zebra, here at the bottom of her garden. Behind it the stand of callistemon, and the beds of flannel flowers and kangaroo paw all around. Was it any less absurd? Intellectually, not. And morally? But the PM could not think about that. She could not really think at all, not while her heart was opening up to the zebra. All she wanted was to keep the animal close by and make sure it was safe.

Right from the start the zebra had held her head high and stared directly at the PM. Zebras had excellent eyesight. Their eyes were positioned wide on the head to give them a great field of vision. And it was said they could see in colour, a fact the PM found comically fascinating, given the zebra's markings.

That morning, as the PM was still looking through books and comparing markings, Malcolm had appeared beside her. The zebra shifted her unblinking gaze to him then turned back to the pile of hay she was nosing through. He pocketed his phone.

'That was finance. I told her you'd call back in ten minutes.'

'All right.'

They watched the zebra chewing for a few moments.

'It's almost enough to make you believe in a god, isn't it?' he said. 'One with a massive sense of humour.'

That was why she found Malcolm so compatible, despite his barely concealed cynicism.

'It's like that joke.'

'What joke?'

'Oh, I'd tell you, but I'd muck it up,' she said. 'Should we get her something nicer to eat? Lucerne, maybe.'

'That might make her shit all green and slimy.'

'You know about horses?'

'I grew up on a farm, just south. The zebra might be different, but I know we had to watch the horses with lucerne. And oats. Too many oats make them frisky.'

Who would have thought it of oats? Stodgy, nourishing food, something one associated with invalids, or babies. Porridge and oatmeal cookies. She glanced at Malcolm. And who would have thought he knew about horses, or zebras.

The garden in bloom was teeming with activity. It was busier than the biggest shopping centre. Noisier than parliament in full swing. More complex and dangerous and intriguing than any section of the city at any time. Deaths, collisions, murders, births. Hatchings and burials and feasts and fights all took place within a deceptive serenity. One only had to sit quietly and gaze into a patch of flowering lavender, wait a while by the rosebushes, stand amid the grevilleas to feel the force of its buzzing, sometimes tempestuous life.

So when, several weeks later, the wind delivered a pale pink bloom from a far portion of the garden, the PM was intrigued. It landed in the grass before her, then danced away, paper thin, before landing again a few metres away. She ran and grabbed for it twice before she succeeded, and when she looked closer at the crumpled petal in her palm she frowned. The peony bed was on the opposite side of the property, part of the showy front garden, but she reached it in a minute, almost running. She stopped, panting, then held her breath. Then cried out in anguish. The damage. The waste.

The plants had just been displaying their first buds. A few, including the one in her hand, had opened up in the days before. But most of the fleshy stalks had still been covered with firm, marble-shaped buds, promising a splendid burst of bloom in the coming weeks. Now the beds, massed in shallow terraces that extended to the north path, were a mess of uprooted stems, crushed and in some places ground to a green pulp, and a litter of buds everywhere. Pink and white cracks in the dark green buds, revealing the promises of pale pink flowers, some so pale as to be cream, others to feature a subtle stripe on the outer petals.

Her first instinct was to blame Billy, the gardener, but for what? Not being vigilant enough? That was hardly fair, and Billy, though silent to the point of unresponsiveness, was a good worker, a decent man. Her second thought was that it was the zebra, but there was not a single hoof mark, and even as she scrutinised the ground the PM felt guilty for considering it.

It was that Kerr. She knew it down to her boots, though it would not do to start making accusations yet. Her neighbour would hate flowers, as he would hate anything that was not considered useful. She had once spotted him removing all the everlasting daisies from the nature strip along the front of his property – the nature strip that was not even his – and he had been observed by Billy and the Bobs clipping off the magnolia blooms from the specimens planted where the properties adjoined. Evergreen trees he tolerated, and in some places encouraged, as they provided privacy. Shrubs he would also tolerate, so long as they were tidy and obliging. But flowers would be a contemptible frivolity. He would abhor them. He would especially loathe their sexy connivances. The way they posed and preened and parted their petals. He would hate the whole scented, blowsy, fecund world of arousal and desire and attraction and disguise that was the flower. The rose unfolding like the vulva, the hairy testicles of the unopened poppy, the polleny, powdered stamen of the lily. And the peony, which contained, it was said, the very scent of a woman. Was it true that their stamens and petals were more genital-like than many other flowers? That the Chinese over centuries purposely bred peonies to capture this?

Long before knowing any of this, the PM had decided this flower was one of her favourites, and the crushed-looking pink blooms of the *Paeonia lactiflora* her favourite of all. The utter perfection of it almost made her laugh.

The PM was not laughing now. She felt close to tears. Her beautiful plants. This would have been the third season they had flourished.

The peony bed was a long way from the southern fence line, but she did not put it past Kerr to come somehow, in the deep end of the night when even she was asleep, with his mattock or pick or whatever tool of destruction he used. Was he not down the back all the time, sawing, chopping, abusing any vegetation that wasn't useful? Had she not just that morning caught him at it? Not that she was certain of the exact nature of his depredations this time, but there seemed to be bush saws and mattocks involved. Had she been able to see into his backyard she would have known for sure, but to do so would have required ladders or upturned crates and an undignified sort of curiosity incommensurate with her position. She imagined the yard was full of severe-level lawn (she regularly heard the lawnmower chewing its way through her Sunday mornings, even from the distance of her bedroom), something harsh and unkind to the bare foot like buffalo grass and probably kept greener than most through illegal use of watering – who would know? The place was such a fortress: the trees guarding the property on all three sides. And as for other plants, nothing that wasn't useful. She expected he planted potatoes and onions, a variety of root vegetables. Serious, filling, carbohydrate-rich vegetables, the sort that required immense efforts with digging and maintaining the soil. Why would you bother when you could drive to the local markets any Saturday morning and buy an entire sack of potatoes or a bag of carrots for less than twenty dollars?

Oh, but she did know why he would bother. It was not about saving money or providing wholesome food for his household, it was far more primal than that. It was about making his mark on the land. The more he cultivated it, the more he controlled it, the more he felt the power that had been denied him by whatever circumstances had brought him to this state: a miserable, antagonistic, abusive balding man in a dirty orange baseball cap, obsessed with her property and violating it by stealth.

She knelt down in the bed, not caring that she soiled the knees of her trousers. One or two plants seemed intact, though wilted. She gathered them close.

The peony was immortal. Unlike more revered beauties of the flower world, such as the tulip, whose capacity for propagation had been diminished down the centuries, the peony could be endlessly grafted and cloned. All the developments in the horticultural world could not make a cornflower or a pansy much more exciting than it was. Seasons and fashions may bring a fondness for streaked petunias or a mania for pink lilies, but little more. A carnation – even a green one – was never going to transcend its status. It would forever be a flower for nervous young men in new suits or old ladies in nursing homes.

But the peony, like the rose, was an open-ended flower. It resisted closure. It contained possibilities that had not been exhausted by generations of cross-breeding, cloning, grafting and other forms of unnatural selection.

Despite knowing most of this, her response to the flower was instinctual. She first loved it for purely aesthetic reasons, only later appreciating its unique design. She loved the way its profuse and crowded petals seemed so accidentally arranged, so messy and wayward, and yet how each bloom was held together by the tightest and strictest of architectures. Its petals were soft and papery, yet they remained strong and erect. They curved outward then inward, and remained upright despite all the laws of gravity that should dictate their falling or drooping. Their arrangement was not entirely circular: the blooms formed a flattened sphere. They were more like little globes than balls. And their central emptiness seemed to be another ingenious paradox. Even the double blooms of the *Paeonia officinalis*, the common European peony, offered a void. The petals clustered around nothing. And yet there was everything in that vacant space. It was the reason the petals arranged themselves so artfully in deceptive disorder.

Billy had helped plant the peonies soon after her first

few weeks of residence. She was delighted that her arrival coincided with the flower's optimum planting time. The dry air and cool soil would provide the perfect conditions for enhancing the flower's beauty. She planned to set up a national competition for breeding the first truly purple peony. For as much as she loved them she felt cheated by the limitations of colour, largely restricted to pinks, reds and whites. The cerise and shiraz colours of the deeper pinks and reds which were often passed off as purple were nothing like the amethyst or iris shades she desired. There were some insipid pinky-mauves. The professional horticulturalists, even the amateurs, she thought, could do better. While she was knowledgeable about much, on gardening and flowers in particular, she was a novice. And she knew in her heart she would always be an amateur, and that she did not have the obsessive personality – or the time – to devote herself to a breeding challenge.

From the time she first gazed on a bunch of peonies, she knew that this flower was exquisite. And that she would have them as much as possible in her life. She was living in an inner city share house at the time. A grateful friend, whose several years' worth of muddled accounts and unlodged tax returns she had sorted with her clear eye for arithmetic order, sent her a bunch. Not only had he not been fined for the late returns, but he had received a tax refund for exactly the amount she had predicted. She hoped he'd not spent too much of it on the flowers, for she had received them fatigued and worn. They had arrived when she was at work, and been entrusted to the care of neighbours, a wife and husband team who made their living from a towing business, and whose truck screamed and clattered under her window late at nights going to and from jobs. When not working, they spent their leisure time in the street, drinking beer and laughing. They both wore the same kind of overalls and had the same short hair and gravelly smokers' voices, and she would have had trouble telling them apart except that the husband had an impressive pornstar moustache. When the woman banged on her door later that evening and shoved the flowers at her, they were well into a slab of VB.

'Here ya are, love. Been mindin' them for ya all day.'

It was before the time when florists started to shroud arrangements in metres of stiff brown paper and preserve stem ends in water-soaked tissue. The blooms drooped. A few petals fell as the neighbour handed them over. But they were not spoiled. And while she hoped they had brought some pleasure to her neighbours' day, she knew they would have lain ignored. She carried them to the sink to untie them.

'Thanks very much. Here, why don't you take some?' The arrangement was enormous. Creamy petals, with a hint of pink. Dark green leaves. All dotted with many more buds, firm and rounded like marbled gobstoppers.

But the woman declined, cheerfully slamming the screen door on her way out and whistling. Perhaps it was best. She imagined their house, which she'd never entered, was a serviceable place. Probably no vases. She herself was having trouble finding a suitable vase. The flowers – she still didn't know what they were – required more room and support than the ones she had, so she trimmed the stems and made do with a storage jar.

When her housemate arrived, she took one look at them and said in delight, 'Oh, peonies. Unusual at this time of the year.'

'Peonies? Is that their name?'

'Yes.' She cupped one of the blooms in her hand. 'I've only seen these growing back home, never here. Do you know what we call them in Japan?'

'I didn't even know what we call them here.'

'They are called the prime minister of flowers.'

'The prime minister of flowers?'

'Yes. They are that special.'

How had the carnage been effected? She could see no evidence of boot prints, or weapons. The dew had already dried. But it had to have been him. Who else would have been up that early, before her? It was probably before dawn. He could have sneaked over the fence and come around the western side of the property. She walked back towards the house, taking the short cut through the pool yard and the kitchen garden, searching the ground for signs of violation, some squashed blooms or clods of soil. Nothing, but she continued striding down towards his place. All was quiet. The fence sat innocently, behind it his trees, also quiet, not even any honeyeaters about. There was nothing to link him to the crime. Still, she glared in his direction.

There was the matter of the fence, which she should do something about, but she could not imagine what. A fence was a fence, and it was not as if her property suffered from losing eight inches. Lately he had also been trimming the prime ministerial trees that extended above his property but she had said nothing, he trimmed them all the time, though strangely left his. The trees were lopsided but seemed unharmed and she had been content for the moment to leave it at that.

She made her way back, and combed through the peony bed to be sure. There were two or three plants left, escaping the assault by accident. She laid them side by side, then picked up the smallest, a tiny wilting thing – and maybe it would not have produced many flowers – but she lifted it out of the soil and, cupping it in both hands, took it down to the garden shed.

'Billy, look at this. The peonies are all destroyed. I need some small pots please.'

He turned around. 'Are you sure?'

'Go and see for yourself.'

He dropped the handles of the wheelbarrow and strode off. She had just found a stack of empty flowerpots when he returned, shaking his head.

'My guess it's that maniac from down the back.'

'Exactly my thoughts. But what are we going to do about it?'

'I'll go and talk to the bastard.'

She considered this. There was not the slightest proof. And there were other factors to consider. Her position.

The dignity of the office. The fact that Billy was an intimidating size, six foot eight in his socks, a former rugby forward.

'No. I'll have to think about what to do.'

As she washed her hands at the tap she wondered if Billy had too much to contend with lately. It was a large property, and while the lawns were mowed and the trees trimmed and the paths swept by outside contractors, perhaps she had made too many claims on him, with her projects.

She would have to be calm, think rationally. Gardening was meant to be calming. The PM felt soothed when she had her hands in dirt, though it had taken her a long time to come to terms with gardening. The ultimate humiliation of her childhood – a childhood so full of humiliations as to seem like one endless hot blush – must have been the news of her mother caught scavenging horse manure from the middle of Sefton Road one afternoon. Three girls from her class at school spotted her mother, shovel in one hand, hessian sack in the other. Shamelessly scooping, ducking in and out of the traffic. Then slinging the sack and shovel into the back of her old station wagon, which was plastered with peeling yet still readable bumper bar stickers espousing the virtues of red meat and advertising the Country Women's Association. Another reason to blush. Anyone could tell at a glance from the high-waisted, faded cotton frocks and the sensible flat shoes that her mother was a genuine country girl, even though her family farm had long been swallowed by the western urban sprawl. More humiliation, of course. In Sydney you could come from anywhere but the west. In the western suburbs themselves, where the PM spent her childhood, the west was especially despised, for there was always more of it. Beyond Blacktown or Londonderry or Toongabbie there was always another semi-rural settlement comprising half-built houses on huge lots. Tiny fibro shacks. Redbrick cottages. Concrete and tile monsters that commenced ambitiously but petered out by the rear half of the house. Testaments, all, to overcapitalisation, mortgages underserviced by the owners' meagre incomes earned at the meatworks, the car yards, the furniture factories.

If she'd had a horse, or even been allowed to ride one now and then, it might have been different. Instead she had a mother who scavenged manure for her vegetable garden. Who, when they were driving to the shops or the library, didn't think twice if she saw a pile of steaming golden shit left in the wake of some lucky carefree girl in the quiet streets where, then, it was still possible to ride out, often with a few envious friends running behind. Her mother would slam on the brakes, hop out and commence shovelling while the same girls were still in view, still able to turn, spot them, and tease her the next day about it. If she had had a grave robber for a parent it could not have been worse.

Humiliation upon humiliation. If it were not the taunts about the manure, it was the teasing about her mother's jam stalls, set up from time to time at the front of the yard. Picking the first raspberries of the season, grown on canes she had set herself the autumn after the election, the PM would remember her mother's berries, remember collecting them in the early morning, when the pectin was at its most intense, or so her mother maintained. The jars they kept in a box in the kitchen until there was enough fruit for a batch. She helped write the labels. Strawberry Jam. Gooseberry Conserve. Marmalade. She recalled the boredom of waiting for people to drive by the stall at the front gate. How on a Sunday afternoon she would disappear down to the local sports field to hang around with the other kids, returning an hour or so later to lie to her mother about there being no customers.

Or worse, she now recalled. Her mother had bred champion boxers and sometimes on the weekend she took them away for shows. She had often used the excuse that Star, the older mother, now a household pet, had barked so much at the front fence, she had turned off customers. It was plausible, Star being so defensive. Her front fence performances were so loud and persistent, sometimes visitors had to yell out to the house from the front gate. In later years, she thought she should have felt guilty in exploiting Star, slandering her like that. But the dog was a nuisance. And a sense of culpability was not something a ten-year-old had in high stock.

The PM regarded the one little peony, wilted in its new pot. Her anger was now steady, focused. She could think properly. She realised now that Kerr's violations – there was no other word for it – had commenced soon after she moved in and she had ignored them all in the belief that he only wanted attention. When he failed to elicit it from her, she believed he would eventually back off. But this was not an annoyance, like his shifty relocating of border shrubs – for at least he let them live – or his nocturnal stealing of her property's quality garden mulch – the pile down past the garden sheds was prone to shrinking dramatically overnight, and could not be ignored. He would have to be dealt with. Confronted. Her forgiving and tolerant nature had probably brought this about. He thought he could get away with anything now.

All the different forms of assault he had inflicted, she now ticked them off. Chopping at the Christmas bushes with an extendable chainsaw, right on Christmas, too, her first in the house. Then the Bobs had reported to Billy, who'd mentioned it to her, an attack on the grevilleas that grew above the height of the fence. Spectacular moon-white flowers had been dropped on the front lawn as an added insult. She should have acted then. She should have brought to bear some law or another. Surely there was a Commonwealth act prohibiting the violation of the national home, the official residence, its fences and flora? Failing that, by-laws protecting the rights of trees? The Arbor Act? The Preservation of National Homes? The Territories Mulch Protection Act? If not she would create one. Create several laws, if necessary, to stop him.

The gravel spat from under the soles of her shoes as she rounded the house. She walked faster, breathing deep, and staying calm, keeping her thoughts focused. Turning a bend towards the entry, she could see down to the front gates. The Bobs had their backs to her, slouching before the weight of the sunlight as the day progressed. She stamped harder. More gravel flew. Kerr had no right to this violation. She was the Prime Minister. The Prime Minister of flowers. She almost tripped as she approached the gates. A root, snaking under the path? She paused and looked around her. Right here at the very front of the property there was an unacceptable number of weeds around the beds of kangaroo paw. And the mulch itself was in need of renewing. And where were the kangaroos? Normally at this hour they'd be dozing in the shade. The beds themselves looked dry, and long untidy fronds, brown and dusty, drooped from the tree ferns. What was happening to the garden? Why was it suddenly falling into decline?

As she approached, the police officers stiffened and looked impassive behind their reflective sunglasses. Bob I was chewing gum. At the start, she'd decided that they would be amongst the first to go. She was not the sort of prime minister who needed full-time police security at her front gate. She had no desire to repel people at her door. But her democracy of care also meant she could not simply sack the Bobs. It was not in her heart to dismiss them. They would have wives and children – preschoolers – mortgages. It was bad enough they'd be doomed to live in the dry, light-bleached suburbs out in the west, where the trees wouldn't grow fast enough to provide shade, where the lawns would be yellow and the fences would always look newly planted. What did ex-cops do? Become private security goons. Bouncers at nightclubs.

Now she looked at them closer. Beneath Bob I's sunglasses, his cheeks were soft, flushed with pink. Bob II had an endearing constellation of pimples just under his jawline. They were really quite young. There was no way she could have sacked them, no way a Prime Minister of flowers could have such an act on her conscience, but now, perhaps, she could find something better for them to do than lounge by the front gates enforcing a languid security.

She was about to speak when she sensed a movement in front and to the right of her. There was that man, still sitting cross-legged a few metres beyond the gates. He seemed not to have moved from the day before, or the day before that. Ever since he had appeared, early one morning, as if he were a spirit from out of the nearby trees, he had just sat there, waiting, head erect. Beside him was a tray of tea and pumpkin scones that Hazel had provided which he had not touched. Did he eat and drink? He seemed not to be wasting away, as far as she could tell. The only thing clear about the situation was that he was not a security threat.

By the time she had organised the Bobs to remove the dead plants and dig over the destroyed bed, she was calm again. Billy brought around a barrow load of wood chips that smelled comfortingly of old wardrobes – the arborists had recently identified a feral camphor laurel which had been felled and mulched – and she began to feel benign. She wondered if this was how her mother had felt, why she was so devoted to her gardening. Perhaps her mother also found simple solace in growing her vegetables. Despite the unattractive utility of the PM's childhood garden, it was possible that for her mother it had been as beautiful as the garden of Eden.

The three of them raked the mulch over and when it was done she sat back on her heels and contemplated the prospect of confronting Kerr. The problem was he was clearly devoted to his property. Perhaps, in his manic, twisted way, as devoted as she was to hers. And there was no proof at all that he had been the culprit. The security cameras swept the entrance to the property, the front courtyard and every entry point to the house but did not extend as far as the peony beds.

She rose to her feet. Thanks to the drama she had missed her lunch appointment with the presidents of three major unions. She would meet them again but not until she had taken the action that she had decided upon while her hands were in the soil.

'Thanks, guys,' she said to the Bobs. 'Take an early break today. And Billy, can you bring a ladder down the back?'

Malcolm appeared, looking like he had scented a wild animal on the prowl. 'A ladder? What for?'

'Because it's either that or climb a tree.'

'What are you talking about?' He hurried to keep up with her as she walked back towards the rear of the house, only pausing to rinse her hands in the frog pond.

'Kerr. Down the back. I'm going to see what he's up to on the other side.'

'But with a ladder? You're the Prime Minister, you can just walk up to his front door, you know.'

'No, I can't. He'd slam it in my face. Tread on my toes.'

'Take one of the Bobs, then.'

'No. Anyway, I want to see into his backyard, not poke around his house.' She walked faster. He seemed to stumble somewhat, trying to match her pace. She expected it was the elegant shoes he wore, smooth leather soles, impractical for proper walking. Hers were sensible, with rippled soles.

Beside her he was chewing his lip with anguish.

'You might fall,' he said. She gave him a look. 'Break your leg or something.'

'Oh, Malcolm, come on. It's just a ladder.'

But he had planted a seed of doubt. That tight spot in her lower back. It might just clench at the wrong moment, let her down, send her tumbling to the ground. Though she suspected Malcolm's concern was not one of altruism. Missing lunch appointments was bad enough, but what would he do if she were truly out of action? That could not easily be accommodated, not with the Treasurer's desire to communicate on an almost hourly basis, these days. Nor with the calls they were receiving, the stream of media queries about the man out the front. And how would he explain such an injury to the nation? The Prime Minister falling while spying on her neighbour. And no doubt it would all be witnessed by the neighbour himself. More crimes for him to taunt her with.

'Let Billy go up a ladder, then. God, he's tall enough, he could practically look over the fence without one. See all the way into the man's place.'

'Hang on.' She stopped, held his arm. Billy was walking towards them, ladder over one shoulder.

'What?'

'There is a better way. Should have thought of it before.' She turned to Billy. 'Sorry, I don't need that after all.'

The man was always home. The Bobs, on duty every day, never saw him leave. Indeed, they only saw him when he appeared to reinforce his fence or otherwise augment his security. The place was always occupied, the property guarded. His front fence was a line of battlements, constructed of brick, cement render and steel slats. He had ignored the city's regulations regarding front fences, building it higher by a good half a metre and bringing it right to the edge of the nature strip. How the civic authorities had allowed this was a mystery. The PM could only assume that his proximity to the official residence awarded him some sort of immunity.

Recently he had replaced his driveway gates. One day the old wire mesh ones, about a metre high, were taken off. Early the next morning, the Bobs spotted him in the driveway with a jackhammer – a jackhammer! he appeared to possess endless noisy tools – pulverising the concrete footings into pieces small enough to be prised out with a crowbar. His letterbox had been removed and now lay on the nature strip like a felled soldier. Parked out in the street was a Handi Skip which he was filling with rubble. Another violation. Skip bins were not allowed to block roads or take up parking space. The PM had glimpsed him that morning as she returned from a walk around the block. He was wearing earmuffs. Sparse curls stuck out under his be-capped head, and he was covered in grey dust. He looked like a dwarf digging for gold.

If only he were that harmless. And if only she had acted earlier to curtail his activities. She should have marched forward, unplugged the jackhammer, ordered the Bobs to detain him and got her gardening crew to clean up the mess. It occurred to the PM that in some ways she was a jellyfish. She had taken on the coalmining industry and the woodchipping lobby. She had ordered the states to cooperate on a unified education system. She had stood up to the gun lobby and the banks. At times it seemed she had shaken her fist at the very heavens – and got results – but right from the start she'd wavered at the prospect of Kerr, to the point that she pretended he barely existed. And now his antagonism had become something more than personal. Today it felt like an attack upon all that she stood for. Today was the day she was compelled to deal with it.

Shortly after, the new gates were in place, solid galvanised steel ones that slid open and shut via a remote electronic device. They presented a blank wall to the visitor, should there be one, who had to press an intercom for admission. His property was more inaccessible, more protected than hers. He had also installed sophisticated security lights along the front and down the driveway to the door. Possums and bats regularly set them off.

The possibility that there might be something valuable, something rare and worth securing, in this curious property of which Kerr was the lord, master, groundskeeper and guard, was slim. Short of sending in the local authorities – for despite the acrimony created by his fence-side taunting and power-tool waving, these were hardly threats to the state – gaining any sort of access while he was there was unthinkable. And investigating while he was absent impossible: the place was always occupied.

He was irascible and irrational. Highly unpredictable. He had never been friendly to her, but the Bobs had experienced the sudden manic gusts of favour and the occasional eddies of good will from his direction. He was prone to yelling out strings of abuse for daring to position themselves too close to his front fence, despite the fact that it was many metres away from their post, in fact around a bend. This did not stop him from coming up to her gate to complain that they were glancing in his direction, which he called spying and perving. Then the next morning after an episode like this he would appear suddenly, waving heartily and smiling as he went about some conspicuous digging, sweeping or hammering. One afternoon he almost spat in Bob I's face with accusations of front-fence violations, then demanded to know why he was stealing his mail. When Bob II stepped in to tell him to cool his temper, Kerr turned and called him a paedophile, heathen, drunkard and dog-murderer. The next day he brought over a bottle of beer in reparation. When both police officers remained silent and impassive, staring out at the street behind their sunglasses, their hands behind their backs, he merely continued smiling and waving as he leaned down and deposited the bottle next to a patch of agapanthus.

'Make sure you drink it while it's cold!' He waved again and walked off.

When he had disappeared, Bob I turned and inspected the beer. Not a brand he liked. He ignored it and the bottle remained there for a week until the PM ordered that they get rid of it. A longneck of Tooheys New in the front garden of the prime ministerial residence was not a good look, even if it was unopened.

She had rarely climbed to the uppermost storey of the house, the third attic level where there were storage rooms and unused accommodation for domestic staff from a former period. And a long window at the end of a narrow passage that opened onto a balcony of sorts, just a patch of asphalt where household staff would once sit and smoke or dry their personal laundry or cultivate a few potted plants of their own. Several weeks previously, she had been inspecting this level with a view to using the empty rooms. With only a little refurbishment they could accommodate perhaps a dozen people, she had thought. The idea had been to set an example to the rest of the nation: no one need be homeless were houses fully occupied.

Now she climbed the attic stairs and went directly to the balcony, pushed up the window and emerged into the sunlight. Leaning on the parapet, she could see down the garden to the fence, and just over it. Kerr's tight plantings of Leighton Green cypresses – a species now banned in many urban areas due to its excessive, view-annihilating growth – meant that she still could not see far into his property. But how strange. There towards her left was the man himself on the rear balcony of his house, elevated into the PM's direct line of sight. He was bending down with his back to her, fiddling with something, the tiles, perhaps?

No, he was painting. She saw him dip a brush into a small tin and bring it up to the railing. Had he turned around he would have faced her, albeit from some distance. They might have stared directly into each other's eyes.

As she watched she saw a child emerge from the doorway that led into the house. A girl, aged three or four, wearing pink shorts and t-shirt. Her hair was a bundle of blonde curls gathered into a ponytail. The child went to Kerr and hugged him, leaning across his back. And then, as if she knew someone was watching, she turned her head, rested it on his shoulders, and stared straight up. Staring right at the PM, she raised her arms and gripped her father even closer.

For he was her father. He had to be. To the PM, the girl's stare was not an unmoving thing. Not an accident. Not the unselfconscious gaze of the innocent who had not yet learned discretion or guile. Simply a child who loved her father. And even as the implications of that flooded through, she observed Kerr absent-mindedly but not accidentally turn partway and place his free hand on the child and ruffle her hair as he continued to paint with the other. Here was a man, a father, capable of gentle affection. Who returned his child's embrace with an ease that could only mean the affection was genuine. That he was devoted to his daughter. Perhaps there were other children, though she could hear no sounds coming from the house. And children must mean there was a mother. A woman whom Kerr cared for. With whom he had lain, and held in his arms. Someone into whose ear, perhaps, he had whispered sweetly. There was in the world some other person who had felt the warmth of his body, tasted the flavour of his mouth, pressed his chest to hers and hugged him tight, and breathed in the same air in the still, close quiet of their bedroom at night.

There was no noise this afternoon. The wind had dropped and the birds were at rest. It was a silent tableau, a story without words, a barely moving picture that said it all. And it was a long story, a narrative captured and spent in only seconds, but speaking of a lifetime. Her heart tilted as she watched the pair, the child holding her father in a tender embrace. The man painting slowly and with exceptional care. The mute communication that flowed between them. The child's unfixed gaze that seemed to say to the PM, this is my father, my comfort, my rock, my world.

What could she do to a man with a child who loved and trusted him like that? She backed away from the parapet and re-entered the house, fastening the window securely behind her. All the measures she had been entertaining to deal with Kerr, from merely exerting her legitimate powers, making the local authorities issue orders to demolish the illegal front gates and remove his feral trees, to full-blown revenge fantasies, commencing with one of those wild, raucous parties that she had never had but about which he was always complaining. Perhaps inviting loud rock bands to perform from the second-floor rear terrace, aiming their amplifiers straight towards his house. Making sure there were plenty of teenagers and other noisy partygoers who had the stamina to keep up the noise level until well into the early hours.

In other extreme and frustrated moments she had considered ordering in wholesale quantities of weedkiller and spraying his place from the back of hers. Or dropping prawn heads into the hubcaps of his car. Firecrackers into his letterbox, and broken bricks onto his front lawn. Late during sleepless nights, high on insomniac frustration, she had pictured herself crawling commando-like into his property and cutting his phone and power lines. Or ransacking his garden shed to remove every tool and implement to prevent the absurd and endless digging, chopping, sawing with which he filled his days, his sole aim that of ousting her.

Now these plans all deflated. She would naturally perform no such acts of vandalism. He should be dealt with in the correct and legal manner, but now she could see that that too was impossible. Kerr was loved by at least one other person in the world. He had his worth. He may have no respect for the PM or for anyone but she would not meet that with a lack of respect on her own part. Instead she would meet his lack, his void, with her own substance. So far she had countered his violations and his abuse with dignified aversion. Now she could see how someone like him could construe that as infuriating passivity. He had regarded her efforts at improving her property with contempt that expressed itself in many ways, from simple verbal abuse thrown over the fence, to the violence of the destroyed peony beds.

It was now time, she decided, to take proper steps. Not to resist him or return his insults, but to set a standard. To take control. To show him she was in charge. To lead by example. To concentrate on his strengths and talents (apart from his excellent capacity for abuse) and show him what he could do with and for himself. And for his family. And his country. To do, in short, what she was employed to do, and be the Prime Minister. His Prime Minister – though he may not want her – as well as the rest of the country's.

Not long before her mother had sold their home in preparation for a move closer to the city, she and their neighbour had replaced the side fence. For most of her life Star had conducted a war with the fox terrier on the other side, a war of sustained barking punctuated by ferocious growling, day after day, year after year, despite the fact that the two animals had never met. The morning the old fence came down, Star and Bullet were engaged in mutual hostilities, running up and down either side of the section that remained, until they came to the gap created by the builder. Facing each other for the first time, they were both shocked into sudden and panting silence. Unmoving, the pair stared at each other for several long seconds. Star panted and drooled and licked her lips. They both looked around. Bullet whined. They both edged back to the section where the palings remained. Then they happily recommenced barking and running up and down the fence, avoiding the gap.

As a child the PM had disliked the boxer dogs that her mother bred in the backyard. They were a nuisance and a shame. They stank, they yapped, they salivated. And they were ugly, even when puppies, when all puppies were meant to be cute. She couldn't even take them for social walks down to the local park. Why couldn't her mother have bred poodles? Silly name but elegant and endearing dogs. Or plain old golden retrievers, which everyone loved. Especially the puppies. No one could resist a golden retriever. Everyone liked them. Even their names suggested beauty and goodness. Golden retrievers were universally beneficent. They were the bananas of the dog world. The daffodils. Disliking them amounted to publicly admitting hostility towards handicapped people, the blind in particular. If only she'd had golden retrievers her social status would have been assured. A warm glow of kindness and charity would have emanated from their family. Had her mother come to weekend netball games with two of them on a lead, then girls – from rival teams too – would have rushed to embrace them. Instead, her mother waited out her daughter's games seated in the old Valiant station wagon reading seed catalogues while Star dribbled at the rear window. No one rushed over to the car park to fondle the dog or exclaim over her good looks.

She was too young to know the difference when her mother had brought the first puppy home. A puppy was a puppy and therefore she loved it. Her resistance was marked from the time, a few weeks later, when she was allowed to hold the dog's lead, and they walked her to the local shops. Outside, while her mother tried to persuade the grocer into taking some of her blackberry jam, she encountered a schoolfriend and her family.

'It's a boxer. Her name's Star,' she announced. Owning a new pup was high on the kudos-scale at school.

Star, who had already slobbered over her bare legs, now leaked urine from excitement. The friend reached out to pat the dog's head but was pulled back by the father, who said he had heard that boxers were notoriously unstable, prone to snapping and biting for no reason.

'She's only a puppy,' she said. 'Don't you think she's cute?'

The friend looked doubtful. The distinctive white splodge on Star's forehead was not enough to counterbalance the excess of undershot muzzle, the frill of black lips, the strings of drool stretching between her mouth and her owner's shins like slimy fishing line. The friend shrugged. 'She's kinda ugly.'

By Monday recess the entire school knew that she owned an ugly, dribbling dog. Over the next few years she became convinced she smelled of dog and dog shit, even though an increasing disdain for the animals meant she rarely associated with them, leaving them to the backyard runs. They were her mother's responsibility anyway, and only when she ruffled a wad of notes in front of her face after selling one of Star's litters, did her daughter see any virtue in keeping them. Motherhood meant Star became quiet, docile. Except for her front fence line ferocity, her bouts of carefully constrained aggression with Bullet, she remained a loyal, gentle animal.

One morning Kerr walked out his back door, yawning, to be greeted by the zebra. She was standing at the step to the patio, her head slightly down. He caught her direct gaze, the expression in her dark fluid eyes inscrutable. As his mouth gaped and before he could utter a sound his eye shifted to beyond the black and white shape of the animal. And then he gasped at the sight – the entire back garden of the prime ministerial residence exposed in the early light. Mouth still open, he swung his gaze to the zebra again, who had not moved a fraction, and did not as he took a few steps across the patio until they were almost nose to nose. She broke eye contact first, turning around and flicking her tail as if dismissing him. She stepped across his back lawn, past the barbecue and pergola and the garden shed, towards the line of cypresses, where until last night his fence had been.

The PM was standing there, in front of the closely massed azaleas on the slight rise of the bottom of her property. The zebra almost brushed her as she passed by, but neither looked at each other, as if they were members of a relay team, and as the PM walked towards him the zebra continued into her property and disappeared.

'Good morning,' she said. She was holding a long roll of paper. 'Now you're here we can get started.' She was accompanied by several people wearing hard hats and hi-vis shirts, a few others in gardening greens with spades and wheelbarrows. 'Oh, yes.' She waved an arm around. 'I had to have the fence removed. Thought I'd get a start by having that done at first light.' (Early that morning? How had he not heard that?) 'I needed the access, you see, and we can't get through the front of your place.'

It was true. The front of his house being so fortressed.

'And it came down very quickly, in the end.' She was holding a lightweight cordless screwdriver, obviously having removed some of the hex screws from the top caps herself. The panels would have slid out easily. They were now stacked neatly in the far corner behind the potting shed. Considering all his long efforts, secretly removing and replacing the fence, section by section, to encroach on her land, the nation's land, it was almost a shame.

'Of course, we can replace it when we're done. Although I never really liked that colour. Do you? Reminds me of warships.'

Speechless still, Kerr almost nodded in agreement. She was now walking across to his garden table. She was walking across his garden. His land.

She unrolled the papers on his outdoor table and began pointing.

'Now these are only rough, and only suggestions, mind you, but I thought we should have something to go on.'

What was she talking about? He stopped staring at the vanished fence, then stared at her, then down at the paper. Plans of some sort. Landscaping plans. He could see his own house sketched in on the left, the PM's residence away to the right, and there in between, right where the fence used to be, was a series of what appeared to be rails snaking back and forth. Then, closer to his house, clusters of round things, coloured blue. Pools. Or ponds? On her side, stacks of blocks.

She was talking again, the irritating woman. Except he did not feel irritated. She had demolished his fence and he should have been assaulting her with a sledgehammer but instead he was standing here calm in the morning sun, as if it were any kind of morning and they were any kind of neighbours, discussing the weather or the football while down at the letterbox.

'Now you have your team and they're all reliable workers. You won't have any problems. Hamish here' – she waved over a man in shorts and boots – 'his team has recently done three child-care centres. And Ashleigh' – a woman in a hard hat raised her hand and waved – 'well, her landscape business has won so many awards, I can't tell you how experienced she is.'

He examined the plans again. At the top was printed: GARDEN FARM PLAYGROUND.

'Oh, don't worry about that,' the PM said. 'It's only a working title. You can think of a better one, when it's done.' She fixed him with her gaze. The same candid, unblinking gaze that transfixed the nation when it appeared in public, or on the television screen. The clear blue eyes that lacked guile. And the steady smile that crinkled their corners. The smile that people found reassuring and comforting for no particular reason. Above her smile the nose that, he conceded, intrigued a nation.

It was the first time he had been this close. The first time he had entered the personal space of the PM, that magnetic field that people found so compelling but without knowing why. And stripped of his tools, without his fence or his front gate, or even his cap.

Apparently he was building a children's playground. He was to be in charge of the project. Apparently he had agreed – had he agreed? – and some of his backyard was to be appropriated for the project, to be added to the PM's property, if not claimed altogether, and it was a good deal more than eight inches.

There was the proposed miniature railway. He could already see how that could be adjusted, to circle around the trees and run through little artificially made hills with tunnels. And the water feature seemed rather basic, just paddling pools. They could include fountains and a lake, and the lake could have ducks floating on it, with a little waterslide for the ducklings; children always loved that. There could be a proper sandpit, with miniature earth excavators and fake buried treasures. A cornfield, an organic potato patch, all growing miniature vegetables, for miniature hands. A dam near the rock wall there, and so partly in the shade behind his azaleas, with tiny windmills that actually worked. Gentle water jets spraying out at intervals. The climbing frame, the blocks sketched in the other side of the railway, would require shade cloth. Maybe it could continue the farm theme. Bales of hay stacked all around.

'The shade cloth could resemble the roof of a barn. And the sandpit could have all sorts of things buried in there. Tiny picks and rakes. Or coins.'

Was the woman able to read his mind?

'But don't let me get carried away.' She held out her hands, palms up, as if disavowing the whole idea. 'It's your project, remember, and basically I'm leaving it up to you.

You're the expert with building and suchlike.' She pointed to his barbecue, elaborate and rather picturesque beneath the pergola covered in wisteria, to the children's swing set which she'd also spotted from the top of the house and which gave her the idea. Except now it sounded very much like it had been his idea.

A slight woman wrapped in a blue dressing-gown had now emerged from the back door. She was looking around with her hands on the backs of two children, the girl whom the PM had seen some weeks earlier, and a boy, slightly older, with the same curly golden hair. They were both still rubbing their eyes.

And up this close, for her part, she could see that Kerr was rather younger than she had thought, prematurely rendered bald. Without the cap he seemed exposed, almost vulnerable. But with his family, who had now moved up to stand beside him, he seemed more of a man. He was a man who had dug and sawed and sworn, who had hammered and shouted and slammed and even stolen, but from the conviction that he was doing the best for them. And he was a man who may even have more children. He would want, she knew, to continue in these endeavours, for them.

She leaned closer to him across the plans. 'You won't let me down, will you, Mr Kerr? You won't let down your own children? And the children of this city? This country?'

Still speechless, he almost shook his head. His eyeballs barely moved while his lower lip twitched sideways.

'No. I was sure you wouldn't. And we shall all be very, very grateful.'

THE TRANSFORMATION HAD been rapid. Lake George was swollen like a placid cow, almost at full capacity. People had commenced taking boats out again, something that few in living memory could recall. On weekends families were now driving thirty or forty kilometres and parking by the lakeside, pitching tents in the free campsites, inflating rubber dinghies or setting afloat canoes and kayaks, and taking to the waters as if they were a cure. Along the lakeside, on the narrow strip between the water and the freeway, small cabins had appeared perched on stilts (the rise and fall of the water was unpredictable), brightly coloured, pink, orange, cobalt blue and banana yellow, some with flags atop like pennants of medieval jousting pavilions or Balinese temples. On the banks were small flotillas of tinnies; out on the water, rafts and paddleboats, churning like crazy. Children ran and splashed and screeched with delight, while the elderly reposed in deckchairs with magazines across their chests. Fish had reappeared, and freshwater crayfish burrowed along the lake's banks.

Motorboats, jetskis and other noisy mechanical toys were forbidden. Waste was all recycled. Sunhats were freely distributed and spray-on sunscreen booths dotted the shores. Ingenious water sports were devised, like giant paddles and great umbrellas of water that spouted high and wide before falling down to the shrieking joy of countless children. A bicycle path stretched the length of the lakeside. There were ice cream booths, gelato bars on trolleys and even a raft where one enterprising vendor was floating around serving slices of icy watermelon directly to bathers.

'They had excellent coffee out there,' Malcolm told her one Monday morning. 'Some guy in a coffee cart. And the weather was perfect. Didn't want to come back to work.'

That was it. As soon as he said it, he realised the source of the nagging unease he had nurtured since he'd woken that day. The afternoon at the lake had been his first away from work since she'd become Prime Minister. Not that she didn't give him days off – he had his fair share, and she was as generous with him as anyone else in her employment – but he found it impossible to stop working altogether when she never did. So he came to work on the weekends, stayed back until later in the evenings, often returned earlier than necessary the next morning. When she, of course, was always up and working. And that afternoon out at the lake, he wasn't really there. He was still observing, not participating. And he was alone. He felt that now, and it was not a good feeling.

As if she sensed this unease, she handed back notes and papers. The latest report from the tax office.

'It's a bird's nest,' she said. 'We've pulled out a few bits and pieces and tidied them up, but what a mess. Enough to make you want to impose a flat income tax rate. Except the conservatives were always keen on that. What if you draft up something after all? Perhaps get an expert in.'

'It's tax. We have a thousand experts. An entire department. We don't need to get someone in.'

'Well, for once I would like some clarity and simplicity from my staff.'

My staff? She meant him too?

Apparently. All day she worked in her office and barely talked to him, and just after 6 pm she walked out. He watched her through the front windows as she made her way towards the path that led to the area beyond the tennis court. It wasn't like her to abandon a task, even one as unexciting as the taxation system.

'You know he fancies you.' Therese placed bread on the table and departed. When she returned with the first course she added, 'Has done for months.'

'Surely not.'

'Of course he does. Pepper?' She waved a grinder over the soup as the PM shook out her napkin. 'It's obvious. He rings you every night, for a start.'

'That's just because he has to, he needs to talk about things.'

'Really?' Therese, hands on her hips, tea towel dangling like a lowered flag, was almost intimidating. 'Then why doesn't he debrief before he leaves every day? Why doesn't he email you if he has to tell you stuff?'

The PM took a sip of the soup. 'Nice. Not pumpkin?'

'Sweet potato and coconut milk. A touch of curry.'

'Why do you stay so late, anyway? You know there's no need.' It seemed to the PM that Therese was in danger of having no life. She started work early in the morning and was often still at the house ten, twelve hours later.

Therese ignored her. 'And if he doesn't fancy you then why does he always ring when he knows you're alone, eating your dinner or watching the news?'

'I'm not alone. You're here.'

'You're not fooling me.' Therese emitted a theatrical, disdainful sniff. 'You realise how much you laugh when you're on the phone to him?'

'Laugh?'

'Giggle, actually.'

The PM did not giggle. Did she? And while on the phone, to her executive assistant? Just the word was bordering on insult. It was saying she was superficial and empty-headed, and susceptible to flattery and deferential to the opposite sex and nervous and kooky and all the things she was not. Children giggled. Stoned people giggled. It was said that the collective noun for schoolgirls was a giggle. Prime ministers did not giggle. Prime ministers aged forty-something especially did not giggle, and certainly not when they were on the phone to their most senior staff, however charming and amusing they may be. She did not do giggling.

'How often?' But Therese had finally gone.

After dinner she brought her coffee back into the TV room and closed the door. She took her mobile phone from her pocket and tapped at the keypad.

'Malcolm?'

'What's up?'

'Nothing. I just wondered . . .' Her question froze on the tip of her tongue.

'Yes?'

'Well. Um. Tomorrow. I thought . . . Look, could you come a little earlier than normal? Say at seven-thirty? There are a few things I need to discuss before our breakfast meeting with the –'

'Are you sure there's nothing wrong?'

'Certain.'

'You sound odd. Is someone there?'

'No one. I'm alone.' Oh. Should she have admitted to that? What if Therese was right and he interpreted that as an invitation to come over? He could be here in five minutes, he only lived at . . . Where did Malcolm live?

But he was already telling her about his evening. Gossiping, or researching, he called it. He regularly spent a half-hour or so at several bars where the best quality information was to be gleaned. Tonight over a glass of wine he had met the sister of the girlfriend of an assistant to the Leader of the Opposition. One of the best sources of inside information, he claimed.

'Anything we should know about?' Keeping the conversation idling along. She didn't especially care about the Opposition. They were a disparate bunch: mavericks, independents, some extremists who had expediently merged as a way of appearing to offer an alternative. No one, least of all themselves, took them seriously.

She put the phone down. There. Not a single giggle. Not even a laugh.

Like many women of a certain age who had become accustomed to irregular or unsatisfactory relationships, the PM was ignorant of her personal attractions. Malcolm was around because of work, that was all. Now Therese's comment was a window that opened directly in her face, letting a sudden shock of cold wind into a cosy room.

Had she ever thought about it properly, she may have believed she was agreeable. Neither ugly nor pretty. With the kind of face and form that blended in, rather than stood out. When she looked in the mirror she saw a deepening line between her brows, the tiniest but discernible start of sagging along her jawline. She failed to notice the clarity of her blue eyes, the fullness and natural rose colour of her lips and the persuasive charm of a nose that was straight until the very tip that softened and curved in a most unusual way. It was a nose that detoured so unexpectedly, yet so subtly, that not even the cartoonists had dared to caricature it. The PM's face resisted the best efforts of the cartoonists. All her ministers and many of her senior public servants came under fire, but for her there remained a no-go zone, a quarantining of her face, so that she was merely drawn, not mocked. In the centre of her face was this nose that defied them. An innocent nose, almost vulnerable. The least nosy nose imaginable. And those drawings, from the lightest sketches to the more substantial feature, revealed a tenderness on the part of the artist, as if even battle-hardened cartoonists of the popular press, numerous scalps under their belt, could not bring themselves to ridicule their leader. A simple nose had defeated them.

Malcolm replaced the phone and lay back on his bed, gazing up. The ceiling in his flat was a textured grey material that looked like sprayed-on dirty foam. He presumed it was for soundproofing.

The PM possessed the most erotic nose he had ever seen. He had long desired to take that nose and kiss it. He wanted first to purse his lips and bestow small kisses on the tip, then open his lips and apply his tongue to it. He would mouth it like a baby at a nipple. He was aware that this was an unhealthy aspiration.

Someone must have actually conceived and designed this ugly ceiling. Its purpose was to offend and repel. It could not be painted, cleaned or disguised: it was a ceiling made to oppress. The whole block of flats had the same utilitarian quality. He turned over on his side.

He had barely touched the PM except to take her arm at moments when guidance might be deemed appropriate. Once they had touched hands, exchanging a document or something, a brief encounter, across the desk. He remembered withdrawing his hand and staring at the side of the palm, as if that moment might have left an impression, a sheen of something emanating from her like ectoplasm. He placed the hand very carefully in his left pocket and when he retreated to his own desk, took it out again to examine in private. Surreptitiously, he raised it to his nostrils. He believed he could detect a scent, something astringent and fresh, lime or green tea, wild thyme or cedar, and yet she never wore perfume. He sniffed again. Her own special scent? The one that would be at its strongest at the top of her neck, where the hair curled in wayward little tendrils? That place he had seen again and again, standing behind her at endless functions where he was required to maintain an attitude of affable neutrality. Which was hard sometimes, as she deplored sunglasses, refused to let her staff wear them except in direct sunlight, as recommended by the Cancer Council. She deemed them intimidating and pretentious. But behind sunglasses, he would have been able to gaze at that spot on her nape for as long as he liked and fantasise about pressing his own nose – nowhere as eccentric and attractive as hers, yet a respectable one, he felt – to the skin there and breathing in slowly and deeply, taking in that extraordinary scent (lemongrass? ginger? passionfruit?) and gently exhaling to make those little tendrils dance like dandelion flowers in the breeze.

When he thought about it like this, it seemed to him that the most erotic places on her body would be the most unlikely. Were he alone with her – not here, of course, not this bedroom with its depressing public serviceability and its ceiling that looked like it would crumble and fall with the onset of any activity more exciting than removing your shoes – he would explore these unexpected nooks and valleys of her body. The inside of her elbow, for example, where the veins lay dark green just submerged beneath the skin. He was sure that spot would be soft and warm under his lips. That ankle. He would stroke that softly. The skin, so thin there, would slide over the bone but only so far, then it would not yield. Then there were the backs of her heels. In summer she occasionally wore sandals. Approaching her from behind, he would be struck by the vulnerable pink of those bare heels, absurdly soft-looking. It was a kind of nakedness. It surprised him that no one else, herself included, considered that she appeared indecorous or immodest. It seemed to him she could not have been more exposed had her shirt gaped to reveal her midriff, or more. Those rosy heels almost demanded that he bring her shoes – her sensible, comfortable, court shoes – kneel before her and, placing his hand to steady first one foot then the other, gently guide the shoes into place to cover up that startling nakedness.

Malcolm sat up. He was some sort of pervert, perhaps, that he had such thoughts about parts of the body as ordinary and unexciting as elbows and heels. Not to mention fantasising about the nation's leader. And yet he was not aroused in a raw, animal way. He was, if anything, touched. And his behaviour, he knew, had always been unimpeachable. He might have brushed her shoulder once or twice, replacing a jacket or adjusting a microphone, but that was all.

He was stuck in this room for the moment, housing in the city being so short. He had taken the only place that came up for rent, and not even the influence of his position had improved the state of that ceiling, or the walls, painted in a cold shade of putty. And he wasn't here that much of the time, anyway. It was convenient. One bedroom, and a balcony that was just small enough to resist the idea of entertaining, were that even possible given the amount of unsocial weather, the infrequency of his days off, and his lack of friends. His mobile phone had a more active social life than he. Why had she phoned him? And she had sounded so stiff. Never laughed once.

Early the next morning the PM was prepared. Malcolm would not suspect she had only phoned him last night for company. No, she had determination, purpose. Imagination and energy. She was the Prime Minister of possibilities and she would surprise him, and everyone else, with her ideas.

'A maze?'

'Right here.' She spread out a rough sketch and pointed to a section beyond the tennis court. 'It's only wasted space at the moment. The grass never grows there properly.'

'There are more important issues, you know. There's that implementation of the education guidelines. And the review of defence funding . . .'

'That's your job. To cool down those debates. My job is to be creative. Show real leadership. And we can do both, you know. Everything.'

'Do you think?' After all this time, he still had these doubts.

'I don't think, I know. And it will give everyone focus.'

They walked upstairs and stood outside on the rear terrace, where she pointed to the site. They could see the zebra, who was wandering around, having left her shed for the morning.

'If a zebra, then why not a maze?' she said. 'In fact the more I think about it, the more it seems that the two belong together. A zebra *needs* a maze. Plus there is that great bare patch down the back, just begging for a project.'

His eye travelled further down to the former fence, where work was well underway on the children's mini train line.

'Well,' he said, 'I guess we have the perfect man for the job.'

Kerr had come into his own. Though still barely communicating, he had commenced work on the Garden Farm

Playground project instantly. Sunrise to sunset, he devoted himself to the job. Within a week he had created a discernible layout and established the sandpit, the garden beds and the tracks for the miniature railway. His capacity for this sort of industry was immense. He had exceptional stamina, working with Billy and the cast of civic gardeners, landscapers and designers. When the PM approached him with her idea for the maze it was almost as if he expected it. He grunted, shoved her papers in his overalls pocket, and within no time had conjured up a set of his own notes.

Now, from the back terrace, she watched him unrolling plans, scribbling calculations, walking along rows, counting and turning, adjusting notes, walking more, pointing and marking the soil. The weather was dry. Rain had not fallen for several weeks, but the ground was still soft and the first few spadefuls were easy work. He took on much of the digging with gusto, demonstrating great skill in the task developed from years of experience. He had a way of slicing into the ground, tilting the blade, and extracting a spadeful of soil so quickly and neatly it looked like he was cutting and stacking chunks of cake. The team had enlisted the help of interested citizens, who would later boast of their involvement like any other community landscaping project. Kerr, rarely speaking, would hand the helpers their spades, point at the ground and move on. The PM occasionally walked out into the grounds for a closer look, wearing her black-and-white striped gumboots and huge Driza-Bone. A waterproof garment was not necessary, but she wore it to keep warm when the wind was chilly, which was often at this time of year, especially in the afternoons. When she attempted to take a spade and dig the ground herself she was gently relieved of the tool and directed to something else. With her on the sidelines, in her striped boots and flapping coat, work proceeded smoothly. Within a month the maze was complete, each row of cunning symmetry an illusion of perfect order. In years to come, she thought, she would look out from the terrace or even the top floor windows and still not see the design. No one would know what lay at the centre unless they succeeded in working their way through.

Wintergreen, boxwood and yew. Privet. Pittosporum and murraya. These had been advised for the best creation of a maze. But many of these were unthinkable. Privet and murraya were intolerable by the hay fever–suffering members of the public. The PM did not suffer herself but understood enough to know that. One of the landscapers had suggested maize but she rejected the idea. It was a worldwide craze. And it would be ephemeral. The trend for maize mazes would soon wane. And the plants themselves would grow, wither and die within six months. While they were being tilled and replanted the site would be a wasteland. The shoots of the freshly sown maize were too tender and vulnerable. She needed something for posterity. Her maze was to last, its evergreen shrubs easily replaceable if and when they died, in ten, twenty, fifty years' time. Kerr had consulted with the team of landscapers for weeks, with designs and suggestions. Native shrubs were her first choice but she yielded to the durability of the many northern hemisphere species, ones that survived cold and wind, drought and frost. She reckoned that if a plant could survive the almost unimaginable cruelty of being smothered by snow, its feet frozen in the earth, and winds that sliced and tore at it for months, it could survive anything. The hardiest of the natives grew in the Tasmanian wilderness, at the bottom of the world, at the top of the mountains. But Kerr had done his research too: such plants, he advised, were either too spindly, too slow-growing, not high enough, not dense enough, or intolerant of the regular pruning needed to keep a maze in shape.

In the house's library she had found an encyclopaedia of native plants published in 1930, and after consulting it she considered banksia. The coastal varieties would transplant well to the inland city, although she was not sure of their tolerance to frost. She regarded the banksia as one of the hardiest of the native plants, not least because they had survived May Gibbs' conscription of them into glowering villains. But was a flowering shrub suitable? Kerr persuaded her not. The species would not like being shaped and pruned. And they would become too leggy.

Bougainvillea, then. But, no, its thorns were far too cruel, and pruning only made bougainvillea grow more exuberantly, making it too fast and unpredictable for a maze. And bougainvillea could not grow this far south and inland; it would not survive the frosts.

The bay tree. It had literary and classical credentials as well as the required height, density and durability. They all tried to talk her out of it but at first she would not be persuaded. It would grow too high, but that could be taken care of with well-planned trimming. And what would be trimmed could be used, the leaves cleaned, dried and packed to be sent to grocery stores and restaurants around the country. The Lodge – one day she would find a way to change that name – could even open a brand of exclusive gourmet provisions, using bay leaves as the focus. Dried herbs, pickles, seasonings and sauces. Perhaps a roadside stall, out the front there, right in the heart of the city. There would have to be parking, a lay-by for safe pullovers. Maybe a coffee cart. Free water, other refreshments. A pit toilet. Sustainability, she declared to Malcolm. Isn't that what every business aspired to?

'You are joking,' he said. They were standing by the marked-out entrance to the maze, where Kerr was explaining where the wicker gate would go. Kerr only glanced at her, as if not quite trusting his own mouth to exercise the compliance the rest of his being clearly desired.

'Security. Traffic. Damage to the gardens.' Malcolm listed all the reasons such an idea was unrealistic. 'And conducting a commercial enterprise is not allowable under the departmental guidelines.'

She sniffed. 'It was just a thought.'

'And in some ways a lovely one.' It was true, she was full of lovely ideas, so many of which had blossomed into actuality. He had visited Lake George again, only that weekend, and felt the bittersweet pleasure of all those couples and families enjoying themselves. How the PM had contrived to bring water and water sports and everything else back to the lake remained a secret to most of the population.

In the end, growing in the native garden at the east side of the property was the perfect plant. And it was Kerr who had spied it one day when Billy was occupied with the removal of a Cootamundra wattle that had died and was threatening white ant infestation. The purple-berried lilly pilly. A cluster of three were growing just above head-height, having been carefully pruned over the years to prevent them blocking the sun from a bed of Sturt's desert peas behind. Kerr had taken out his secateurs and snipped a small length, then walked all the way up the garden, into the house and along the ground floor corridor to her office.

'What about this?' He held the stem out as she rose from her desk.

Kerr was quite right. The lilly pilly had small glossy leaves that changed colours as they matured and so provided a polychromatic effect. And its foliage was dense but not impenetrable.

'This variety's called Resilience.'

'I think it will be perfect,' she said.

'Maybe you could still have your stall,' he said. 'The berries make good jam.'

She looked at him. His face was deadpan. It was possible Kerr was mocking her, or that he shared her keen sense of enterprise.

'And they grow fast.'

'How fast?' she said.

'I reckon in two months it'll look like a proper maze.'

As he walked to her office door she said, 'Kerr?' He turned around.

'This is the first time you've ever been inside this house.'

'Yes.'

She came out from behind her desk. 'Well, you're very welcome here.'

He stared at the floor. 'Right. Thanks. Ah, back to work then.'

She watched him leave. *Thanks*? It must have nearly killed him.

The evening phone calls diminished. Malcolm made a point of summarising matters before he left for the day. Sometimes he sent her a final email updating her, advising on what to expect first thing the next day. Now the long nights were made longer by the absence of that chirpy ring. Night followed night with the phone soundless in her pocket, beside her chair, on her desk. The PM discovered an anguish that she never knew existed, an empty gulf made all the more bleak because there was no one to tell, no one with whom she could discuss it. *He fancies you, you know.*

Therese's words, which had slid out the side of her mouth as she left the room one night, had become the opening lines of a narrative, a long delicious fiction in which she and Malcolm gradually came closer and declared their feelings and in which she, the heroine of this narrative, overcame all the practical difficulties of this unlikely relationship – the age gap, the fact she was his employer, the contempt of her colleagues, the ridicule of the press, her long working hours, the alienation of the electorate – in this one long tale of desire and devotion, longing and love and lust. In this fiction she envisaged all the ordinary things too: takeaway pizzas and late-night movies, browsing through the weekend colour supplements together in bed, arguments over the toilet seat left up. The story contained everything overriding the dignity and good sense that she had carefully nurtured for so long in order to preserve herself against the unbearable weight of love gone wrong, and becoming yet again that most abject person of all, the spurned woman.

But how could she have been so stupid! So guileless. And so vain. To think even in the darkest, least accessible nodes of her brain that he might have been interested. And to betray those thoughts so artlessly when on the phone. Giggling, if Therese was right, and no doubt she was. She had denied it but of course she would have been giggling. She had probably been simpering and blushing too, twisting her hair in her fingers and swinging her legs like some schoolgirl in love with the captain of the team. To imagine that a man like him – how much younger, a good ten years? – would desire a woman like her.

One evening, after switching off the television, having watched three current affairs programs in a row and registering none of their contents, she could bear it no longer. These thoughts were rotating like lottery balls in a barrel. She had to do something, at least assess her situation. She went to her laptop, opened her emails, clicked the icon to order the messages by correspondent, and scrolled through. Nothing to Malcolm that was not work related. Some friendly, some informal, many brief, but none that could be interpreted as flirtatious or as an invitation to something more. Then her text messages. Again nothing, though that was to be expected, since her messaging abilities were restricted by her lack of patience with the medium. No other forms of correspondence that betrayed her feelings, her hopes. That left the phone calls, the face-to-face conversations, through which she raked again and again. The last time they spoke during one of his late-night calls (how long ago was that?). But nothing.

The last time they spoke that afternoon, before coffee, when he was ushering her out of a press conference. He'd handed her something, what was it – that's right, a file that she'd placed in the pile on her desk. She went and retrieved it. A thick document outlining the proposed water resources policy, the one to capitalise on the excellent rainfall and take the country through the environmental crisis, indeed make it a leader in a grand global sustainable future.

Crisis. What crisis. She tossed the paper aside and flicked through the remaining pile of folders and documents. What did she care for water resources or any resources when her heart was gripped so tightly? This was a real crisis, her whole being abased. Shamed. She shrivelled under the force of her own disgust. Look what she had become, a bell curve of expectation and disappointment, an index of overworn emotions and fatigued hope.

She paced the room. Unsleeping was familiar to her, but unsleeping with all her nerves feeling like their outer sheaths had been peeled away, leaving them exposed to the brutal elements of her emotions – this was not familiar. She paced and paced. She would ring him, and put an end to this misery. She would not ring him. What would she say? Hello, Malcolm, just wondering if you were watching the eleven o'clock news bulletin? She glanced at the clock. It was 10.10 pm. And it would only be plausible if there were a link to something affecting her or the government. She would not ring him. She paced; she nibbled the tip of her left thumbnail. She would ring him. She would ask if he had remembered to organise the steelworks visit for next month. She would ask him to remind her of the schedule for that week; she would pretend she had something else on that required urgent discussion. What could she pretend? A distant relative's ongoing illness? Not plausible. A friend's family crisis. He knew enough about her to know that she didn't have friends like that. What did she have on that would require a discussion, and at this time of night? There was nothing. The most significant thing she had on that week was her period. And search her brain though she did, she could not come up with a way to work that into a conversation about the national iron and steel industry.

She would not ring him, she would not. She could not.

Oh, but she could. Sort out your ideas by going on a walk, her undergraduate philosophy lecturer always advised. Pacing stimulated her creativity and so she had a brilliant idea. She would ring him. She could. She could ring his landline and block her identity, and then at least see if he was home, and if not then she would know he was out somewhere (but where? what would be open so late and on a weeknight?) and if she didn't want to speak she could just hang up. Or maybe she would be inspired with the perfect reason to call him at this time. But if he were out? And with whom?

She would not ring him. That would impose an added torment, wondering if he were in an intimate bar with a woman. Who would be, unquestionably, much younger than her.

She paced. Before another string of thoughts could knot themselves together, in one movement she flicked through her phone book and reached for the phone, then quickly tapped at the keypad as she sat upright at her desk – if she were seated here it would be a professional call, it would have to be – and breathed in two very deep breaths as, at the other end, the phone buzzed once, twice, thrice and was then picked up.

'Hello . . .'

A woman's voice. The PM slammed the receiver down.

This was nonsense. She was making herself unwell. Late as it was, she had to get out. She was halfway along the drive when she realised that would not do. The night security staff, John and Hazel, would wonder what she was doing. They might talk. People could gossip. The word would spread that the PM was disaffected or unstable, given to aimless nocturnal prowling. Well, she was disaffected, seriously so, but she would overcome it on her own. She turned and walked down the side of the house to the rear instead.

The property was not in complete darkness. The moon shone on the lily ponds and made silvery shapes of the trees, showing the way through to the maze. The entrance was marked by a pale wicker turnstile and the maze itself was faintly lit with small solar lamps set into the side of the path at regular intervals. The lilly pilly shrubs were now just past head height, making adventure into the maze a genuine challenge even in daytime. There was just enough light for her to make her way through without stumbling or groping, although she should, she thought, be able to make her way through blindfolded if necessary.

Obviously there would be a woman in his life. Malcolm was personable, even charming, at times outrageously witty, good-looking but in an undramatic way, with regular features, reasonable skin and, so far, an unreceding hairline. He was fit. He was well informed. He was in his thirties. Well educated. A dog lover. The fact that he had never mentioned a woman, that a woman had never appeared at any of the numerous social functions he had attended as her adviser, was explicable, the PM supposed. She would expect that he would keep his private life separate from his professional one.

She reached the centre, and spotted the sundial. The moonlight glinted off the surface. She held her hands out and reached to either side of the dial, leaning into its face as if it were a magic mirror in which she could divine the future or read the secrets of the hearts of others. The segments were marked in roman numerals and around the edge was the inscription, *Gather ye rosebuds while ye may.*

A movement behind her made her turn, alarmed. The PM did not have a nervous disposition, but this night she felt especially vulnerable and miserable. A dark mass moved forward from the gloom of the hedges and she instinctively stepped back, feeling her heart beat faster, for two, three seconds, until the mass took shape and the zebra emerged into view. She sighed, relieved, and held out her hands. The zebra ignored them. She stopped on the other side of the sundial and raised her nose to sniff the night air, whisking her tail back and forth.

It seemed that the zebra had become more independent lately, as if she ignored the rest of the world now that she considered herself adequately housed. At the end of each day, from wherever she had roamed – here into the centre of the maze, or up at the main gate – the zebra would make her way back, unassisted, through the grounds and into the stable beside the potting shed and the compost bins. Rarely did their interaction progress beyond a few quiet words on the PM's part and a gentle snorting and tossing of the head on the zebra's. Now that she had found her perfect home the zebra was if anything more aloof, less grateful. Or maybe that was the PM's clumsy reading of the animal's personality. Perhaps the creature was simply and perfectly content, and therefore in no need of displays of affection or dependence. At least she comforted herself with this explanation. Any other would have meant a form of rejection that she found personal, more personal than she cared to admit. It would not do to be spurned by a zebra, especially a zebra that she had rescued from euthanasia – if Mr Beamish were to be believed – and fed and sheltered in the most important house in the country.

The zebra tossed her nose as if to say, *Let's go*, turned around and commenced walking back through the maze. Feeling oddly comforted, the PM followed.

Malcolm was restless before the day hit 9 am. The PM's office door was ajar; he wasn't even sure she was in. He'd been at work since seven-thirty and seemed to have achieved nothing, not even the consumption of the morning news, which he normally digested like baby food. A walk, some fresh air, then he would return to face the task of appearing normal for the remainder of the day. The maze was perfect for this. It was like running the brain through a workout, though less physically demanding. He would return to his desk glowing, not sweaty. He knew the maze well, though it always seemed like a new puzzle, having followed its paths since the day they were first marked out, that day the PM stood there with Kerr and his crew of landscapers and gardeners, in her raincoat though it was not raining, and those ridiculous striped gumboots. Zebra stripes too, of all things. Thinking of things like that only made his heart sag a little more. He would have to learn to live without the sight of the PM, oblivious, uncaring, unfashionable woman that she was. How much he would cherish all that about her, if he could.

Last night, talking to his sister who had dropped by with a casserole, he had realised there was no alternative but to move on, in fact move right away. His sister's talk of her husband and two children, her happy chatter about their friends, their latest family holiday, their plans to get a puppy, all made up his mind. He would have to crush all feelings for the PM before he started hatching any foolish ideas for that too, something approaching a normal family life, even if it were just him and her. When the phone rang while he was in the kitchen, and his sister told him it was a wrong number, he felt unaccountably forlorn. No calls from her, no calls from anyone at all. Yes, definitely time to move on.

He first went to the stable, the corner of the garden shed which Billy had fixed up for the zebra, not that she had ever needed it; she had never needed any confining. But she was not there. Her stall was empty and her feed scattered around, though that was not unusual. Partly eaten carrots and chunks of apples. Since people had been coming out to feed her she had become casual in her eating habits. Lately she had been flinging hay around, and half-chewing mouthfuls of lucerne before dropping the remainder. She nibbled at vegetables then spat them out, nosed through buckets of apples. It was as if she was becoming both finicky and profligate with her food. Or rather, Malcolm thought, she was simply being fed far too much, the result of constant unchecked visitors. They should curtail the animal's eating habits, if not put her on a proper diet. He was sure she had gained weight in the last few months.

Nor was she in the corner of the property that she favoured on sunny days, down under the eucalypts past the native garden. He had walked back past the stand of callistemon, wondering if she had strayed around the front. It was rare that she did, but occasionally she had visited the Bobs, surprising them out of their postprandial reveries by silently approaching and nosing one or the other in the back. Then he reached the entrance to the maze. It was quite possible. She had hung around the maze often enough and several times entered for a few minutes before returning with her head up and her tail flicking, as if to show she had considered it and decided going further was an unnecessary distraction for an animal of her standing. And yet she was the most curious of animals, so compliant but remote. Malcolm would have said tame, except the word did not encapsulate the creature's immense reserve and independence. *Tame* implied a bending to human will, a compromise of her wild nature, a meek or cringing acceptance of behavioural boundaries. The zebra was nothing like that. It was almost as if she had arrived here as a result of her own decision, not that of Mr Austin Beamish.

He walked more slowly as he approached the centre. Nowhere along the paths did the zebra appear, until he turned the final corner and there she was, right behind the sundial. He stopped short, shocked and open-mouthed, still staring as he made to turn around and race all the way back through the maze and up to the house to bash on the PM's office door and bring her back to show her what he'd found.

But she was already there, not five metres away, approaching him almost at a run, hair ruffled and face slightly flushed. Just in time, Malcolm stopped the instinctive lift and curve of his arms to scoop her close, as she ran right up to him but not to him at all, to pause beside him, gazing just as he had with open-faced wonder at the miraculous sight of the zebra and her newborn foal.

Delight. Sheer child-like joy. And laugh-out-loud amazement. For it was not just any foal, it was a mongrel, a freak, a *lusus naturae*. The absurd little creature that was already wobbling on its chopstick legs was a zonkey, a zebronkey, a zebadonk, a donbra, a donkra, a call-it-what-you-will – one of nature's most improbable things, the baby of a zebra and a donkey.

'I suppose,' she said, when they had stopped exclaiming, 'it was another reason Mr Beamish was keen to get rid of her. Maybe the main reason. But isn't it just the perfect thing?'

The foal looked like two different animals had been cut up and reassembled by a blind person. A striped head, a grey-white body, a large patch of stripes on its flank in the shape of Victoria, and four white legs, three of which ended in striped socks.

'It's a freak, a folly,' Malcolm said. 'In a maze. Of course it is!' Then he laughed, really laughed. A laugh that began low in his stomach and rippled up through his body, throwing his head back and making his teeth shine in the morning sun.

The PM watched him instead of the zebra and her foal. His tongue was very pink. He already loved the zebra as much as she. He had also thought Stubbs's painting of the zebra in the English park was as absurd, as funny, as endearing as she had. Now he shared her joy in the unexpected appearance of the zebra's foal, and what a foal. Oh, to know a man who understood! Who shared her sense of humour. Who laughed like that. Perhaps she could tell that joke after all, the one about the zebra asking god if he were black with white stripes or white with black ones, if only she could get it right. Jokes were like sonnets, they had to be pitch perfect. She stepped closer and smiled directly into his face. She almost reached out for his hand, almost leaned up to kiss him. A man who didn't need words to explain all that, who shared her thoughts without needing them expressed, except by his merriment. He continued smiling.

Somewhere she had once read that if you think too hard about how to kiss someone, you are bound to make a mess of it. It had been one of the few aspects of cultural theory that she remembered. It made no sense that a theorist should also be cautioning against over-stretching the mind, but it contained an irresistible logic, an implicit prioritising of the instinctive. She thought about how she had always thought too hard, about everything. She would not think too hard about what to do next. She would not think at all. She settled back on her feet. He leaned forward. Still smiling.

It was only the prelude to a kiss. And if they were to kiss, it would be a short brush of lips against lips, then a drawing back. She would be surprised to discover that his would be warm and soft because Malcolm's cynicism, his wry humour, his perpetual air of mocking the world and everyone, including her, suggested that his lips would be firmer, or cold. Up this close she noticed they were fuller than their rather pale colour first suggested. Some people had very rosy lips. Others had bloodless ones. Some men of a certain northern European complexion had a fairness that lent itself to a pasty colourlessness around the mouth and eyebrows. The PM had never gone for these men with ill-defined features, with eyebrows bordering on baldness and lips that looked like they were permanently swiped with zinc cream. She preferred a more assertive eyebrow, a mouth with colour and movement. Even so, she knew that colour could be deceptive. Her first real boyfriend had, she thought, the most beautiful lips. Before she even spoke to him she used to admire them from across the room in their undergraduate social work classes. Instead of concentrating on the social and justice policy integration process, or on community work theory, she daydreamed about how it would be to kiss those lips. They looked moist and warm. They would taste sweet. And so it was a great surprise, when they did first kiss, awkwardly and almost accidentally, to discover they were cool and salty. She had licked her own lips in the safe dark of wherever they were (the back seat of his car? the porch of his house?) and tasted the disappointment of finally touching those luscious-looking lips, before warming them herself with her own mouth and making them as kissable as they looked.

Malcolm's lips invited her again, curving to a smile. As did his eyes, now crinkling at the corners. Smiling herself, she allowed her face to approach his again. He leaned down as she stretched up.

But no. She stopped reaching. She was no good at this. She never had been. Kissing was an art she had never mastered. In kissing she was a hopeless amateur, a weekend dabbler, capable only of producing clumsy blurred messes.

If she kissed Malcolm now their lips would do more than brush, they would touch, firmly, then press together. What happened then she knew would be a disaster. He would think her ridiculous or disgusting. He would push her back, hold down her arms, smile yet not conceal condescension, and turn around. He would walk back down this final stretch of the maze, turn the corner to the left, then follow the gravel path through the rows of lilly pilly hedges all the way back to the entrance, push through the wicker gate and exit. Anyone might be out there, all the people who waited around a politician hoping for handouts and tidbits, the journalists and other media people, publicists and hacks and hangers-on and everyone, who would be waiting to hear the story of their leader's most abject humiliation, the woman who couldn't even kiss. She would be left standing here with an indifferent zebra, not even the birth of its foal to comfort her, here in the centre of her maze, her folly. She glanced at the zebra again. It was nibbling at the new mauve tips of the lilly pilly, something she had never done before, as if having produced such an extraordinary infant it was entitled to these privileges.

She held out her hands. 'Malcolm . . .'

He said nothing. He was not good at leaping into the empty spaces of an awkward conversation. And he was still smiling down at her.

'I . . . I'm . . .'

Still he smiled and did not speak.

She looked away, then up at him, then away again. The zebra was placidly chewing while its foal butted its nose against her side. Was it a colt or a filly? She would have to have a closer look. And were zebra/donkey cross foals even called colts or fillies?

'I can't . . . I don't . . . I'm no good at . . . I don't know how . . .'

How stupid to be admitting she did not know how to kiss. As if he was expecting a kiss, in any case. Of course he was not, and to blurt out this nonsense would only make her more ridiculous in his eyes.

But his face was expectant, his eyebrow raised. He was waiting for her to finish what she'd started to confess.

'You're no good at what?'

She swallowed. Looked around. If only there were someone nearby to whisk her away, a posse of media demanding her attention, a car waiting to drive her off to some urgent appointment.

'Telling jokes.'

'Jokes?'

'Yes. I'm no good at telling jokes. Never worked it out. A great handicap, you know, in my position.'

'Well,' he said after a moment. 'There's no need, really, what with warm-up people. Hosts. You know.'

'Oh, yes, that's right.' Could she have sounded more stupid? 'No need at all.'

She straightened her spectacles, not that they were crooked.

'I'm going back to the library. To research zebra foals, see how to look after them.'

'Right. Good idea.'

She turned and walked up the path. One turn to the left, and she and the moment would be gone, forever gone.

He called out. 'Wait.'

'Yes?'

'Maybe I'll give the vet a call. Or the zoo.'

'Oh. Yes. Thanks.' And then she was gone, around the corner of the maze.

He went up close to the zebras, hands in his pockets. He was such a fool. She wasn't interested in him and he was blind not to have realised it. For a moment there he had thought they might be going to embrace and kiss. He would have loved to hold her close and brush his lips against hers. He was so happy, having found the zebra and her preposterous foal. They had both laughed aloud at the unexpected discovery and he couldn't remember feeling quite so happy about something, about anything. If he could have just held her, placed his arms around her back and gazed straight into her face. They did face each other, closely. Smiling. They could see the simple joy in each other's eyes. For several giddy, delicious seconds he had thought he might lean forward, down, and meet her smiling lips with his own. Then he would draw back, gaze into her eyes again, place the tips of his fingers and thumb just under her chin and draw her closer as he pressed his lips upon hers again. Harder this time, longer. He would not have forced her mouth. No tongue. Not yet. Kissing was an art. A good kiss took time. He would wait for the kiss to evolve as it needed. He was sure she would be marvellously kissable.

Her lips would be warm and sweet and moist. They would soften when they met his. And then, after three or ten or seventeen or a thousand and fifty-six of those little opening butterfly kisses – whatever it took, he could wait – their mouths would slowly open, their kisses taking them deeper into the endless world of new love. He would hold tighter her body to his. Life to life. Love to love. At some point he would kiss her excellent nose.

But kissing was evidently the last thing on her mind.

LAKE GEORGE WAS not the only water paradise. The Murray–Darling was now flowing again so reliably that entire fleets of paddle steamers were making their way up and down the old routes, taking tourists as well as transporting stock, grain and other agricultural goods. The old steamers, restored and proud, along with newer craft like ferries and barges, began responding to a growing demand for honeymoon tours, for the Murray–Darling river route, with its lazy pace, its illusion of travelling in a timeless world, its soft breezes, soon became the favoured destination for newlyweds. Some fortunate couples went on board in the High Country and travelled the Murray through to Wentworth, then followed the Darling north all the way to its source, loitering in the lake in Menindee, passing Wilcannia, Wilga, Tilpa, then turning around at Brewarrina to do it all again, for the waters were so plentiful, the birdlife so colourful and spectacular, the banks so green and fresh, the trip so relaxing and stimulating, it was the best way to start a marriage, or so the couples said.

Retired people abandoned the trend for camping trips across the Top End or along the Great Ocean Road, left their campervans and took to the inland water routes instead. At Echuca, Swan Hill, Mildura, boarding houses and bed and breakfasts had opened in formerly abandoned homes. Hotels were refurbished, rooms that had barely been occupied for decades were now full again, and the dance halls, the bars, the cafés and the movie theatres were alive in the evenings with visitors from the ferries and steamers that stopped for the night.

Koalas began to come out of their trees, and to amble across parks and around reserves as if there had never been the spectre of extinction, there had never been threats from hunters or foxes or four-wheel drives.

The platypus was regularly seen in creeks and billabongs and not just by naturalists or wildlife specialists on secret expeditions.

Down south, sightings of thylacine were now confirmed.

And the PM was not happy. All the time she had attended to the rest of the country and her own modest estate within it, the nagging thought that these changes were barely enough had become an obsession. And the growing realisation that for all her or anyone else's zeal, passion and fair-mindedness, she would only ever, as Prime Minister, be patronising. Relief work was not the answer. Charity an insult. Housing plans, educational programs, health initiatives and work schemes, despite their evident well-meaning, forever doomed to be the plans of those in power over those in need.

Here she was, mucking around with kisses (or not) and mazes and weird mongrel animals. Meanwhile the country was taking care of itself. The fertile land, the swollen waterways, the abundance of wildlife, all proved that. She needed to get out, away. She had been in this house for too long. Telling herself that she needed to reform this and that and basking in all the successes, from improvements in children's literacy to the increased participation in music, dance, drama, juggling and all the things that she believed added up to some greater whole – the reduction of the use of cars, stimulation of higher, more satisfying employment, eradication of hospital waiting lists and public service excesses – all this had only made it possible for her to avoid her real responsibilities, to confront the greatest challenges.

Success, popularity. They were all just peony flowers. Remarkable, even stunning, and doomed to wilt, then crumple, turn brown and fall. She would be a pile of compost soon enough, and before that happened she needed to expose herself, almost literally. She realised what had once sustained her now held her captive, and before it suffocated her she needed to get out and away. And she needed to do it soon before another encounter with Malcolm, before she dissolved into some abject creature, some cringing, shrunken half-person obsessed with her own status and comfort, the sort of despised political animal she had observed in the past, before she became PM, and had determined never to become.

She had become too comfortable. She had been sleeping, these last few weeks, sleeping like a koala. It had happened slowly and incrementally. What had happened to her? She had not slept like this since she was a child. Then it occurred to her that this recent restlessness coupled with sleeping meant something more significant.

Across the country, her country, a child was in jail somewhere for stealing a chocolate bar, and she was *sleeping*? That man camped at her gates was here for a reason. She had remembered the joke, the zebra question, and one might laugh but it was not a funny joke at all, it was sadder than sad. And here she was, comfortable in this bed, this room, this house.

She would have to do something, go out into the world, take some action. There was nothing more she could do here at the house. But where would she go? And how?

The PM woke early. Five am. That was not unusual. But she had woken from a deep sleep, one that had brought a dream. In fact she had been dreaming about being asleep. She had been asleep! She had slept.

Sleeping, again, and she an insomniac. This had been happening for too long. She threw the covers back, sat on the side of the bed and checked the clock again. She remembered turning off the light soon after eleven. Nearly six hours.

She slipped into a pair of shoes and, still wearing her pyjamas, left the bedroom, passing down the stairs, along the hallway and, aided by the dimmed night lights, through the doors leading to the kitchen and then to the rear of the house. If she went out the back she would remain unobserved, and John or Hazel wouldn't be alarmed or think an intruder was about. She unbolted the door that led to the courtyard off the kitchen, and opened it to a chilly freshness, the beginning of autumn. She walked softly across the paved square, unlatching the gate, past the kitchen garden to the gravel drive and down to the small flight of steps and the path that led to the tennis court and, behind it, the maze. A pale glow was spreading low in the sky. She stayed on the path, unwilling to leave footprints on the damp lawn, not quite understanding how she had almost overnight begun to feel like an intruder in her own home.

Since the birth, the zebra had chosen to stay in the maze, keeping her foal close, accepting apples and handfuls of grass from visitors who made it to the centre with the same enigmatic demeanour she had exhibited from the moment she stepped out of the back of the horse float and into the PM's life. This morning she raised her head and sniffed then stared at the PM as if to signify something was in the air, was not quite right, and what was the PM going to do about it?

She went over and placed her hand just below the zebra's neck, the only touch that the zebra tolerated, but the foal came closer and nudged her with its moist nose, snuffling into her shirt, hopeful and eager. In the gloom it was hard to tell but she thought the creature's leg stripes were becoming more prominent, contrasting with the grey-brown of its body. She rubbed its head with her free hand, then gently scratched in the velvety place under its chin, while it trembled with pleasure. When she stood back, the foal attached itself to her mother and commenced suckling. The zebra lowered her head, sighed and nosed the foal, an attitude of contented resignation.

As she walked back through the maze, she noted the lilly pillies needed trimming, the crushed gravel paths a sweep. She made her way up to the wicker gate, pausing to brush away leaves here, pick up twigs there, break off the occasional untidy sprig. Constant work, a garden, especially one like this, with all its features. But Kerr would clearly be up to the job of supervising the entire property – how much she had achieved! – since despite all that bad history, his diligence and hard work could not be bettered, and his tenderness towards the land and its plants more than evident. She could leave the place in his hands and be confident it would be tended well. She wondered now if he really had been the one who destroyed the peonies. They had never discussed it.

She gazed up towards the house, looming brighter through the dawn. She had loved and nurtured the house, transformed it into a true home. And all her housekeeping, her good order, her sensible decisions, the harmony and joy that had rippled through the rooms like the laughter of elves had extended past the house, outside the grounds, beyond the neighbourhood, through the city, and flowed past the borders, across the states, the whole country.

The Lodge had become a place for the people, but she had not taken it far enough. In short, it didn't lodge enough people. There was one last important step to take, and it did not involve finding the right name for the place. That was why she had not been able to settle on a name, for a name was the least of it.

As she realised this she heard soft thuds behind her, and turned to find the zebra with her foal at her heels. They both followed her through the gate, which swung back to shut after them with a click. And then the zebra pushed the PM with her nose, pushed her on the arm, gently and firmly, and, as if propelling her back towards the house, walked close beside her all the way. The PM raised her hand to pat the animal, then, inspired, daring, placed her arm around its neck. The zebra did not resist, and the odd trio walked all the way up to the gate into the kitchen courtyard, which the PM had left open. After she went through, she turned around at the door to the house and stared at the zebra. And the zebra stared at her, head high, eyes unblinking, for a long time. The PM wondered what she would do if the zebra wanted to enter the house. She even stepped back from the entryway and held the door wide open. But the zebra only stared for a few moments more then tossed her head, whinnying faintly. She swung around and walked away, her foal trotting behind. She did not turn towards her stable in the garden shed, nor did she take the path back to the maze. Instead, she continued walking around the house, turning left onto the path that led to the driveway out to the street.

She fetched a glass of apple juice and sat at the kitchen table. People had told her she had changed their lives, and that the country was a kinder, gentler, more prosperous and peaceful place than ever. That it was the best country in the entire world, blessed and bountiful, warm and welcoming. She felt a prickling of disgust. She was a fraud. If it were true she had achieved so much, more than anyone before her, she had done so by accident. Freakish coincidences had conspired to bring her to this role and all she had done was wave her hands around and order this and that to be done; she had conceded nothing of herself, given over to the country and its people not an iota that implied sacrifice, commitment or discomfort.

It had all been too easy.

There was her maze, with hundreds of visitors each week marvelling at the deviousness of the design and delighting in the experience of being lost then found, all in the safety of the gardens of the PM's home. The zebra had been sent to her; she had done nothing to earn it, indeed had at first denied the initial requests to take her. And as for her hybrid foal – cunning Mr Beamish, if he had known – the PM had suddenly become something of a celebrity amongst animal lovers and wildlife groups, as if she herself had been responsible for the foal's existence. And now it appeared the zebra was going. Moving on. Relocating.

The only thing that had given her real grief was her slightly crazed neighbour, whom the PM and others believed had succumbed to her charms, but she knew that was a lie. Kerr had merely been provided with the right context for his obsessions, and received a proper acknowledgement of his skills. She had not vanquished the man. She had only exercised patience.

How that would read in the history books to come she could not imagine. If a more passive approach to reform could be found, she was not sure where. The history books remembered prime ministers who confronted wars in distant lands, who stayed up every night waiting for overseas bulletins on the teletext machines, now from the satellite, the internet, text messages. Who broke strikes or put an end to conscription or wrestled monopoly from the banks. Who disdained the loopy left but protected the rainforests, restored the wetlands, and saved from extinction the orange-bellied parrot. Who barked commands and were loud, imperious, sarcastic. These sorts of prime ministers may not have been loved, or even liked, but they were always admired. They were remembered for saving iconic national brands, for making the public service shiver in its boots, for inaugurating vast ambitious projects, like dams and mines and hydro-electric schemes, and for never taking shit from the unions. Her industrial relations improvements had been so successful that the unions, recently revivified, were fast becoming obsolete. She was not sure now that was a good thing.

Late the day before, she had walked down to the Garden Farm Playground. Not the most ambitious construction project of her career, but one of the most satisfying. Now the place was looking almost worn in. Gardens were like that, shrubs and climbers growing, in the right conditions – and the weather had been perfect – at fairytale rates. Like the Hardenbergia, which had scuttled across the roofs of the little toy tractor sheds like it was on a mission from god – and weeds sprouting through the pine-shaving mulch while you glanced away. She recalled now that her final thought last night, before falling into that remarkable sleep, was that her mother would have been proud. Had she seen the results of digging and composting, the jars filled with berries and honey, the buckets of new potatoes crusted with soil, her mother would have noted approvingly and understood that her only child had achieved something important in her life. And it was perhaps more important than the PM had intended, more than she herself realised.

She did not consider herself a religious person, but she realised Kerr was like the one lost sheep in that parable, for whom the shepherd searches high and low, all through the night, until finally he brings it home, safe and warm. He was not perfect – he could still lose his temper and make mistakes and stalk off back to his own home and slam the door from time to time – but the deep-seated nurturing qualities that had previously manifested as manic fence-building and obsessive digging and planting were now given their natural expression. She had created the right place, in every way, for him to bloom. She had allowed him to be a man, the sort of man that at the time even he hadn't understood he needed to be. Perhaps in the end Kerr would stand as her greatest achievement. He was her national green energy scheme, her harbour tunnel.

As for him, he had gained the precious experiences of countless children who had come through the place, played in the miniature cornfield and got dirty digging up his perfect Dutch cream potatoes or presented sticky hands to their parents at the end of their adventures, having picked strawberries – actually growing out of straw! – and mulberries, and followed bees from the flowering melaleucas to their hives and then helped while the warm, cinnamon-coloured syrup dropped from comb to jar, flowing in a lazy, drowsy way as if time stood still and waited, which in fact, for children, it did. And it was the children, only the children, who had managed to elicit any response from the man keeping vigil out the front. He had accepted their gifts of fruit, their bowls of honey, their grubby corncobs.

Of course, she should have realised by now. Yesterday, the man out the front had been packing up his few things. She had been too preoccupied to pay any attention when the Bobs reported some activity, a tipping of tea dregs into the bushes, a neat stacking of a few plates left by the children. It was not too late. She raced upstairs to her bedroom, where she changed into jeans and walking shoes, threw a few things into a backpack. It was just breaking dawn as she slipped out the front door and set off up the driveway. If she walked fast enough she knew she could catch him up. Perhaps they could both follow the zebra and her foal.

But he hadn't left. He had packed up, but was standing there waiting by his swag and a milk crate of belongings, waiting as if by appointment, as if expecting her. As she approached she smiled and waved, and he only nodded, not friendly, not unfriendly. That was right, she thought, he had no need to be grateful for anything. When the idea struck her it was so logical she might have been planning it for months, indeed for her whole prime ministership. It was as if this moment were the entire reason she had entered politics, been elected, come here to live. The very reason for her existence in this world.

Instinctively she patted her pockets for a key, before realising she had never had a key to the house, never had the need for one.

Nor did he.

'The back door's unlocked,' she said. He nodded again. 'Clean sheets on all the spare beds. Plenty of milk and bread in the fridge. And I think Therese's made a lasagne.'

As he hoisted his swag she thought she caught a flicker of a smile. After he passed her she turned and watched him stride towards the house. She hoped he would rename it. She wondered what it would be, then realised that it was none of her business now. It was his business, his and all his people's. She assumed they would all move in quickly, the relations.

Her chest felt light; she was breathing better than she ever had in her life. She would walk as fast as she could, and might even catch up to the zebra, and follow her wherever she led. She adjusted the backpack and took out her mobile phone. As ex–prime minister she could do whatever she wanted now, and as she pressed Malcolm's number she smiled. She might even allow herself to giggle, or to laugh.

Acknowledgements

EARLIER VERSIONS OF some of these stories have been published previously. The author would like to acknowledge the following publications, and thank their editors:

'How to Mend a Broken Heart', in *Good Weekend*, *Sydney Morning Herald* (January 2011).

'The Master Shavers' Association of Paradise', in *A Country Too Far*, edited by Rosie Scott and Tom Keneally (Viking: 2013).

'Nourishment', in *Kill Your Darlings*, Issue 10 (July 2012).

'Welcome to Country', in *The Intervention*, edited by Rosie Scott and Anita Heiss (concerned Australians: 2015).

'Festive Food for the Whole Family', in *Southerly* (vol 77, no 3: 2017).